THE MECHANICS'
ISSUE 12 AUTUMN

The first Mechanics' Institute in London was founded in 1823 by George Birkbeck. "Mechanics" then meant skilled artisans, and the purpose of the Institute was to instruct them in the principles behind their craft. The Institute became Birkbeck College, part of London University, in 1920 but still maintains one foot in the academy and one in the outside world.

The
Mechanics'
Institute
REVIEW

The Mechanics' Institute Review
Issue 12 Autumn 2015

The Mechanics' Institute Review is published by MA Creative Writing, Department of English and Humanities, School of Arts, Birkbeck, Malet Street, Bloomsbury, London WC1E 7HX

ISBN 978-0-9575833-4-4

"Item, One Tortoiseshell Bag" © Marina Warner. This story first appeared as "The Tortoiseshell Bag" in *AnOther Magazine*, Issue 27, Autumn/Winter 2014.

Project Director: Julia Bell

Editorial Team: Matthew Bourn, Livvy Brinson, Cristina Chira, Judy Hepburn, Melanie Jones, Sophie Morgan, Tamara Pollock, Miranda Roszkowski, Carmel Shortall, Luke Terry

The Editorial Team would like to thank Julia Bell, Sue Tyley and Anne-Marie Taylor for making this project possible.

For further copies or information, please contact Anne-Marie Taylor, MA Creative Writing, Department of English and Humanities, School of Arts, Birkbeck, Malet Street, Bloomsbury, London, WC1E 7HX. Tel: 020 3073 8372. Email: a.taylor@english.bbk.ac.uk

Website: http://www.writershub.co.uk/mir.php

Printed and bound by Berforts Limited, 17 Burgess Road, Hastings, East Sussex TN35 4NR

Cover design, quotations design and typesetting by Raffaele Teo

The Mechanics' Institute Review is typeset in Book Antiqua

TABLE OF CONTENTS

Introduction: The Age of the Short Story

JULIA BELL

The literary novel is, we are constantly reminded, by both pundits and publishers, in crisis. It's no longer the dominant cultural force it once was as everything is driven by the bottom line of what will sell (plot), and as books are overtaken by, or turned into, TV series, and challenged by the changing landscape through which text is mediated. Readers are more impatient, less willing to give latitude to the difficult or the demanding, especially now that they have shiny smartphone screens to distract them.

Where, then, can readers discover new perspectives, and writers experiment and find their voice? Where does the literary impulse live on in contemporary culture? In my experience it's in the form of the short story where a prose writer is most able to try new things. Its portability suits the distracted temper of the times and some of the best exponents of the form can deliver as much of a punch in a few thousand words as many mediocre novelists achieve in several hundred thousand.

The novel was born out of the leisure hours of the emerging middle classes of the eighteenth and nineteenth centuries; it was something that took time to read and to write. Whereas the short story emerged from the oral traditions of folk and fairy tales, often taking the form of the parable or cautionary fable. These stories were part of cultural traditions, too, narratives that were told and retold at festivals, rituals and feasts.

In this context, not only is the short story a more ancient tradition, it is also a more flexible one, and one perhaps better suited to our interesting times. A short story can be a few hundred words long and have the density of a poem. Or it can be a complete life story wrapped up in a few thousand. What matters is the internal coherence of the writing, the velocity of the language. A reader will have more patience with a disorienting or difficult piece of work over ten pages than they might over several hundred. Also, for a writer, if the story ends up in the recycling bin, it's only a matter of hours or days that have been wasted rather than months or years.

But brevity does not mean a loss of depth, either. Many short-story writers attest to the months spent revising their stories. Often the best collections are works of accretion, with versions of stories appearing over time in magazines and journals that can be very different to the stories in the finished volume.

Kevin Barry, winner of almost every prize for the short story there is, acknowledges the amount of work that goes into his collections in a recent interview with the *Paris Review*: "just one or two of every ten stories I write is good enough for me to send out. That's the kind of proportion I'm dealing with, maybe one or two out of ten. Hopelessly uneconomical. So I could only do a story collection every five or so years, I think."

At Birkbeck we are committed to the short story as a form, and teach it partly in order to address matters of technique without having to wade into the depths of a novel, but also because we are committed to its continued existence as a literary form in its own right. A separate entity from the novel, with a different aesthetic weight and shape.

Chekhov wrote of his own practice in a letter to his friend A. S. Suvorin, saying that a writer must not confuse "the solution of a problem and its correct presentation. Only the second is incumbent on the artist." This notion of the "correct presentation" of a problem is what a story can achieve so well, a task that is much more difficult for a novel. Over length it's harder to maintain focus and consistency; a short story can be polished until it shines.

The increasing popularity of the short story seems to be reflected in the culture. The emergence of more and more well-funded prizes for the short story (*Sunday Times* EFG, BBC, Bridport,

Manchester), and even of its own bespoke festival (London Short Story Festival), confirms the fact that the form is finally getting its cultural moment in the spotlight. Publishers might say that stories don't sell, but for a short-story writer it's perfectly possible to make a career from winning prizes for volumes of stories, or from winning competitions – just ask Colin Barrett or Kevin Barry.

Writers exist alongside publishers, not because of them – ask any poet. The writing is done because it is the work that must be done, the story that must be told. The market is erratic, and most often conservative, so in this sense the short story is the form of the purist who does it for the sake of it and lets the publishers catch up, as they always do, eventually.

So to *The Mechanics' Institute Review*. Each year we publish a curated collection of stories from current students and alumni to offer a showcase for the variety of work that has emerged from the creative writing programme over the past now twelve years. Some of the writers in this volume graduated several years ago, but they are still writing, still using fiction as a way of talking and thinking about the world. We are proud to be a part of this new Age of the Short Story, and in the following pages you will find a rich selection of different voices, styles and subjects that attests to the continued vitality of this, the most open and exciting of all the literary forms.

"It's none of their business that you have to learn how to write. Let them think you were born that way."

Ernest Hemingway

Kate Bush
DEBORAH MARTIN

When you were four years old, for around a year or more, Kate Bush turned up in your life to terrify you on a regular basis. You had no idea why she did this – all you knew was that you wanted her to stop.

You would be playing quietly in your room, carefully laying out the pieces of your plastic tea set, when she'd burst shrieking out of the toy cupboard, dark hair billowing, red dress streaming, mouth stretched wide open in a ghoulish pantomime of alarm. Then you'd scream and press your hands tight against your eyes until your mum rushed upstairs to see what was happening.

But by that time, Kate Bush would be gone. Perhaps she'd climbed out of the window and scuttled down the oak tree to the garden – you couldn't be sure. At any rate, you soon learned that she was as much a mistress of wily exits as she was of sudden, unwanted appearances.

Once, when you were looking under your bed to find a dolly's shoe, you spotted her crouched there in a thin black leotard, hair in a ponytail, legs curled tightly beneath her. She winked at you and you sprinted away in terror, her laughter following you all the way down the stairs. And for a long time afterwards, you'd refuse to get into bed until your parents had checked underneath.

Other times, when you were walking down the street with your mum, Kate Bush would be there too, following you. You'd hear a certain unearthly chime of music and, looking round, you'd see her peering at you from behind a wall or through a cluster of trees. And though she wore a hooded cloak on these occasions, you still recognised her from the pretty white nose, the scarlet lips, the puffs of dark hair.

But even if you'd had any doubts that it was her, these were soon dispelled when she whipped open her cloak, arms outstretched dramatically and thigh thrust out defiantly, to briefly reveal the scanty gold bikini underneath. Then you would squeal and tug on your mum's hand but by the time she turned around, Kate Bush would be gone.

These visits continued long enough for you to develop a terror of any woman you spotted walking down the street with dark billowing hair and the hint of a maverick pout. It was also enough time for you to take to screaming and sticking your head under a cushion every time she appeared on TV, much to your parents' confusion.

But eventually, as is the way of these things, Kate Bush's visits fizzled out. She faded from your life like a phantom wisp of silk or stage smoke, and by the time you started school she'd become a fragment of the filmy past, that season of life recalled much more in feelings and impressions than in clear memories.

Your life moved on to other things: to lukewarm school milk spurting from a straw, to off-white training bras lining the laundry basket, the ashen haze of your first cigarette and the messiness of your first kiss. There was the thin scroll thrust into your hand when you graduated from university and the warm piles of paper that churned from the photocopier in your first job.

And there was meeting someone, moving in with them but it not working out; then stuffing clothes quickly into a suitcase before leaving the flat for good.

And where are you now?

You are back at your parents' house. It's late and you're unfolding your nightgown in readiness for bed. The sight of this unchanged childhood room brings back memories of the dark Gothic diva who once haunted you. And as you glance out of the window into the garden below, something about the moonlit oak tree brings back smudged recollections that you can't quite grasp.

For there's a memory that's teasing you, one folded deeply in the tissue layers of time. And slowly it unwraps itself.

You are four years old and you've suddenly woken up in the middle of a warm night to find yourself standing on the back lawn in your nightgown, feet bare on the grass, stars winking above. You've been sleepwalking again, you've done it before, although this is the first time you've ever wandered outdoors.

And Kate Bush is there too, across the lawn; she's standing beside the oak tree in her black cloak. She's staring above her, an archer's bow in her hands, poised to release an arrow into the sky. And you know, without being told, that she's aiming for a star.

She turns to look at you, and at first you're terrified. But this time she doesn't scream or smirk or laugh. Instead, she holds the bow and arrow out to you and nods, as if to say, your turn.

And you want to say yes, but you find yourself turning and running back into the house, pounding up the stairs at full speed and crawling into bed to hide under the covers till morning.

That was the last time you saw Kate Bush. Though her perfume – a mulled, musky fragrance – lingered here and there for a while. And, some time later, you found a red silk scarf abandoned under your bed, mingling among the dust motes.

Now, climbing into that same narrow bed in the corner of your childhood room, you wonder what would have happened if you had taken that bow and arrow from her.

And you realise that for your whole life long you've been holding your breath, waiting for the lady in the red dress to come rushing towards you once more. Waiting for Kate Bush to return.

"Everybody walks past a thousand story ideas every day. The good writers are the ones who see five or six of them. Most people don't see any."

Orson Scott Card

Item, One Tortoiseshell Bag
MARINA WARNER

. . . rectangular, with deep lid, chrome clasp, two
curved handles and four internal compartments.
Parisian manufacture, c. 1954

The glowing, mottled panes of my mother's evening bag were
puzzling; my pet tortoise was dry and dusty all over, its dark
shell grooved and grainy as old timber on a breakwater above the
waterline, where the waves never splash to make it gleam in the
sun. The pattern on the animal's carapace was squared off, the
sections bulging more towards the dome, but neither this mottling
nor the shell's lustreless texture looked in the least like the honey-
and-toffee translucent dapple of Beata's prize possession.

The animals were cheap at the pet shop in the bazaar; they
weren't protected yet. The shell, by contrast, was a luxury material
– like ivory, crocodile, or shagreen. But when I say "my pet tortoise",
it's misleading because I had a series of the creatures, each one
disappearing in turn. "It's gone into hibernation," Beata would
reassure me, "it'll show itself again when the weather warms
up." A tortoise never becomes a pet, not really: petting is limited
to tickling it so it'll poke out that troubling ancient head with its
dinosaur eye, dull and mineral as a diamond before polishing, or
coaxing that low-slung, narrow and lipless mouth to ruminate on
leaves. But no tortoise I had ever uttered a sound. Could a tortoise
bark? Could it squeal?

The tortoises of my childhood were baffling – perhaps they
gave me my closest encounter with the state of bafflement.

Yet, from this gloomy, lumbering creature in its mute pathos,

9

its almost unfathomable antiquity, came the translucent and luxurious material of the brushes that Francis kept on his dressing table and the combs Beata wore in her hair.

The bag was a love gift from early on in her marriage. Francis had bought it for her in a rare moment of largesse from a boutique under the arches of the rue de Rivoli; it was her birthday – her twenty-sixth, I think. If I hadn't been told otherwise, I would have thought it was made like the windowpane sugar on Beata's crème caramel, or a slice through agate – gilded sweetness fused with light set hard through fire or ice long ago. But "bag" really isn't the mot juste, since it suggests something soft and shapeless, whereas this objet de luxe is rigid and architectural, like a jewel box or some kind of superior picnic kit, but wonderfully delicate: an ornament, a centrepiece, an exhibit to add to the display she'd make every evening she and Francis went out into the Cairene social round.

I prised up the catch on the clasp, the chrome a little peppered by age, and lifted the deep lid on its tiny hinges of copper – one screw has worked loose over the years and the shell has warped a little – and from the empty and silent box rose the hubbub of a warm summer night in Gezira, laughter and snatches of talk, whisperings and exclamations, the clatter of china and chink chink of crystal from the drawing room, blurred names being called out at the door by the suffragi, a car door slamming in the street below, more laughter, the curtain on a veranda slapping in the night breeze from the river below, the shout of a carter with his donkey caught in the melée of the traffic, the patter of casino chips and ricochet of the ball against the rim of a roulette wheel, the spurt of a cigarette lighter being lit, a guffaw from Francis, a car starting up and driving off, at speed, slower traffic from the street moving haphazardly towards the Qasr el-Nil Bridge, the evening call to prayer from the mosque across on the other side, distant music from the barges moored downstream on the left bank of the pulsing river, stars falling into the dark water, Beata coaxing and Beata cooing, Beata waving, flutter flutter, swish swish, with her Japanese-style fan, smoothing the folds of her dress, the rustling cream organza over layered petticoats of tulle, scattered with sequins she'd stitched in arabesques that curled up the bodice and picked up the glitter from her eyes. She had her admirers – she called them cavalieri serventi – and all the time I was still living at home there was always someone in her life who came and went, and Francis sometimes loved him too, but not always.

After Beata died, I heard from Selma, who was her confidante from those days and afterwards, in London, that at one time my mother had come very close to leaving Francis, but that she had stayed with him for my sake, for my sake and my sister's.

"Who was he, Selma?" I asked. "Please think back."

"He was quite a high-up, and seemed a bon parti. He was doing some business in Africa. He was mad about her. Everybody was mad about her. But this time it was a near thing, I'm telling you. Thanks be to goodness your mother thought twice about it. He went to the bad. I heard that later he was put in gaol."

"You must remember his name! What did he do? Who was he?"

"It's all too long ago." Selma shook her head and gave me the names of some old friends to ask. "If they're still alive," she added.

A few months ago, before I'd sorted all her possessions and before I felt able to give away her clothes, a flyer came through the door saying that the *Antiques Market* telly programme was to come to our area, and would be setting up shop in the local library, and we could bring along any mystery objects for the experts to identify and value.

Tortoiseshell is now an illegal substance, its export prohibited under severe penalties, as notices at airports constantly warn travellers. At Gatwick and Heathrow there are those dilapidated Wunderkammern, with their dusty and higgledy-piggledy displays of conch shells and crocodile skins, pelts of rare cats and snakes, ivory tusks and carvings – they also include, often enough, turtle shells and a few gnarled objects made out of them. I wondered what Beata's evening bag would be worth these days, or if it would even be seized.

The programme's young researcher thought the bag was sufficiently unusual to be featured, and I was taken to meet the expert who'd conduct the interview on camera later. She was a young woman called Dido, very long and slender with her red hair in a colourful bandana tied up with a flourish; she had a funny deep voice that made everything she said sound italicised and bristling with exclamation marks.

"Ooh! Vintage contraband!" She picked up Beata's bag, and ran her long hands with their slender fingers tipped in green lacquer over the smooth surfaces. "Gorgeous! Glamorous! Almost edible, no?" Her fingertips were remembering, through the unexpected temperature, neither cold as metal nor warm as amber, this material's reptilian origin. "Delicious – but only as a dragon or a python might be. A strong taste. A very strong taste. A fashion accessory for a woman of style, a sensational woman . . . your mother? Wow, this was your mother's?

"Well, I can see her now in you, yes, that's it.

"A museum – and that's really the best place for such a piece – a real talking point. To explore bespoke artisan industries in Paris couture. On eBay, you'll probably get £200, £300 if you're in luck.

"But I'd keep it if I were you. Take it out now and then. Like a musical instrument, such an item needs a bit of TLC.

"Meanwhile, for the rest of us, faux tortoiseshell, Bakelite best of all, passes all right these days– like faux ocelot, faux zebra. You take your pick, and no harm done!"

She asked me about Beata and Francis and I spoke a bit about them, the life they led in Cairo where my mother would wear her special evening bag from Paris to the tea dances and cocktails and soirées and charity galas and other dos they went to every evening. I brought out a photograph of a Christmas staff party with Beata in the foreground wearing a paper coolie hat with a streamer and smiling in unself-conscious gaiety at the camera, which must have been held by Francis, as he isn't in the picture.

About a month later, a handwritten letter arrived, forwarded from the television company.

The writer had seen the programme and wanted to tell me:

> I recognised the bag – it all came back to me, the parties, the fun, that time I was passing through Cairo on my way back from Addis where I was teaching English literature at a school there. It must have been 1954, and your mother – and your father – were wonderfully kind to me.

You reminded me of her – may I ask, is she
still alive?
She was a marvellous free spirit.
Yours, with best wishes,
Ronnie Quigley

The writing paper was quality rag, the address – in Jane Austen's village of Chawton – nicely set out and embossed, the hand shaky but shapely.

On an impulse, I did not write back a routine acknowledgement as I would normally (if I got round to answering at all), but rang the number included in the address on the headed paper. A quiet, agreeable voice; old but not entirely moribund. We talked a little; the dates fitted, it seemed to me, and from what he said on the phone he'd led an adventurous life, mostly in Africa. He invited me to lunch at a small place he knew in St James's; he would come up to London from where he lived in the country to meet me again, he said, as he had known me when I was a little girl.

I arrived first, on purpose as I wanted to see this old admirer of my mother's, Ronnie Quigley, come through the door, and, if possible, take stock of him before he saw me. It was almost certain he'd be the only guest of his age arriving at the restaurant. But what did I want, now? What did I expect? Did I want him, this one, to be the one for whom Beata nearly ran away from Francis, but didn't because of me and my sister?

This old man, now giving our order to the waitress – two Kirs to celebrate, trout paté for me, soup for him, then Dover sole for two with a bright Pinot Grigio? ("Yes, perfect," I murmured) – is tall, bulky, with ruddy colour on his veined cheeks and hands; hooded, colourless eyes; leathery jowls; careful good clothes, the collar and tie knotted high to conceal the tortoise neck; but swollen feet in orthopaedic sandals. A widower, he informs me; he clearly has savoir faire and old-world gallantry, he is suggesting the opera, talking of his neighbours in Hampshire, and the gardens that open to the public in his village; this old man in his old school tie is in his mid-eighties, florid and dilapidated, but still, doing well for his age, not altogether implausible in the role of a romantic adulterer in the tropics many decades ago; his old flat clumsy feet mourn the dancing partner who

13

took Beata by storm. Clark Gable, Cary Grant, they were her idea of a man: a certain caddish allure, the effrontery of their self-delight. But then Leslie Howard and, later, Anthony Perkins moved her to tears: the "gentle" in "gentleman" matters, she would say. Ronnie Quigley here at the restaurant, drinking his soup with as little mess as possible, could never have been as suave as Clark Gable or as sweetly cissy as Tony Perkins, but you never can tell.

"Could you bear to hear the story of my . . . friendship . . . with your mother?"

"Yes," I said. "I'm grown-up. She's dead. She died five years ago."

"On a scale of one to ten, how much of the truth can you take?"

"I'm not sure," I said. I was startled. "It rather depends what it is. But I would like to know."

I'd expected the reminiscing to be nostalgic, tender, but I straightened up as Ronnie Quigley was holding a tight smile on his dry, narrow mouth.

There were many things he began saying that matched what I know about those days:

"We first met at a terrific bash your father gave. At the Sporting Club, at Gezira. I was teaching, but I was considering the business I then took up – educational publishing for Africa. So I'd met Francis, of course. We'd common interests, and he invited me along. He was very hospitable. I was immediately overcome by your mother – everybody was. She was – well, you know. Who would have ever imagined a man like your father would be married to such a stunner!"

I shook my head, drank my Kir.

"She sent a note round after that first evening, asking me to come to tea. So it began. She was a free spirit. Your father was so much older, you know that. She was frustrated, stifled – she needed someone younger. I was younger. And more virile. I was that, too. I had the impression they had not been . . . well . . . lovers for some time when we met."

I winced, I nodded, I chewed on a piece of bread and paté.

"She was very direct. No, feisty. She was feisty." He brought out a clipping from a newspaper. "Look, here's a piece in *The Times* I cut out which talks about the meaning of the word 'feisty'.

"Your mother all over."

Over the next few years, work brought him back to Cairo at intervals, he said, from Botswana and Kenya and the Sudan where he was supplying schools and the universities that were just beginning throughout the continent. He'd visit Beata in the afternoons.

"One time, she sent me a note saying she was taking the boat from Alex and to meet her there to see her off. You were there, you were a little girl then. She told you to go and play on the deck where there were quoits and other games, and then she and I . . ."

I was following, making pictures in my mind as he was speaking, and they kept assembling and disassembling, between what I remembered of Beata, what I never knew, what I might never have known about her except for this old man with his lightless eyes, who was drinking and eating with appetite as he talked.

"There in the cabin, you know, I showed her ten inches of hard young male, which was much to her liking, and we did it there, in the cabin."

"No more!" I waved my hand at the old, bluish, dry lips, the rheumy, slightly bulging eyes. "Please."

It made no sense; I couldn't bear it to make sense.

There were some corroborating circumstances:

"Your father helped me out, one time. Good chap." Later, over the Dover sole, Ronnie Quigley went on, "I'd run into a spot of bother in Addis with the authorities. The Consul there got in touch with our man in Cairo, and he fixed things, but there was some money involved. Francis stumped up, you know. He said he knew Beata liked me."

But there were also discrepancies: the timings, the places. For one thing, Beata suffered horribly from seasickness: she never travelled anywhere by boat.

And there were other sides to the story Ronnie Quigley told me that veered wildly from what I knew; some won't bear repeating. For she was never bold, my mother, never direct, hungry, never ever "feisty". Weepy, guilty, whispering her prayers every Sunday, fastidious and full of decorum, however flirtatious.

I told Ronnie Quigley he had things all wrong, but he said he had told me everything, just as he remembered it.

That was a few months ago and now that I have had time to gather my wits together – and rinse my mind of the confusion and distaste he caused me – I can look at what he told me in a number of ways:

I can give him the benefit of the doubt, and imagine he has simply mixed my mother up with another woman, or with other women who he's been entangled with in the course of what has been, according to his own boasting, a very long and adventurous life.

Or, his mind is going: like a demented and senile ape he's trying to stir up his dead embers by talking dirty to strangers.

Or, he's made it all up: he's discovered a clever way of dating women who catch his eye on television – especially ones who might have a background with nice things. After he told me his so-called memories of my mother and I rebuffed him, he simply returned home and waited for another possible candidate to appear, to whom he could write a charming and mysterious letter suggesting he had known her mother rather well. He could take up Facebook, Facebook dating for Bluebeard, online lonely hearts for senior citizens.

Or I can believe him. I've heard from friends how retrieving the past can lead to disillusion. One young woman I know went looking for the mother who had given her up for adoption – but the first thrill of the reunion soon faded and perplexity set in, with the added sadness of entering a deeper level of estrangement based now on choice, not fate. Recognition in real life feels very different from that enthralled bliss that sweeps over dramatis personae and audience alike when the curtain falls on the foundling refound, the lost mother regained. My mother didn't give me up – she held on, against her own interests perhaps. But meeting her in Ronnie Quigley's story brought me face to face with someone I don't know. The family romance itself sours – the other family whose true child I am or might be brings nothing but disappointment in the end. And besides, when it comes to a stepfather manqué, another father who never was, the romance quest leads astray. My attempt to understand Beata's unhappiness will never be complete. It is possible that it's inspired not by what happened to her, whatever it was, but by my need to find she was more fulfilled than it appeared because she so often seemed deprived, constrained in her marriage to my father, and consequently envious of the freedom that life had lavished on me and my generation.

Or I could be looking for Ronnie Quigley, I could be inventing Ronnie Quigley, because he'd give me a reason not to feel guilty about that unhappiness of hers, that gaiety of hers that had so little chance for expression, guilty that sexual liberation came easily for me in my time and not for her in hers. Even though it would still be my fault that in the end she didn't run away.

"the simple, if
guilty, hope that in
the abyss that lay
between his dream
and his failure there
might be something
worth reading in
which the truth
could be felt"

Richard Flanagan

Joe the Crow

TOM C.B. WILLIAMS

When Joe the Crow finally turns up, he's face down in Jawbone Creek. He didn't show for the teardown in Penton, so we figured he'd flown the coop. That kid was flighty, and these things happen – every once in a while someone decides they've had enough and leaves. But we get enough suitcase acts over the season for the numbers to balance. So when Crow upped and vanished we all just kept moving.

Don't get me wrong, we were sad to lose him, but the show's gotta go on. Next town on the route card is Caster's Fields, last one of the summer, and this time we've struck oil. The fancy girls are having a good time, and their clean-shoed men spend big on games they'll never win. One week here and we'll be good through winter. Then the Penton cops catch up with us, and that's when we learn about Crow. Some kid playing hookey from school found him in the creek. No signs of foul play. Cops reckon he'd been drinking, probably slipped and drowned.

That don't sound much like Crow – he'd never slip and fall. We're talking about someone who could do a triple with no net. Not much of a drinker either. Anyhow, since I'm the closest Crow's got to any next of kin, turns out it's my job to haul ass back to Penton and identify his body.

Bones offers to drive me in the pick-up. Says he's fine with me smoking so long as he can whistle. He's special like that since his fall last season. Well, a deal's a deal, so we hit the road with the windows down, Bones whistling the theme tune to *Rawhide*.

"Hey, Cogs," says Bones at some point. "How come you don't drive?"

"Who says I don't?" I tell him. That gives him something to chew on.

We park up at Penton morgue. Bones tells me he wants to wait outside with the truck. Says morgues give him the shits ever since he got trapped in a freezer as a kid.

So I go inside and take a ticket, and when my number's called they point me downstairs. A white-coated lady asks me for ID. She's attractive without smiling, but I can't shake the thought that those fingers touch corpses on a daily basis. Under other circumstances I still probably would – but let's not forget that this is about Crow.

The lady mortician hands me a bag of Crow's personal effects – wallet, watch, keys, and that old brass Zippo lighter with the initials D. C. engraved on the front. He always carried it, even though he never smoked. This one time it was stolen from him, but Crow didn't get mad. He just set about investigating in his own silent way. And when he tracked it down to one of the sledge-gang giants, Crow waited for his moment and then stole it right back. Afterwards he told me that the lighter had belonged to his dad, who he'd never met. He didn't even know what the initials stood for, but it was all he had to go on.

I slip Crow's bag of things into my pocket, and then I follow the mortician along the corridor and into the chiller. When she slides the long drawer out of the wall, the cold pours down like stage smoke. Looks like she's performing a trick, but then she unzips the bag and there's no hiding the fact that the bony white corpse inside belongs to Joe the Crow.

His shins are covered with stake bites, just like mine, but that big old scar down the middle of his chest is Crow's alone. His lips are bloodless and smiling, like he died knowing something that no one else ever will. Kinda peaceful-looking, too.

"Mr Cogman," says the lady. "I'd like you to confirm the identity of the deceased."

"That's Crow all right," I tell her.

"Could you please confirm his full name?"

"Sure I can, he's Joe the Crow."

Her face tells me she's not the sort of woman who's ever been skinny-dipping.

"Joseph Nathaniel Lewis," she says, over her glasses like a teacher. "According to his driver's licence. Does that sound correct?"

"Whatever you say, lady. The kid was an enigma."

Because that's exactly what he was. He just appeared one day out of nowhere, and straight up asked if he could join us. He was a funny-looking kid, thin as a wire, home-made tattoos on the backs of his hands. His clothes were all black and way too big, so when the wind blew it looked like he was gonna fly away. Told us he'd train-hopped his way across the country and wanted something new, preferably paid. I asked him about his tricks but he had none, and he was way too small for the sledge gang, but something about this kid told me that he had potential. For what, exactly, I couldn't tell you, but potential nonetheless. And I was right – Crow turned out to be the best damn aerialist any of us ever saw. He was strong and light and totally fearless. I taught him everything I knew, but it turns out nothing teaches you to hang on better than the gap between railroad cars.

The lady mortician clears her throat and asks me if I need help with funeral arrangements. Penton is a small enough town that the morgue doubles as a funeral home, so then she starts going down this long list of expensive caskets with add-ons like mother-of-pearl inlay and crêped interior. I can see the coffers emptying right before my eyes. Seems there's good money in dead people.

I'm good at making decisions, so when she tells me she's heading back to her office to fetch a catalogue, I know what to do. Sorry, Crow, but you'd do the same.

Outside in the parking lot, it's hot as a hay harvest. Clouds are stacking up overhead ready to explode. Bones is leaning against the truck, picking his nose and whistling *Blackbird*. You should see the look on his face when he turns and sees me coming over, carrying Joe the Crow in my arms.

I hide the body in the bed of the pick-up. Bones knows not to ask any questions when I take the keys and get in the driver's seat.

Rain is coming down like a cow pissing on a flat rock. Halfway back to Caster's Fields we pull off the highway. Crow needs to be out in the open. There's other reasons too, but that's what I tell Bones. Given the conditions I'd say we gave him a respectable resting place. You try gravedigging in the pissing rain, headlights blinding, shoes not right for the job, mud falling back in the hole as fast as you can shovel.

We wrap Crow's body in a tarp and then tip him into the muddy hole. For a moment I think about throwing the old lighter in there too, but then something tells me I oughta hang on to it. Maybe one day I'll meet D. C. and give him back his Zippo. Stranger things have happened.

I scratch Crow's name into a rock with my pocket knife, and I stand there, hunched to keep the rain off my neck, while Bones whistles this long, sad song. Then right on cue, from far beyond the woods, comes the horn of a passing freight train.

Pelt

LOUISE SMITH

Today it's too hard watching everyone eat lunch so I slip out of hall and run down empty corridors, sliding on tiles, catching corners to brake, peering round in case Liam is waiting. I go out to the deserted playground and sit under the physics lab roof, picking the scab on my knee, tarmac cooling my shrinking thighs, enjoying the lightness in my head.

"Sarah," she whispers.

I leave my scab half lifted like a piecrust. Dawn is leaning against the side wall of the next block, holding some Tupperware. Ever since I started here she's been following me around.

"I want to show you something." Her hooked nose and lopsided grin promise danger, like when Punch creeps up on Judy in the puppet show. I don't move so she hunches down beside me, pulls off the lid and holds up something small and furry, the size of a coaster.

"What is it?" I ask.

"One of my gerbils died." She lays the skin on my hand and strokes it. "Beautiful, huh?" Her black eyes glint like coal.

I try to imagine the gerbil when it was alive, nestling in sawdust and nibbling on seeds, doing gerbil things, contented.

"My others died too." She puts the box in my lap. Inside are many skins, grey, brown and white, overlaid like carpet samples in a shop.

"How do you do it?"

"What?"

"How do you get the skins so perfect?"

"Practice." She puts the lid back on the box. "Do you want to go to the fair tomorrow?"

"Sure," I say, glad to have someone to go with.

The lesson bell goes.

Maths is OK because Tammy is in my class and she is much fatter than me. Still, I hang back at the door, waiting for Mr Miles to arrive. Liam and his friend Spencer clap and shout, "Dance, Tammy, dance," and Tammy, standing on her desk high above everyone, wiggles her feet, her doughy face searching for help. With her short blonde curly hair, she looks like a giant Tiny Tears doll someone put a uniform on. Liam is small so if she sat on him she could easily crush him. But she just blinks at him, as if she really is a toy and that is all she can do.

"What are you waiting for?" Mr Miles shoves me into the classroom. "Tammy, you stupid lump, get down. See me after for a detention ticket."

I don't know how I know but I know Tammy's parents are deaf and I wonder what sign language is for "I got a detention."

Hot wind licks my skin and the earth, wet and muddy from last night's thunderstorm, is trying to suck my pumps from my feet as I trudge across the common to the fair. My stomach growls at the smell of fried onions and spit floods my mouth. I wonder if it has any calories and pop a strong mint, concentrating on the heat rising through my cheeks, causing my head to ache. The gravity cage starts up, spinning slowly, then faster and faster, until it's a blur. Pantomime laughter booms from the ghost train, drowning out the pop songs and the yells of the ride hands. Screams rise and fade in the air.

Dawn is standing by the waltzer where she said she'd be, scratching the eczema on her neck, which is brown and crispy like the toffee apple she is crunching.

"Want some?"

I step back, but not before she's waved it under my nose and I get a torturing whiff of caramel. "No thanks."

She shrugs, tossing it half eaten onto the grass. An old man holding a goldfish in a plastic bag shakes his head and glares at her. She answers him with a sneer, pumping her hand fast like she's wanking a boy off.

"Disgusting," he mutters, turning away.

I'm glad I'm with Dawn because she doesn't seem afraid of anyone.

"Come on," she says.

I follow her over the wooden floor to the nearest carriage. She smells of wee, as though her clothes haven't been aired, or maybe it's old sweat trapped in her fat rolls. I shift away, watching the man collecting the money. It's important to act scared so he'll spin you.

The platform turns, the tiny wheels under us screeching in their brackets. I imagine being flung out and smashed. The man is here, blue tattoos on his red arms.

"No, no," I plead and he grins, yanking us round hard like I want. I have to grip the bar so I don't touch Dawn. She's screaming her head off already. I'm praying she doesn't throw up on me when she elbows me in the ribs and points at the shooting gallery. Liam is handing a rifle back. Spencer is struggling with a black-and-white pit bull tugging on its lead.

The ride stops but the world is still spinning as Dawn pulls me off the waltzer, following them.

"I want to go on the gravity cage," I say, wriggling, as she drags me into a gap between the ghost train and a trailer.

"We should teach Liam a lesson," she says.

"How? He doesn't care about anything."

"What about his dog?" She pushes me forward so I can see round the corner of the trailer.

The pit bull is pogoing, attacking a swirl of candyfloss Liam is holding out of reach.

"I want to go on the rides."

"Come on. Let's take his dog. It'll be a laugh," she insists.

"But it hasn't done anything wrong." I stare at a used condom wrinkling in the mud.

"It's only a dog," she says. "He would do it to you. Don't you want him to leave you alone?"

"I'm not bothered," I lie. I want that more than anything.

"Look, they're over by the dodgems. Get on."

I think maybe I should just go home, but I don't want to be there either, so I do as she says, running out in front of them.

"Dollop woman, dollop woman. Ha, ha!" they shout.

I get into an empty car and grip the wheel, feeling sick. Spencer ties the dog to a post and jumps in next to Liam who is reversing his car to follow me. Panic makes me drop my coin. As I fumble for it under the pedals they judder closer. Fear squirts through my bum. I find the coin, drop it in the slot and drive away. I let them corner me against the barrier. They ram me hard, reverse and ram me again, laughing. Behind them Dawn unties the lead and skips off with the dog. When she's gone, I jump out, run to the House of Fun and hide behind a line of parents queuing with their kids.

Liam dashes to the post then punches Spencer in the head. I follow them as they circle round the fair, Liam calling out "Tyson," over and over, until it grows dark and they give up.

Monday breaktime Liam has me cornered by the tuck shop. He spits on me.

"That's for making me lose Tyson, you stupid fat bitch." He has a black eye. I wonder how he got it.

Dawn is behind him, sitting on the bench, sucking a green chewy stick, Tyson's lead hanging out of her pocket. I shake my head at her. Liam looks over his shoulder. I get ready to run, but she winds it in with a magician's speed, smiles at him and carries on sucking her chew.

"Are you fucking stupid or what?" Liam spits at me again. "I said that's for making me lose Tyson."

"I'm sorry you lost your dog. Maybe he'll come back."

He runs at me but I swerve him.

"You think you're fucking clever? Spencer, kick the stupid fat bitch."

Spencer lunges but the tuck-shop lady sticks her face out of the window, so he shuffles back, head down.

"You wait, we're gonna do you properly, you ugly dollop bitch," Liam hisses.

The other kids just stand there staring. Then the bell goes and everyone except Dawn wanders off. Two girls I don't know from the year below look back and whisper. I wait for them to turn away again before shaking my hair to get rid of Liam's gob.

"Put it in his desk after school." Dawn hands me the lead.

I curl my fists tight. "I can't, he'll know it was us. Where's Tyson?"

"In my dad's garage." She traps the chewy stick between her teeth, pulls it into a long strand and slides it down her throat like a big snake swallowing a small snake.

"Doesn't he bark?" I pick up my backpack, trying to remember what my next lesson is.

"I took some chloroform from the biology lab."

I picture Tyson sleeping peacefully between a bike and a lawnmower, having dog dreams. I decide he could be more comfortable so I add a blanket, a blue tartan one, a window, and then a sunbeam coming through the glass, warming his head.

My bag is on my back now so I can't stop her putting the lead in.

"Look, stupid, he knows it wasn't you because you were on the dodgems. That should make you want to hurt him more."

Mr Miles makes me sit next to him so that he can help me with algebra. His hand brushes my knee, the hairs on his knuckles tickling me in a way I don't like. Because I'm trying to decide if Dawn is right about Liam the symbols swim before my eyes. Instead I watch Katy. She's the prettiest girl in our year and she gets top marks for everything. Liam is leaning over to her, trying to see her answers. She shifts, covering her book, so he leans back against his chair and gives me the finger. The bell goes.

With everyone gone, the classroom is stuffy, like how it must feel to be inside a coffin. Liam's desk is a dustbin: sweet wrappers, an aerosol can with no lid, a big tube of UHU. I pick up an empty Sunblest bag but drop it because it's all sticky. On the underside of the desk lid is a Polaroid of Tyson as a puppy, lying in a bed of yellow flowers, head between his paws. On the bottom border are the words, "Tyson my champ". I take a felt tip out of my bag and write on the top border, "Tyson, our hostage", drop the lead and go home.

I hate French. Because it's Tuesday Mr Raymond is asking us questions about our weekend. Katy's parents took her to Alton Towers for her birthday. Typical. There's a fair in town and she gets the luxury option. Dawn's next. She smiles at me and for a second I think she is going to tell him what we did.

"*J'étais malade. Je suis allée chez le médecin.*"

She's a good liar. I'm looking forward to more details of her illness.

"*Ou le vétérinaire, peut-être?*" Mr Raymond cocks his head.

Katy starts giggling and everyone joins in, like it's the funniest thing they've ever heard.

Dawn just sits there grinning, scratching the scabs on her neck, drawing fresh blood, which drips, spotting her collar.

For the rest of the lesson I think about the rumour that Mr Raymond is shagging Katy. It makes sense. She looks kind of like Brigitte Bardot.

Walking to our next class, Liam grabs Dawn's satchel, empties it, sending her lunch box spinning. Spencer lobs her apple onto the playing field and chews her sandwiches with his mouth open, showing us the mess behind his rotten teeth. Mr Raymond walks past towards his clapped-out 2CV, swinging his old leather briefcase. I leave Dawn picking up her stuff and go to Geography.

Wednesday lunchtime, I'm warming myself under the hand drier in the girls' toilets. Katy and her friends, Beth and Joanne, are putting on make-up in front of the mirror.

"Jamie's bound to ask you out," Beth says to Katy.

He's the best-looking boy in our year so it makes sense for him to be with Katy.

"Do you think so?" Katy brushes her long golden hair, smiling in the mirror like she can't help flirting with herself.

I look out of the window. Liam is chasing Tammy, whipping her sweat-drenched back with the chain part of Tyson's lead. He corners her by the bins but I can't see any more because other kids are crowding round.

"Are you going to the disco?" Katy is talking to me but smiles at her friends.

"Why would I want to listen to the shit music you all like?" I say, turning from the drier and walking to the door. "Anyway, there'll be no booze. Can't think of a more boring waste of time."

"Can you get us some?" asks Katy.

I stop. "Maybe. Depends what you want. There's a bottle of Malibu in my mum's cupboard."

"Yeah. That'll do. Bring it tomorrow."

I've started walking home to lose more weight. It takes two hours but it's OK, no one knows. Dad goes to the pub after work and Mum is always in bed when I get home. The tablets for her depression make her sleepy.

When I check on her she tells me to get her a beer. In the fridge, besides her cans, there is a hard corner of cheese. I sniff it. The tangy smell of mould makes me gag and forget I'm hungry. I have a swig of Malibu and put it in my bag. Mum won't say anything because she'll think she finished it in a blackout.

I'm washing my uniform dress in the kitchen sink when the phone rings. It's Dawn. She tells me that Liam and Tammy have been suspended.

"What are you going to do with Tyson?" I'm sitting on the bottom stair, stroking the smooth scar on my knee, feeling sorry the scab has gone and I can't pick it just right so it doesn't bleed.

"The chloroform's running out. We need to decide soon," she says.

"So what are you going to do?" I ask again.

"What do you think?"

"I don't know," I say. "You wanted him. Are you going to keep him?"

"I can't. My dad doesn't like dogs."

"So we should take him back, then."

"Can't you have him for a bit?"

"I have a dog," I lie. "Maybe we can leave him at a refuge?"

"No. Not yet. Liam still needs to learn." She hangs up.

"What are you feeding Tyson?"

Dawn and I both have a free period on Thursday afternoons so we're sitting on the tennis courts with our skirts hitched up, tanning our legs.

"Scraps from the bin. There's not much, though. My dad hates waste. If I leave dinner I have to eat it the next day. You any good at shoplifting?"

"Never tried."

"See if you can nick a can of dog food."

"We can buy it."

"If you really cared about Tyson, you'd steal it. Do you want him to die?"

"You got that Malibu?" Katy walks onto the court.

Dawn stares at her as I get it out of my bag.

"Thanks." Katy stares back at Dawn, looking her up and down, smirking and twirling her hair. "You coming Saturday night, then? You can both hang out with me if you bring more booze."

Dawn watches Katy go. "Why you bothering with her? She's just using you."

"Why don't you come? We could get pissed. It'd be a laugh." I zip my bag shut.

Dawn stands up, stretching. "Maybe."

"I'll take Tyson to the rescue home on Sunday morning. I can collect him if you tell me your address."

She stands closer, blocking out the sun. "No, you'll be too tired after the disco."

I think the rescue home is a stupid idea anyway. If nobody wants him, they'll have him put down. "Liam's learnt his lesson."

Dawn scratches her neck. "Why do you even care about him? He hates you."

"I don't care."

"You really going?"

"Yeah."

"I can't come. Got nothing to wear."

"We can go shopping Saturday morning. I'll do your hair."

"I don't want you to do my hair." She walks off.

The next morning, Dawn is waiting for me at the school gates. She hands me an envelope with Liam's name on. "Tyson's claws were too long so I clipped them."

When I shake the envelope the claws rattle like drawing pins.

"Tonight we are going to put it through his letter box," she says.

"Can't we just put it in his desk again?"

"Where's the fun in that?" She laughs, swinging her satchel above her head.

"How do you know where he lives?"

"I've been watching him."

I'm late for assembly so I stand with the big girls at the back and wonder if it will be better when I'm older like them. Mrs Shaw, our headmistress, is speechifying. She will not accept violence in her school, she had no option but to suspend Liam and Tammy; no drinking at the disco; well done to the rugby team for another win; let's sing *All Things Bright and Beautiful*. Everything goes black.

"You fainted," the school nurse says. "It's probably the heat."

"Can I stay here?"

Her office is bright and cool and white. It smells of antiseptic, like a hospital, only nicer because there are no patients.

"Come on, you look sturdy enough."

On my way to English I decide I won't even have a Weetabix with water tonight. I'll have a cup of OXO instead. I read in my mum's *Woman's Own* magazine there's only twenty calories in an OXO. I weighed myself in Boots last night and I've lost another half a stone, but it can't be enough because no one's noticed.

After school, we're on the bus, heading to the east side of the city, the poor end, where all the immigrants and dole scroungers live. Dawn eats a family-size bar of chocolate, not even chewing the chunks, just swallowing them whole. Roads narrow, houses shrink, trees disappear. We get off. She hands me the envelope.

"I'm not doing it," I say. "It was your idea."

She ignores me and turns into a side street. She points to a house with an old washing machine in the front garden. "If you don't do it, I'll knock on the door and tell him you made me take Tyson."

The garden isn't very long and the curtains are drawn. I grab the envelope, drop it through the letterbox and run after Dawn who is already halfway down the street, laughing.

Back in town she says goodbye. "You're all right, you are." She hugs me so tight I can't breathe. "Maybe I will come tomorrow."

I follow her, but at a distance, worrying she'll hear me even though she has her headphones on. She stops at a big ivy-covered house and lets herself in. I can't see the garage. It must be at the back. I inch over the gravel towards the metal garden gate and peer over. At the far end is a rotten shed with boarded-up windows, its door flecked with blue paint and fastened with rope. I hear Dawn whistling and duck. Through the gate keyhole I see her walk across the grass to the shed. She is wearing a helmet with a lamp on it like potholers wear. Thinking of Tyson lying on his own in the dark for a whole week makes me feel so sad I decide to wait so I can take him to Liam tonight. But Dawn is in there so long my knees go numb from squatting and my feet get pins and needles. I rock back on my heels. An old lady is watching me from the upstairs window of the house next door. I jump up, pull my bag over my shoulder and ignoring the stabbing pains in my feet, run off.

Dad's whisky and Mum's cans are clinking in the carrier bag as I walk across the park to the war memorial. I'm wearing the new dress from Miss Selfridge that I bought this morning with the twenty quid I nicked from Mum's purse. I love the design, a Native American print with a fringe of coloured feathers round the neck. It's this summer's look. My flat, black school shoes don't match but I didn't have enough for the moccasins the shop girl tried to sell me. I spent hours braiding my hair into tiny plaits, following the instructions in *Sugar* magazine. Now I really do look like the squaw in the picture.

It's quiet, just some old people walking their dogs. A scruffy terrier bounds over and sniffs at my ankles. I pat him too hard and as he shrinks, I remember to set my watch alarm for 4 a.m. so I can get Tyson before anyone is awake.

I read the names of dead soldiers carved on the stone: Leonard, Arthur and Stanley. Names only old people have now. Stanley was seventeen, three years older than me. I wonder if he was handsome. And then Ian, the boy I like, is in my head, charging with a bayonet through a smoking field.

Katy and her friends are passing the Malibu as they walk. Beth is wearing the same dress as me. Katy's dress is suede, with tassels, the most expensive one in Miss Selfridge. She is wearing the moccasins I couldn't afford. I swig some whisky and wave.

"Your hair looks nice." Katy sits down next to me. "Give us some of that."

I pass the bottle over and pull the ring on a lager can, forcing myself to swallow, hating its malty taste.

"You can't come," says Beth to me, "not wearing my dress."

"Shut up," says Katy. "It's not like she looks better than you."
They all laugh.

I take another swig. Beth's brown hair is in one thick, single side plait. She looks more like the model in *Sugar* than me. "Yeah, don't worry, you look really good," I say, thinking that soon I'll be thinner than her.

"I'm not worried." Beth bends down and snatches the can from my hand. Lager slops onto my dress.

They talk about the boys they're going to snog. I touch the scar on my knee that I've tried to hide with make-up. Joanne says Ian's been asking her out for months but she's not sure whether she should kiss him because he's shorter than her.

Even if Ian asks me to dance I won't now because it will piss her off.

"You've lost weight," Katy says. "What's your secret?"

"I think it's the heat." I'm really happy that she's noticed.

"My mum's put me on that SlimFast diet," she says. "It's wicked. I lost four pounds this week. How much have you lost?"

"I dunno, probably the same." I'm hoping Dawn doesn't come now.

When we arrive, Mr Miles is alone in the middle of the hall, wearing a pink Hawaiian shirt and dancing to *Like a Virgin* like he's having a fit. He's still wearing his thick glasses and grey nylon trousers so he looks like a mad person dressed from a charity shop. He waves at me but I pretend not to see him. We sit down. Katy opens the Coke bottle she mixed the whisky into and tells Beth to get some paper cups from the buffet table. She nudges me.

"What do you think of Paul?"

"He's all right, I suppose." I don't really think anything about Paul except he's not Ian, and his hair is brown, not blond.

"He'll dance with you if I tell him to."

"I don't feel like dancing."

She struts to where Paul is standing with Jamie, Ian and the other boys by the speakers. They are all wearing jeans and T-shirts, looking nothing like the male models in the *Sugar* Native American spread. They crowd round her in a scrum.

Prince Charming starts. Paul walks over and pulls me up from my chair. Everyone dances in lines, like in the video. I look around thinking Adam Ant would be really impressed and see Liam at the front, really going for it, eyes glazed, singing. *Don't you ever, don't you ever, stop being dandy showing me you're handsome.* They must have let him come because he's in the rugby team and the disco is a fund-raiser for their French tour. Paul can't keep up because he's watching Katy dancing next to Jamie and trying to edge closer to them. The DJ, knowing he's on a roll, plays *Kings of the Wild Frontier*.

Katy goes back to her seat and because her friends follow, I do too. It's a boys' song anyway. They jump up and down to the drums, flinging their arms around, looking more like proper Indians now. I sing along – *A new royal family, a wild nobility, we are the family* – but trail off when I see Dawn at the doorway. She looks amazing; hair a massive Mohican and warpaint on her face. She is carrying a toy bow and arrow. She holds it up and pulls the string tight, aiming the plug to where Liam is dancing, landing kicks on the other boys. It bounces off his head unnoticed. I gulp down my drink and go over.

"You came."

"Do you like my dress?"

I don't really see her dress because I'm staring at the braid around her neck that is threaded with small fangs. I realise looking at Dawn that *Sugar* was right: accessories make all the difference to an outfit. She looks way better than me. I'm annoyed I couldn't afford any of the jewellery in Miss Selfridge but I force a smile anyway. "You look really great, like a chief's wife."

"Here." She reaches into her dress pocket. "I brought you these for being such a good friend." She puts a pair of earrings in my hand, like the fangs on her necklace, only bigger.

"Thanks." They're heavier than I expected, like stones.

Dawn takes one from my palm. "Let me," she says, and as she reaches for my ear, an odd smell stings my nose.

I know it and try to think where from. As she's fixing the other earring, my eyes start to burn and stream. Then I remember. It's the same smell that flooded the biology lab that time the specimen jars fell off the shelf and we all had to be evacuated.

Love Story
HEIDI NORDMANN

Middle

Silence had penetrated Gustav and expanded inside him. The white walls of the house reflected the sun and blinded him. There were anemones in the field surrounding the house, and it all became a blur. For this reason, Gustav's egg was brown. He held it between his forefinger and thumb and gradually applied pressure until it broke. Yolk ran down his arm. A drop reached the garden chair before he captured the spill with kitchen towels and disposed of them in a half-full bucket. He took up a new egg, closed his eyes and clenched his buttocks simultaneously with the pressure he put on the shell. *Crack.* Lasse leaned towards Gustav and put paper towels over his lap, spilling a glass of milk in the process. Full-fat milk seeped through the table and onto the wooden deck. Jocko grabbed the kitchen paper and unrolled it across the tabletop, patting it to speed the soaking-up, while Lasse dried the milk off the floor with his socks. They looked at each other and sighed.

"Gustav, we disapprove of this waste of eggs," Jocko said. "There are a dozen good omelettes in that bucket, a hundred grams of protein, at least."

The sun shone behind passing clouds, flirting with Gustav, caressing him like a woman's soft fingertips every time it came out. Gliding from his hands, up his arms to his neck, it made his body hair rise. With sticky fingers, Gustav stroked his skin.

*

The man with feathers glued to his naked body didn't notice that people were laughing as he focused on releasing the raw egg from his rectum without causing spillage. A mother killing her offspring before its birth was still taboo and not an issue the man aimed to address but he had overestimated his own capacity to handle stress and shortly after he had inserted the egg his muscles contracted. Yolk ran down his thigh.

The nemophilists had brought their binoculars, and were looking for wildlife as they waited. Children ran between the carved trolls in the open area where trees had been cut down for wood. One tree lasted a household the year, and new spruce were planted in replacement. The stumps remained, and the local woodcarver had busy summers turning them into trolls and goblins. The forest was full of such figures and had recently been discovered by tourists who came all the way from Japan to the little village to look at them.

The queue at the lake was long, and Jocko and Lasse passed the time gossiping, about tourists with strange habits, the new abortion law, and the naked maniac who had dressed like a chicken. Jocko cringed. When they reached the front of the queue, they filled their bottles and buckets with water, reported ten litres to the minute-taker, ran to the tree where Gustav had been tied to a branch, and climbed up to him. Jocko washed yolk off Gustav's body, and the blood from the rope burns, while Lasse held a bottle of water to his mouth so he could drink.

Beginning

A virtual seam in the sea, separating the green and the turquoise water, showed the guys where it was safe to sail and where it was shallow. They never crossed the line as they traced the coast and navigated away from the bay. Gustav leaned over the side and wiggled his forefinger in the water, creating the pattern of a sea snake following the boat. The snake shook its tail, blurring the line between deep and shallow, and Jocko told Gustav to sit back up in the boat so he wouldn't fall out.

Half a kilometre from the coast there was only an onshore wind, so the sails were down. Gustav's hair flapped in sync with the Norwegian flag at the aft. The humming from the engine and the squawks from the seagulls were isolated by the trees on the shoreline. The *Møyfrid*, a twenty-seven-foot Albin Vega, was the only boat on the water.

Gustav ordered Lasse and Jocko to take off their shirts.

It was low tide; algae had washed up and dressed the rocks in green. Steam rose from the reef and the air looked hazy. The smell of seaweed and saltwater blended with the smell of coconut sun lotion. Gustav drew a heart of sunscreen between Lasse's shoulder blades. Lasse shuddered when the cold cream touched him. Gustav rubbed the lotion in, applying pressure on the muscles on either side of the spine, from Lasse's lower back up to the knots under his shoulder blades, and from his shoulders up his neck to his head. Gustav applied more sunscreen and rubbed Lasse's neck with his thumbs, in deep circular movements. Lasse's jaw unclenched. Gustav rubbed his temples. The wrinkles between Lasse's eyebrows softened, he closed his eyes and sighed.

Lasse's frame was smaller than Gustav's and Jocko's, but his back was full of tension and Gustav's hands soon got tired.

Gustav shook out his hands and applied sunscreen on Lasse's arms. Lasse grabbed Gustav's wrists. He took the sun lotion from him, squeezed a drop onto Gustav's palm, and massaged his hands, between his fingers, the fingertips. They looked at each other and smiled. Gustav reclaimed the sunscreen.

"Give me that, Freckles," he said, and continued massaging it into Lasse's skin. He looked at the birthmarks on Lasse's shoulders and back, and applied another layer.

Gustav stepped over to Jocko at the rudder, drew on his back with sun lotion and giggled. Jocko looked back at him and smiled. Gustav stroked Jocko's wide shoulders, and tickled the sides of his neck. He felt the texture of Jocko's defined muscles under his fingertips, the hair on his upper back, a few lumps on his shoulders. Lasse took a palmful of sunscreen and positioned himself behind Gustav. Lasse rubbed Gustav who rubbed Jocko. The water sparkled and reflected the sun, and Jocko reached for his sunglasses. Lasse hugged Gustav who hugged Jocko. Jocko shook loose, gave the rudder to Gustav and stepped to the outboard motor.

Two men were fishing on an islet. They looked at the boat and Gustav waved at them. A fish jumped out of the water. Jocko shifted gear on the engine, and they steered further out from the coastline.

Cumulus clouds created a vegetable garden in the sky. Small formations of cauliflowers crept close, and formed a thick band over the shoreline. A kilometre from land, the air was colder. Gustav stroked his fingers over the surface of the water. It was lukewarm.

"It's just the air that's cold," he said. "We can swim here."

A gust turned slightly to starboard, but the sails didn't get a hold of it. The guys' nipples hardened and Jocko's chest hair rose. Gustav handed them life vests and they put them on.

"Actually, it's probably warmer in the water than above it," Gustav said.

The clouds drifted further out to sea, and the gusts came at regular intervals every five minutes. They raised the sails.

They sailed around an islet, scouting it out. No people, no boats, only seagulls. Jocko switched off the engine. Gustav let go of the rudder, stripped down to his boxer shorts, folded his clothes neatly and went inside. He appeared in the doorway, dragging a long plastic bag after him.

"Open it inside the boat," Lasse said.

Gustav went back inside and pulled the bag while Lasse pulled out the contents, smashing Jocko with the fish fin, and laid it out on the floor, half of it sticking over the side of the boat. A one-and-a-half-metre-long mermaid tail encased in silicone glistened in the sun. The shell sparkled and nuances of green, blue and turquoise rolled over the tail. Gustav came outside with baby oil and lotioned up. He stroked the shell, and the colours of the rainbow washed over it. He smiled. The silicone was smooth. He felt the texture of the fin and traced it down to the tip of the tail. A zip was hidden on the belly side of the shell. He opened it and put the tail on; Lasse helped him close it.

"It feels stiff," Lasse said. "Are you sure you can swim in this? Or at least, avoid sinking?"

Jocko grabbed Gustav around the waist and lifted him to the aft.

"Hang on to the boat and see. The suit is pretty heavy," Jocko said. "You should wear a life vest."

"Mermaids don't have life vests," Gustav said and lowered

himself from the dock ladder and into the water. He let out a squeak.

"Cold," he said.

Jocko threw out the lifebuoy.

"Just hang on to it," he said.

Gustav hung on to the ladder and wiggled his tail. The *Møyfrid* moved and the guys laughed.

"Should've put you in the suit earlier, Gustav, saved us the petrol," Lasse said.

Gustav moaned and struggled with his technique, slowly manoeuvring the boat. Lasse put on swimming trunks, sat down on the ladder and put his feet in the water.

"Iiik!"

Gustav splashed water on Lasse's legs and laughed. Lasse wrapped his feet around Gustav's waist.

"Try to hold on to my legs instead, and see how it feels to swim," Lasse said.

Gustav held on to Lasse's legs and let go of the boat, but Lasse slipped under the weight and landed on his back in the water.

"The lifebuoy!" Jocko said and reached his hand out to the guys. Lasse grabbed Jocko by the wrist and got a hold on the ladder. They laughed.

"Probably best not to swim in that thing," Lasse said. He put the lifebuoy around Gustav and climbed back into the boat, while Gustav held on to the ladder.

The water vibrated, and they heard the sound of an engine. They looked around.

"Gustav, stay in the water," Jocko said.

The sound grew louder, and a small fishing boat appeared. Gustav gripped the ladder, pushing himself down in the water so only his face from the mouth up was above it. The boat drew up alongside the Albin Vega. A man and a youth came out. Jocko nodded at them. The youth nodded back. The man and the youth looked at Gustav in the water, and Lasse positioned himself in front of him.

"Out fishing?" the man said.

"Just enjoying the sun," Jocko said.

The man sought eye contact.

"That's a shame," he said. "It's a good day for fishing. I hear there are large fish to be caught today." He looked at the youth beside him. "We're going for the big fish, aren't we?" He nodded to the youth, who held a harpoon.

"Fuck yeah," he said. They grinned.

Jocko took a step towards them.

"Well, don't let us scare the fish away from you. I'm sure you'll have luck at Vatlastraumen." He looked at the man. "We're just here to relax."

The man went inside the boat, watching Jocko through the window. The boat circled around them before it headed off, keeping in sight of the Albin Vega. Gustav stayed in the water for forty-five minutes, until the fishing boat left. The guys helped him onboard and out of the costume. He was shaking, his fingers too cold to dry himself, so Lasse dried him, helped him put his clothes on, and wrapped him in blankets.

They sailed past barren islets and an empty fish farm. The lighthouse was dark. Next to it, in a once yellow house, the windows were barricaded and the paint peeled off.

They approached Rondalen and the wind got hold of the sails. It raced down the windward side of the mountain, and died out when they sailed past the mountain's highest point. They reached the dale, and the *Møyfrid* sped up again. Five boathouses stood on the shore, and tiny red farmhouses dotted the top of the mountain. There was a tractor in a field, but no people or animals to be seen.

Gustav looked up at the sky. The clouds were getting darker. In between the cauliflowers, Gustav could see that they were white, but the sun shone down on them, and the clouds devoured the light, leaving the underside grey and gloomy. Jocko looked up from the GPS and laughed.

"Ten knots," he said.

The coastline merged with the sea. Dark-blue water turned black turned grey, tracing up a tall cliff to the charcoal sky, and a circle closed in on Gustav. The sky was the sea and he was in it, the horizon a drain and he was running down it.

The *Møyfrid* tilted sideways in a wave, and Gustav bumped into Lasse who grabbed him. Something inside smashed.

"Heads down," Jocko said.

The guys ducked and Jocko tried to tack, but the sails lost the wind and flickered. Lasse and Gustav tried to move the boom manually, but the wind was too strong.

"Stop, stop," Jocko said. "You'll be tossed overboard."

The boat continued to lean sideways in the swell. Jocko started the engine and steered towards the cliff. They rode the waves and moved slowly nearer, hearing the splashing get louder as the breakers hit the wall of rock and bounced back. Closer to the cliff the waves were standing, pulsating like one big vein, and the boat dipped up and down without leaving the spot.

"Fuck, man. We're stuck," Jocko said.

It started to rain.

The *Møyfrid* keeled forty-five degrees to each side. Inside, bags and cups scraped the floor. A bucket of water for flushing the toilet had spilled, and the floor was soaked. Outside, the waves hit the deck with force, sounding like whip lashes. The ropes creaked. Gustav went inside to secure loose items, struggling to keep balance. A can of chickpeas hit him in the thigh. Spare socks and home-knitted jumpers lay in the water on the floor, and the sofas were drenched.

It rained horizontally, and the boat kept careening. Jocko tried to steer it to meet the waves, but the wind pattern was unpredictable and the waves were messy.

"Get the mainsail down so I can steer," Jocko said.

Gustav and Lasse loosened the rope, but it got stuck. The sail smacked the air. Lasse and Gustav both pulled the rope, but it didn't move. The fishing boat appeared a kilometre away, and Gustav pointed at it.

"Maybe it can tow us," he said. The boat careened and he fell to the side, grabbing the backstay.

"Fuck that," Jocko said and waved the guys away.

Lasse took the rudder, and Jocko grabbed the rope. Lasse tried to meet the surf, but a two-metre-tall wave rose and threatened to bury them. It towered over the boat, and looked as if it would pull them down and put a lid on the sea, or send them into the wave in front of it. The guys screamed, but the Albin Vega rode the swell. Jocko yanked the rope free, and took the sails down.

The fishing boat drove away, and was reduced to a speck on

the horizon.

The air filled with vibrations, and a low rumbling sound lingered. Gustav looked up, rain hitting his face and making it difficult to keep his eyes open. The clouds seemed to have lowered themselves from the sky, and were closing in on the boat.

"Please tell me that was the rope," Lasse said.

Grumbles came from above.

"Nope, that was definitely –"

"Thunder," Lasse and Gustav said.

The sky changed from ash to white, and an electric worm wiggled between two clouds.

"Gustav, go inside and get the box from under the galley," Jocko said.

Gustav retrieved the box, opened it, took out two jump cables, screamed and threw them back inside the boat. Gustav and Lasse looked at Jocko.

"What the hell?" Gustav said. "Thunder, water, electricity. What's the logic here?"

"Lightning rod," Jocko said. "Minimises the damage if the boat is struck."

"Won't it make it more likely we get hit?" Lasse said.

"Yes," Jocko said.

Lasse hid his head in his hands.

"Veto," he said.

"Hang on, wait," Gustav said. "Will we get hit either way? I mean, what are our odds?"

Jocko looked around. Away from the cliff the sea was open; there were no other boats in sight, no mountaintops or islands nearby. Just the Albin Vega, with its seven-metre-tall mast.

"I haven't a clue actually," Jocko said. "But if I'm on deck steering and we're struck . . ."

"No one stays on deck," Gustav said. "Come on, we're going inside."

He took Jocko's hand, but Jocko shook it off. He gave the rudder to Lasse and went inside, but came back out with the jumper cables.

"You wanna drift further out? And be inside the boat when we tilt?" He got out a knife and started de-insulating the cable.

"I'm the captain. VHF radio and phones off, and go inside," he said.

Lightning struck inside a cloud above them, followed by a rumble. Jocko dropped the knife and looked up. Three successive strokes of lightning hit the water in the same spot on the horizon.

"Holy fuck, we're in line with the storm," Jocko said. "Maybe it will hit the fishing boat." Thunder rumbled and he shouted, "Someone time it."

"Fuck timing it, we're standing in water," Lasse said. "We need to go inside. All of us."

"The lightning rod," Jocko said.

"Standing in water, Jocko," Lasse said.

He looked at Gustav who nodded. They grabbed Jocko and dragged him with them inside the boat, taking the jumper cables with them.

"The headsail," Jocko said. "We've got to take it down. We'll capsize. We'll drown."

Lasse closed the hatch and locked it while Gustav held Jocko down. They lay on top of him on the sofa until he stopped resisting.

The sky turned white outside the window, and it sounded like a ton of rocks were dropped on asphalt from the sky, and kept falling in smaller and smaller loads. Jocko tried counting the seconds between light flashes and the thunder. The guys held each other, but the boat careened. Gustav looked around.

"I used all the rope to secure loose items," he said.

He stood up to untie a bag and was tossed against a cupboard on the other side. He slid down to the floor, and the guys sat down with him. Gustav had a cut above his eyebrow.

It sounded like a gun was fired outside, and the shot echoed. The guys flinched.

"Oh my God, it's the fishermen coming to off us," Gustav said. His nose stung, pain shooting up his sinus to his head, and tears streamed. He wiped his eyes and smeared blood across his forehead.

"It's just the lightning," Lasse said.

He raised himself onto his knees and reached for the rope, but fell down again when the boat tilted. He waited till they were between waves, and stood up to continue untying until he got the rope loose. The guys crawled up to the cabin and into bed. They took off their wet clothes and wrapped themselves in the blankets, tying the rope tight around them. They rolled from side to side in the waves, hitting the walls. Sandwiched between Lasse and Jocko, Gustav could hear their heartbeats and focused on counting them. He closed his eyes.

Gustav looked at the ceiling and realised that his face was jammed between two pillows. For a second he didn't remember why he was tied together with Lasse and Jocko. He wiggled and the guys woke up. They untied themselves and got out of the cabin. It was dim and Lasse reached for the light switch, but Gustav stopped him. The air was cold against their clammy, half-naked bodies. Their clothes lay wet on the floor, and they wrapped themselves in the damp blankets they'd slept in. Looking around, they saw that nothing important seemed to have been broken.

They went outside.

The wind had died down. The boat had become an ingredient in a steaming bowl of fish soup between the mountains. Mist blurred the line between sea and land, and condensation covered the boat. Lasse started laughing. He grabbed Gustav's shoulders and shook him. They hugged. Jocko looked at the GPS.

"If this thing still works," he said. "Guys, we're in Vatlastraumen." Gustav and Lasse cheered. "Down with the sail," Jocko said. "Gustav, take the rudder."

"The aim is not –"

"I know, that's why the sail's gotta come down. Shit," Jocko said.

Jocko and Lasse took the sail down and put the lanterns on. On the coast, green trees, red boathouses and a yellow cabin faded into grey. White clouds from the water blended with the sky. The trees and buildings disappeared and only the contour of small islands carved into the fog.

"Now what? Do we sail blind? Do we anchor?" Gustav and Lasse looked at Jocko.

"Sail by GPS. Anchor. Shit," Jocko said. "We turn a hundred and eighty degrees." Jocko looked at the GPS.

"Are you serious?" Lasse said. "We're almost home." They looked at each other.

"When the sight is compromised, the only safe route is where you just came from," Jocko said. "If we follow the coordinates . . ."

"Back out?" Lasse said. "Back out to the waves and the stalker boat?"

Gustav touched Lasse's shoulder.

"The storm has passed," he said. "Otherwise there wouldn't be fog. As far as the stalker goes, he could be here right now and we wouldn't know it." Gustav laughed, but stopped when he saw the guys' faces. "I'm sorry," he said. "But Lasse is right, we are close. Jocko?" Gustav looked at Jocko.

"I'm tired." Jocko's lips quivered. His eyes were red and he wiped his face with wet palms. "I'm sorry," he said. "I know I'm the captain."

Gustav and Lasse embraced Jocko and held each other tight.

"The rudder," Jocko said.

"I'll steer." Gustav took the rudder. "You go inside and warm up. Go on inside, both of you, and share body heat."

Jocko sniffed. He nodded and Lasse followed him inside.

Lasse came back out with coffee for Gustav, and wrapped another blanket around him. With the sails down and the engine off, the boat hardly moved, but Gustav followed the GPS and steered in the direction of home, until the fog cleared and he could see where he was. The current had taken them close, and they would have to start rowing or they'd drift past the bay and out to the open sea. The air was cold on Gustav's cheeks, and he felt his throat swelling. He knocked on the hatch and shouted to the guys that they were a couple of islets away from the pier. Jocko emerged in his boxer shorts followed by Lasse. They got out the oars and started rowing. At last, they rounded the corner of an islet, and saw the fishing boat moored in their berth. The captain stood talking to their neighbours while the youth unloaded boxes of fish.

End

So many times will my child come home that I'll buy a hundred-pack of toothbrushes.

Coltsfoot and bluebells shared a field and slow-danced with each other in the warm wind. Children ran barefoot, and picked flowers for their elder siblings to weave. Adolescent boys and girls avoided eye contact as the girls, in their best summer dresses, whispered amongst themselves, and the boys, with borrowed hair gel, did tricks with a football, moving slowly in the girls' direction.

The sheep had moved up the sides of the mountains, and blended in with the snow patches. The ringing from the lead sheep's bells melted with the humming voices around the long table being set. A waterfall in the distance played for the church gospel choir rehearsing.

Two cars drove up and down to the end of the grit road where men waited to carry chairs, tabletops, and trestles to the field in which the long table grew into a horseshoe seating two hundred, and a smaller one took shape beside it. The tables were dressed in white linen, and children, proud to help, put flowers in empty jars. The smell of fat and coal oozed from the kitchen tent. Someone carried a keg into the tent, a dozen men followed, and there was cheering and laughter.

A woman sat in the grass where the children ran, producing coronets for whoever brought her flowers. She watched the children, but failed to notice their mothers watching her. A man half her age walked over and picked up his toddler.

"It takes a village," the woman said, but the man and the toddler left.

The woman had deep wrinkles around her eyes and mouth, pointing downwards. Her red eyeballs were draped in excess eyelid skin. She cradled the bag in her lap and gazed at the sheep while she rocked back and forth. A teenage girl walked towards her. The woman turned to her and laughed.

"I think it's time I cut my hair," she said. "I'm not a youth like you. A woman my age with long hair." She smiled.

The girl screwed up her face and reached her hand out to a young boy who took it. They walked away.

The gospel choir sang the national anthem. A boy kicked a football at a group of girls, and it hit one of them on the head. They screamed and giggled. The boy walked over to the girls and picked up the ball. He rubbed the girl's head. The other boys watched and whispered before they, too, walked over to the girls.

Two men sat down with the woman. She looked at them.

"Jocko," she said, and touched his suit and tie, her hand gliding up to his shaven chin. "Lasse." She turned to him. "My, you look handsome today."

Jocko hugged her and she shook. Lasse put his arms around them and looked at Jocko. A scar in the clouds bled sunlight on them. Lasse took off his suit jacket. Birds twittered and people laughed. The woman looked up from Jocko's shoulder and fumbled in her bag.

"Almost forgot," she said. "I've got something for you." She took out a plastic bag full of toothbrushes and handed it to Jocko. "I thought you could make use of them."

A bell rang and people streamed to the table. The adolescents gathered at one end of the horseshoe, away from their parents. Beer was poured from kegs into jugs and passed down the table. The cook cut up the roast, his biceps contracting as he carved the stringy meat, and placed a central piece on Lasse's plate. The smell of meat blended with the smell of the flowers on the table. Lasse and Jocko downed their pints and poured new ones. Toddlers sat on their parents' laps. Mothers watched youngsters on the children's table next to the horseshoe struggle to carve their food, resisting the urge to help.

"Ew, it stinks," a girl said. "You said we were gonna have chicken."

A woman frowned at the child. A teenage boy tried to hide a jug of beer under the table, but was seen, and mineral water was passed down to the underaged. The humming of voices died down when a knife clanged on a glass and the cook announced that the gospel choir would sing for their supper. The choir sang, and Lasse and Jocko held hands under the table, squeezing each other's fingers until they were numb.

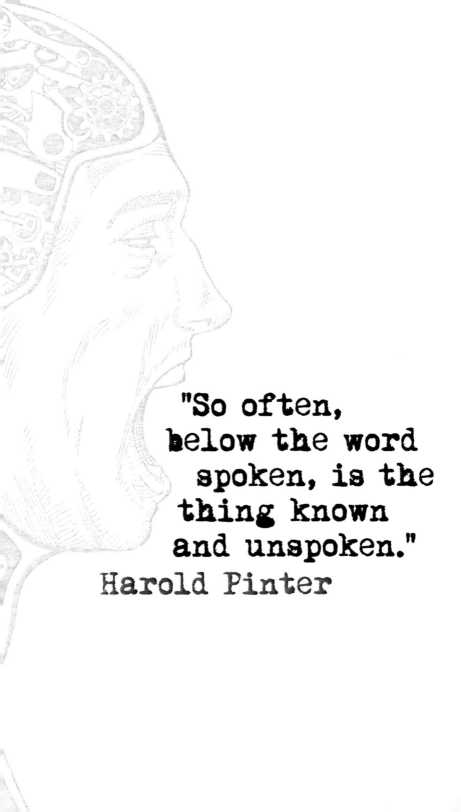

"So often,
below the word
spoken, is the
thing known
and unspoken."
Harold Pinter

Stag

LOUISE LEE

Portopiccolo Sistiana, Italy

I am outstretched on a sunlounger, one arm gracefully above my head. My free hand holds aloft a copy of *The Hitchhiker's Guide to the Galaxy*, officially the most brilliant book ever written. You should always have vast tracts of it memorised. Boys *love* it. If they don't, they're wrong.

Literature to avoid when courting male attention:

Anne Frank's diary. All prose with a religious bent – *The Book of Mormon*, for example; or the Qur'an. Self-help books. *Men Are from Mars, Women Are from Venus*.

The reasons why *The Hitchhiker's Guide to the Galaxy* is an excellent precursor to flirting-proper:

It's science fiction *and* it's comedy.

I'll be brief.

Sci-fi addresses philosophical issues whilst engaging the mind in an abstract way, i.e., the way in which men deal with emotions best, i.e., not head-on. Add a comedic slant and they're hooked, because laughter releases nervous energy in the exact same way as anger and fear – a giggle being a lovely adrenalin rush that peters out before it becomes a fight or flight situation.

That's a male happiness fact.

So I know that when Freddie – his name is Freddie – spots my choice of book from his side of the infinity pool, he'll experience

49

a warm rush of nostalgia. He might recall his first read, or watching the repeats with his parents, or feeling failed by the film adaptation. Whichever, he'll be luxuriating in another moment in time facilitated entirely by me.

That's assuming he stops playing on his smartphone.

Sit up and stare at this place, Freddie. It's not as if you holiday like this all the time.

The location is breathtaking. A six-star coastal development popular amongst the Italian glitterati – uber-cool pads and pretty stone houses nestle into a hillside that overlooks the Adriatic Sea. Sumptuous yachts bob within the pebble walls of a marina. Discreet designer shops, impeccable eateries. Acres of glass, marble, walnut and chrome. At night, halogen lighting invades every nook – from a distance Portopiccolo Sistiana twinkles as though Bulgari-encrusted.

Come on, Freddie, forget Candy Crush. Glance around you. Take in the backdrop. The people, they're definitely worth a look. The woman sitting opposite you – especially her.

Like all Cancerians, I have a soupçon of telepathy. For a moment he stops playing on his phone, laughs at something his friend has said; a swift swig of Peroni and he resumes his game.

I've watched Freddie from afar for the past forty-eight hours. Today is the first time I've placed myself in plain view.

I'll set the scene.

Freddie is one of an athletic trio. They're all attractive, but most would single out the Stag first.

Enzo.

He plays football for the local team, Udinese Calcio, which is a big gig. In his spare time he enjoys standing up and admiring the Adriatic whilst enabling the widespread appreciation of his physique, tattoos and gladiatorial aura. It's a shame perfection isn't my bag – not his kind, anyway. Enzo's too whittled, too mahogany. I imagine it would be like making love to a totem pole.

If I'm being truthful, Freddie's not my type either – though his physique is consummate, he remains a little too "fun-sized". Like a very pretty whippet. One who lacks the statuesqueness of his normal-sized cousin, the greyhound.

Freddie's a footballer too – that's how they met, he and Enzo, playing for a youth team in Bristol. Freddie now coaches disability football. He earns a month what Enzo earns a minute. Suffice to say, this jolly is c/o the Stag. Which is just as well. The sunbeds are extortionate – eighty euros for one day by the pool. Admittedly you get a changing hut with that. And a fluffy towel. And very cool Italian waiters.

Mine promptly arrives with a bowl of olives.

"Can I get you some lunch?" he asks.

I confide in him. "I'd kill for a Lobster Fra Diavolo, but the boss is a tightwad."

"Mine too." He laughs just like a jazz musician I used to know. I feel a crushing sadness; it refuses to scram.

"Just a Peroni, *grazie*." I force myself to concentrate on the third and final member of the stag party.

Jamie.

He's more my type. Strawberry-blond curls, some meat on his muscles, freckled shoulders that glow an angry red in the lukewarm sun. He reads *A Pair of Blue Eyes*, by Thomas Hardy. The glasses that sit on the end of his broken nose are grandfatherly. He reminds me of an introspective polar bear, one who in an ideal world would give very sincere hugs. I don't know what Jamie does for a living, but I decide to put *A Pair of Blue Eyes* on my reading list. Hardy is a wrist-slitting read; I'm intrigued as to why a boy would choose this book on a stag do.

I remind myself of the job in hand. Direct my attention back to Freddie – the one my boss has asked me to assess.

When I say assess, I mean entrap.

And when I say boss, I very much mean client – a client who is thrifty to a fault.

When I asked her for permission to hire a sunbed, she said: *I'm a receptionist not an oligarch. Do they do half days?*

My response was blunt: *During cases of entrapment, never, ever do things by halves.*

Because if you're going to do something this extreme, go for broke. The matter will be settled once and for all, which, categorically, is *the* point of a honeytrap.

The waiter arrives with a Peroni. He also slides a small plate of Lobster Fra Diavolo onto the glass table beside me. He winks.

His eyes are luminous green, his eyelashes black and dense as tarantula fur. I do an unexpected giggle.

Nothing tastes as good as free seafood. I eat it with relish. The fresh bucatini is exquisite. I can taste every last ingredient in the sauce – San Marzano tomatoes, brandy, kosher salt, the lobster pot's rope mesh and timber frame. My stomach hums contentedly – it's almost post-coital. Instinctively I reach for a Marlboro and take a nip of the beer, which tastes insipid, like soapy Prosecco, but the rules are thus:

Sup what your target is supping – it helps with the process of subconscious coupling, assuming he is aware of his surroundings and not glued to a phone app.

I feel a sudden sense of doom for Freddie. Whatever the outcome of this case, he is fucked, what with his girlfriend having such worrying baggage.

Freddie looks up. Sees me watching him, which is rotten timing. You can't appear to have noticed them first. Neither should you be caught looking sorry for them. There's nothing erotic in being made to feel self-conscious and slightly patronised.

I style it out. Pretend I'm in a daydream; one where your eyes get progressively larger until you snap yourself out of it. I then do a carefree little yawn and, ensuring my sunglasses are squarely on my nose, I swap my cigarette for *The Hitchhiker's Guide to the Galaxy*.

Operation Freddie Butcher is now off the ground.

I switch to peripheral vision. Mine is astonishing. Freddie does a double take, followed by a series of manly flexion stretches and concluded by a thoughtful gulp of Peroni. He, like me, retrieves his sunglasses from the side table, positions them carefully on his ears and sits back in the sunlounger.

The difference between us? My sunglasses record in colour and have a memory card the size of a lentil.

"Bingo," I mumble into my book, because look how he's repositioned himself, assumed the pose of spectator. His legs straddle the chair. Subconsciously he introduces his manhood.

This is how I encourage him:

1. I ignore him completely.
2. Now and then I dive, ensuring the manoeuvre is

balletic and involves minimal backsplash.

3. I don't wear ear plugs or a nose clip.
4. Neither do I smuggle a towel to the poolside. I must be on full and proud display.

Between you and me, there are many procedures I'd have had done were I less concerned about dying under the anaesthetic. But we're not talking about me. We're talking about this job. Perfection is beside the point – you need simply to be so sexually charged you crackle like an electricity pylon. An Ursula Andress bikini will help here. Go for one in a peachy colour to replicate the tones of pubescent labia. It suggests youth and the promise of propagation. Men don't realise it, but they are innately drawn to the connotations of the colour peach.

A final note before I wrap this shift up.

There's a very strict chronology to a honeytrap: Two Bumps and The Money Shot. This afternoon Freddie will not get a whiff of interest from me – this allows him to believe that it's fine to include me in his fantasies, because nothing will ever happen.

He's right. It won't.

Not this afternoon anyway – this afternoon is simply about planting a seed in his head.

At 2.45 p.m., I wrap myself in an apricot kaftan, pack my belongings into an Armani tote and leave the pool area.

With varying degrees of interest, all three men now watch me. When I walk past them, I kick over Freddie's Peroni.

"I'm a klutz," I apologise, briefly touching Freddie's shoulder. "I'll get you another."

"No, babe, it's fine. You're all right." He's unable to maintain eye contact – an excellent sign.

Jamie, on the other hand, watches me solidly over the top of his grandpa specs.

Rigidly, I smile at Freddie. "I insist." Then I leave him and his friends to the rest of their afternoon, on my way out, asking the waiter to send over a fresh drink.

"Shall I put it on the tab?" He winks again. It's *such* a winning wink; however, now I stand beside him, I see he's two inches smaller than me, which is a crying shame.

"You must really hate your boss," I say, smiling.

"He's my dad."

"Ah." I get it. Father-son relationships are thorny. The time-worn lion. His restless progeny.

I nod at Freddie. "The football lot over there. Where do they go at night?"

"Drinks and food here between seven and ten, then into town."

This tallies with the information provided by the client.

"Shall I get them all a drink?" he asks.

"Good God, no. I'm going for friendly insouciance. Just the whippet."

By the time Freddie receives his Peroni, I'll be long gone. Yet every soapy swig will leave the aftertaste of me.

And that's that. Bump #1 is complete.

It's a ten-minute walk to my bike, which is attached to railings just outside the resort walls. My civvies are in a carrier bag tied to its handlebars. Converse, cut-downs and a T-shirt. I put them on over my soggy bikini, tie the beach bag around my shoulders, push the bike quickly into the road and do a running mount.

Damp hair blowing in the wind, I cycle home furiously. It's normally an hour's ride to Ronchi dei Legionari. Today I do it in fifty minutes flat. Because I'm late for a phone call. A biggie. It's a conversation I have every Friday afternoon and under no circumstances can I miss it.

"Stag" is an extract from *The Last Bigamist* (Headline, 2016)

Epicentre

SIMON TOWNEND

The crack in the centre of the lounge floor is growing. Finn steps over it now, afraid the floor could collapse at any time. He should have done something about it. Alex was always nagging him to get it fixed. She said it was one of the reasons she left him. He knows the real reason was Jonathan, the man she moved in with. Although, she denies anything happened before they split up.

When Alex left, Finn bought a rug to hide the crack. Now the crack has got so long, the rug is not big enough to cover it. The only way Finn can avoid the crack is to avoid the flat. He spends as many hours at work as he can. So much so, there is talk of promotion. After work, he goes out with friends or, when no one is around, on his own.

The effort of spending so much time away from the flat is taking its toll. After a week of long days and a weekend of all-nighters, Monday is a struggle. It's late when he gets back from work. Up three flights of stairs, unlocks the door, flicks the light switch. Nothing happens. Behind him the communal landing is still lit; no power cut. He crosses the hallway and tries the lounge lights. Nothing. In the dim light from the street, he can see the rug has shifted. It has sunk in the middle. Pulling the rug by its edge, he slides it away. The crack is now a hole. A soft yellow glow emanates from it. Finn retraces his steps. He goes down to the flat below and knocks.

Sam, the man who lives downstairs, answers the door. Alex used to call him Sad Sam. She made her blowfish face whenever they passed on the stairs, and when Finn laughed she threw him a disappointed look. "Don't encourage me," she would say. He understood her, even when she didn't make sense. He misses her sense of humour. He misses her.

"Hi, Sam, how are things?"

"Yep, good. What can I do you for?" Sam asks, holding the door.

Finn leans forward to look around Sam. The apartment is fully lit. Sam follows Finn's gaze before turning back.

"You got any problem with your electrics?" Finn asks.

Sam shakes his head.

"Or the lounge ceiling?"

"Everything all right, Finn?"

"Right, OK, no worries. Cheers."

Finn bounds back upstairs. The hole is bigger, the glow stronger. He takes off his suit jacket, hangs it over the corner of the door, then lying down he slithers to the edge of the hole. Fucking hell. Visible through the gap is an exact copy of the living room he is currently lying in. Well, almost. The large rustic oak furniture – table, chairs, bookcases, too big for an apartment this size – is all there, crammed in. The artwork on the walls is his: a Jackson Pollock print, a hung-over purchase from the Sunday market; the Lichtenstein reproduction, a present for his brother, never given; and the abstract painting he and Alex bought in Barcelona as a memento of their first holiday together. There's no rug, the leather sofas still shine, their surfaces yet to be scarred by use. Alex's ornaments are there – the stuffed owl, the large porcelain ginger cat, the dreamcatcher (a present from Sophie, her hippy little sister). He rolls onto his back, trying to make sense of what he has seen. He is wrestling with all the possibilities when he is disturbed by noises from below.

Someone is down there. A woman walks out of the kitchen. Dark-red suit, skirt, jacket, hair tied up. She stirs something in a bowl, which she holds under one arm. Finn's stomach tightens as he realises who it is. Alex, making her Thai chilli fishcakes, Finn's favourite. He almost calls out to her, but catches himself. He regrets not telling her how much he liked her cooking. He still misses her so much after six months. Every cell in his body hopes this is real.

She walks over to one of the leather sofas and picks up a mobile phone from the arm, chooses a number and hits Dial. Finn edges forward, hoping to see who she is calling, when he is startled by the phone in his pocket vibrating. Trying to be quiet, he takes out the phone. Incoming call. He squints. *Alex mobile*. Finn thought he'd deleted her number. He stares at the phone, too scared to answer. The call goes to voicemail.

"Hi, darling, hope everything's OK. I was expecting you home by now. Let me know if you're stuck at the office. Love you," says Alex. She drops the phone back on the arm, sighs and returns to the kitchen. He wonders how many nights he left her like this. He regrets every one of them now.

His phone vibrates; he's got a voicemail. He hits the button.

"You have one new message . . ." Beep. "Hi, darling, hope everything's OK. I was expecting you home by now. Let me know if you're stuck at the office. Love you . . ."

He ends the call and shakes his head, trying to get things straight. It's no use. Moving to the sofa, he alternates between listening to the message and staring at the hole.

Finn sinks to his knees and pulls at the floorboards. They crack and splinter under the attack, until, finally, the hole is big enough. He turns and lowers himself through, feet first. He hangs for a moment, dangling, before letting go. Falling further than expected, he crashes to the floor, collapsing in a heap. Alex walks in and looks at him lying there.

"I didn't hear you come in. You OK?" she asks.

He bounces up and straightens his clothes. The flat is just the way it was before Alex walked out. The vases, the Indian puppets on the mantelpiece. His suit jacket is hanging on the door. He looks up. No hole in the ceiling, not the slightest crack.

"I was just . . ."

"You ever going to do something about this?"

Finn has a foot either side of a crack in the floor. Just a small crack at the moment. He stands there staring. Alex walks back into the kitchen.

"Spoke to Gemma today. Her and Michael are still up for

Saturday, even though the others can't make it," Alex shouts.

Finn goes to the bathroom; he needs time to think. Splashes cold water on his face before slumping on the edge of bath. Gemma and Michael came over a couple of weeks before Alex left. The evening was a disaster. The subject of Jonathan came up and Finn's jealousy ruined the night. It was the first time Finn had heard about him, the first time he had realised there might be someone else. Looking for a distraction, he takes Alex's toiletries out of the bathroom cabinet and inhales, eyes closed. This was the moment things started to go wrong between them. Someone has given him another chance. He's not going to blow this one. He's got two weeks to change things.

"Good. Great. Sounds great," he says, going into the kitchen.

The blind is up and he can see the full moon in the clear sky. He slips his arms round Alex's waist from behind and kisses her on the neck. She wriggles a little, laughing, and then gives in.

"I love you," he says, "and I love your cooking."

She twists round in his arms to look at him.

"You sure you're OK? Something happen in the office today?"

He watches her cook her wonderful fishcakes.

"Why don't we sit at the table to eat?" he suggests.

"Do we have to?"

"Come on, let's make it date night."

"Really?"

"I'll make it worth your while." He winks.

She laughs and looks at him for a moment. She nods. Finn goes to the fridge for wine. He recognises one bottle, still sitting in his fridge six months into the future, waiting for a reason to celebrate that has never come. A present from a client. A vintage bottle from an ancient vineyard. When he was given it, he'd planned to cook Alex a special dinner to go with it, but other things always got in the way. This time's going to be different. He takes a corkscrew to it.

Sitting at the dining table, he's so excited he fires questions at her. Question after question.

"So how's work?"

"What would you do if money were no object?"

"What are the five things you really have to do before you die?"

"Who would you bring back to life if you could?"

Like when they were first together, he wants to talk to her as much as he wants to sleep with her. They move to the sofa and rather than switching on the telly, he continues his lines of inquiry. He wants to know the answers; he needs to know everything about her. He wants to learn again.

"What's got into you this evening?" she says, smiling at him.

"Why? What's wrong? Have I upset you?"

"No . . . It's nice. It's been a while since you . . . I mean, we, talked."

He leans in and kisses her. A spark in his stomach ignites a warm rush through his body. As the evening progresses, this rediscovered love is slowly replaced by lust as it mixes with the wine and tickles his loins. Finn takes Alex's hand and leads her to the bedroom. Tonight he will do everything he knows to pleasure her, trying hard not to think of his own satisfaction. Later she falls asleep in his arms. He promises the darkness this time will be different. He can change things. Two weeks is a very long time.

The next morning they breakfast together and walk to the station. Finn holds Alex's hand. She turns to look at him, but doesn't pull away. Later, sitting on the train, he talks, entertaining her. He knows she is thinking, processing his new attentiveness, his caring. He hopes it will make a difference.

Finn walks into the office with a bounce in his step.

"Someone's happy this morning," says Mark.

"And why shouldn't I be? Everything's great," Finn says, beaming at Mark.

"Have you forgotten about the Core Tech account? Art's going to blow his top if we don't get something to him for the end of the day."

"Oh shit . . ." Finn had forgotten. The account was a mess. He'd been working on it when Alex left him, and then they'd lost the account as well. Another opportunity to learn from his mistakes.

That evening Finn arrives home later than he planned.

"Sorry I'm late . . ." he shouts. No answer. He checks their calendar in the kitchen. Written in pencil for tonight, *Alex – Work Do*. It's a punch to the stomach. Finn has no doubt that Jonathan will be there. He tries not to think about it; he is not supposed to know about Jonathan yet.

He gets changed, makes dinner and watches television. All the time the voice niggling in the back of his head: "She's with Jonathan. She's talking with Jonathan. She's laughing with Jonathan. She's getting drunk with Jonathan. Jonathan. Jonathan. Jonathan."

Finn paces the flat, sits, rests for a moment before pacing again. He notices the crack in the floor. Could it be longer?

He is still pacing the flat hours later when he hears a key in the lock. He throws himself onto the sofa and uses the remote to start the television.

"Thought you'd be in bed by now." She kicks off her shoes and drapes her coat over the arm of a chair. She has brought in the winter night, and Finn can smell booze and cigarettes.

"Where've you been?" Finn asks.

Alex frowns. "Work do. I told you that. It's on the calendar," she says, going into the bedroom. She comes back in pyjamas. "We need to get that sorted. I'm sure it's getting worse . . ." She points at the crack, before disappearing into the kitchen and coming back with water and headache tablets. "I'm going to bed."

He waits for her to finish in the bathroom, then follows. Alex is snoring within a few minutes. Finn lies awake, eventually falling into a fitful sleep, plagued by dreams. He, Alex and Jonathan are the last people on earth. Sitting round a campfire in a post-apocalyptic world, Alex and Jonathan whisper to each other and laugh at jokes they don't share with Finn. When the alarm goes off, he wakes in a sweat.

He does his best to be pleasant and attentive as they get ready for work, although the voice in his head is digging away and makes it difficult to concentrate. "Why don't you ask her about Jonathan? What about Jonathan? Is she seeing Jonathan? Is she falling in love with Jonathan?" On and on it goes. He can't face the break-up again.

"How about I make us breakfast?" he offers.

"Sorry, love, I've got an early meeting. Got to dash," she says, kissing him on the forehead before rushing off.

He sits at the kitchen table with his head in his hands.

"Idiot. Core Tech don't want this rubbish. Turn something decent out, or get lost," Finn shouts at an intern, whilst colleagues look on. Shouting is a distraction. He texts Alex mid-morning. *How's it going? Fancy doing something tonight? F x*

He spins the phone between his fingers, convinced the quicker he can do it, the sooner the reply will come. The phone doesn't beep until after lunch.

Sounds good. Bite to eat?

At a local gastro pub after work, they make it through the starters before the conversation peters out.

"Why don't we get away?" Finn suggests.

"I thought your work was really busy at the moment."

"Yeah, but it's been a while, hasn't it? We don't spend enough time just us. Come on, a long weekend somewhere hot . . ."

"Why don't we wait and see. You know, maybe after –"

"How about Morocco? We always talked about Marrakesh."

"It's just that my work's busy as well and Mum's not great . . ." she says, looking away.

"Live a little," says Finn, smiling. Her face changes and he knows he's made a mistake.

"That's a tad rich coming from you, isn't it?" she spits.

Before he can apologise, the waiter arrives with their mains. The first few mouthfuls are eaten in silence as Finn composes his apology. Before he can deliver it, her phone beeps. She smiles as she reads the text message.

"Anything interesting?" Finn asks.

"Huh?" Alex says, looking up. "Oh, no. A colleague from work."

"Anyone I'd know?"

"Jonathan. Don't think you've met him."

"Jonathan?" Finn grips the edge of the table.

Alex looks back at her phone and then puts it down.

"He's a good guy, you'd like him."

"I don't think I would," Finn says.

Few words are exchanged for the rest of the meal. Finn walks ahead of Alex all the way from the station.

In bed, they lie facing away from each other. Finn wants to reach out to her but the heavy feeling in his stomach holds him in place. He knows he has to get her back; he has the chance to, but the weight of it is suffocating him.

In the morning, Alex rises early. Finn listens to her get dressed, saying nothing. He is still in bed when she leaves. The days begin to blur. The two weeks become ten days, nine days, eight. Finn doesn't know what to do. He is losing her again, but doesn't know how to stop it. He buys her flowers.

"Thank you," she says.

"Your favourites. Thought they'd cheer you up."

She smiles weakly.

He feels a future misery make its presence known.

They eat together and watch TV together, Finn thinking all the while, trying to solve the problem of their failing relationship.

"Did you think any more about the going away?" he asks.

"I'm not sure now would be a good time." She doesn't even look at him.

The weekend arrives. Saturday morning, Alex goes for a run and comes back in an infectiously good mood. Finn suggests breakfast at the café; she accepts. He watches her reading the papers. Uncomfortable with the silence, his mind races with infinite possibilities, all leading to one outcome. Afterwards they shop for the dinner party with Michael and Gemma.

The evening's proceedings start well, before Gemma unknowingly lights the touch paper.

"So how's everyone at work? I hear Jonathan's left Annabel," Gemma says.

"You didn't tell me Jonathan was leaving his wife," Finn says, staring at Alex.

"They weren't married. Besides, you don't even know Jonathan," Alex says, quietly.

"I heard it was messy. Rhona thinks there's someone else."

"She's such a bitch, bet she's just jealous."

"Jealous?" Finn's stomach lurches, his head swims.

"Who's Jonathan?" asks Michael.

"You've met him," says Gemma.

"Well, at least someone has," says Finn.

"Blond guy with the beard?"

"No, that's Ashley. Jonathan's the good-looking one."

Finn knocks his chair over as he jumps up, rushes to the bathroom. Door bolted, he sits on the edge of the bath with his hands pressed into his eyes. It doesn't stop the tears from coming. With the tears goes some of the anxiety and he gets a hold of himself. He dries his face and heads back out.

Finn says little more for the rest of the meal, just glares at Alex. As soon as pudding has been consumed, Michael and Gemma make their excuses.

"Need to get home, busy day tomorrow."

"You can stay a little longer, can't you?" Alex pleads.

Gemma looks at Finn, who looks away.

"Have you got a cab number?" Gemma asks.

Following Gemma and Michael's departure, a wave of claustrophobia envelops Finn. He gets his coat and goes for a walk, leaving Alex with the clearing up. He walks and walks, until he is lost. When he gets home, all trace of dinner has been washed and tidied away. Alex is in bed.

"I love you," he whispers into the dark of the bedroom. There is no reply. He goes to the lounge and stays up, watching nothing on telly.

The next day, Alex goes to see her mum and doesn't get back till late. There is no confrontation, no accusation, no discussion.

At work on Monday, Finn decides tonight is going to be special. He will cook a magnificent dinner and apologise to Alex. He is going to make it up to her. It is not going to be like last time.

Ignoring the Core Tech account, he searches for recipes to impress; takes an extended lunch break purchasing supplies – sea bass, fennel, broccoli, new potatoes.

He goes home early, giving himself plenty of time to tidy the flat, get everything ready, cook the food, chill the wine. He lays a romantic table, flowers, candles, the good cutlery, even napkins. Alex should be back about six. Just before, he puts the fish in the oven and waits. Half six – still no Alex. At quarter to seven he gets a text. *Running late. Stuck at office. Don't wait for me to eat, we're getting something in.*

Finn pictures Alex and Jonathan sitting in a boardroom, eating takeaway, drinking wine and laughing, his hand on her shoulder, firing off compliments. He throws the fish in the bin. He takes a large swig from the wine bottle, gags and pours the rest down the sink.

Reading the text again and again, he fails to think of an appropriate reply. All he wants to ask is if Jonathan is there, but he knows he can't. Defeated, he slumps on the sofa, waiting in silence and staring at the crack in the floor.

Hearing the key in the door, he quickly switches the TV on. As he is rushing back to the sofa, Alex walks in.

"Did I catch you in the middle of something?" she slurs.

"You're drunk."

"No . . . No. I just had a couple of drinks after work. We've all been working so hard. Jonathan wanted to thank us . . ." She notices the table with the candles and flowers. "Oh, sweetheart . . ."

"Fucking Jonathan."

"What is that supposed to mean?" She wobbles, trying to take her shoes off. "Sandra, Alison, Tony and that bitch Rhona were there. Is there an issue?"

"I don't like you spending so much time with Jonathan."

"What – you want me to change jobs? Or maybe you'd prefer it if I didn't work at all. In fact, how about I stay here chained up in the apartment."

"I'm not the one going off with someone else," he mumbles.

She storms to bed, leaving Finn on the sofa to make the next move. He falls asleep, still undecided.

In the morning Finn showers, dresses and leaves, ignoring her. He focuses on work, trying to block everything else out. He continues without a break until everyone else has gone home. In the semi dark of the office he lays his head on his desk and cries.

The flat is in darkness when he gets home. He walks around, switching on the lights, the television; he needs company. She doesn't get back until the early hours. They don't talk.

Wednesday and Thursday the silence grows, and with it the

pain. Finn didn't notice the silence last time, but this time it crushes his heart.

By Friday Finn is broken. Coming home early, he can sense something is wrong. Propped against the unused candle on the table is an envelope. He opens it.

> Dear Finn,
> Please know how much you mean to me. We've had great times together. I will cherish those for ever. But things have changed. I don't know what is wrong with you, but you are no longer the man I fell in love with. We did things together, we went places, you cared about things. We were a couple once. At some point it became all about you. I look after you – I cook, clean and wash. What do you do? The crack – I've been asking you to fix it for months – nothing.
>
> And when did you become so jealous and possessive? I'm a person too you know. You don't own me. You don't control me. You're not the only one with a career. You don't even know that I've had a promotion. Why don't you care?
>
> Maybe we've just lost our way. Maybe some time apart would help us see things more clearly.
>
> I'm going to stay with Sophie for a little while. I've taken most of my stuff and I'll let you know when I'm coming back for the rest.
> Take care.
> Alex

Finn has read this note. He knows she is never coming back, not for her stuff and not for him. The tears stream down his face as he goes to the fridge for some wine. It doesn't take him long to finish the first bottle, which quickly goes to his head. He texts her.

Can't believe you cheated on me. You'll never know how much I loved you.

He drinks more, waiting for a response. When it doesn't come, he texts again.

I thought you were something special. How wrong I was.
More drink, more tears and no response.
Fuck you. I hope you and Jonathan are happy.
More drink and a little regret.
Sorry. I love you with all my heart. F x
He sends this text once every five minutes, until he passes out.

The morning sun shining through the window wakes him up. Tired, hungry and hung-over, he makes no effort to do anything. Still lying there at lunchtime, he stares blankly at the crack in the floor. He'll have to get a rug for it soon.

As the sun sets the idea occurs to him. With a sudden burst of energy, he springs up and rushes to the cupboard in the hall. He empties it, throwing everything everywhere, desperately looking for what he needs. He takes a large, heavy claw hammer into the lounge. He smashes it against the crack. Again and again, trying to break through.

Shadows

FRANK T. SAYI

Sometimes you could hear it in the night, the soft whimper of it. Swooshing sounds like the rising tide rushing in and out of a hollow cave. And the fishy smell, a pungency of raw eggs and unripe pumpkin. The door slightly ajar, and through the crack, the shadow of the moon. My sister slept at the other end of the room. I lay on my side with my small head on the pillow of my arm as the shadows entered, casting darkness against the beam of light resting between the door and the wall. After a while, I smelt guns and the smell turned into an acrid taste of cordite, oil and forest on my tongue. It came from the shadows visiting the girl in the room.

There were rumours of war, of course. Careful and hushed voices bringing news from afar, saying that death was on its way, with each person painting their own versions of terror. They said there were echoes in pit latrines, in mine shafts and shallow graves; voices that remained in the wilderness. And Grandma's prayers intensified. How could they not? The preacher, the one who showed Thabo's sister stars behind the rocks, said these were the end of times. He hallelujahed and quivered in front of the congregation. But we watched him under the faithless African sky as his buttocks gyrated behind Thabo's sister and she reversed back into him like a dog in heat. She writhed like a caterpillar and he pushed her forward like a wheelbarrow full of sand. Then he went into spasms like he did in the pulpit in church. Grandma said that what has horns cannot be hidden in a sack and that one day the birds of the forest will sing what happened in the shadows. The lying owl threatening other birds with fake horns will one day meet his demise.

When rumours of war were still an embryo in the whisperer's belly, we played under the moonlit midnight sky with bats, singing childhood songs. We hitched rides on the backs of tempestuous donkeys and played football made from rags on makeshift pitches with thorn trees for spectators. Each strike of the ball a thwarted opportunity for the big toe to thrust against fragments of rock, tree stumps and shards of glass. In the afternoons we scoured the forest for wild figs, cherries and *matamba*, and we drank water from virgin streams.

But now, the small brook behind our house had dried up and the last time I went there for a walk I saw catfish swimming with frogs and tadpoles. The water was moss green and smelt like rotten leaves. Grandma said not to drink it. She said that catfish and frogs and tadpoles swimming together was an evil omen.

Beyond the small brook was the house of the man who crushed ten puppies from a height with big rocks because he had nothing to feed them with. War had killed his heart. Grandma said we mustn't kill things that don't speak unless we were meant to eat them. She was like that. In her heyday she herded cattle like the boys, fought like a man and had the fierceness of a wounded bull. When she milked cows, she struck their calves so hard with the back of her hand that they sneezed a tremulous liquid. But she would leave sufficient milk in the udders for each calf and afterwards stroke them gently, enticing them to feed once more.

Next to the house of the man who killed the puppies, behind the tall mahogany tree, was Thabo's house. Thabo's mother had died, as well as his two brothers who were buried together in a shallow grave. His younger sister cooked and cleaned during the day and at night she became his mother. She had inherited her mother's death bed and all the woes that afflicted her mother when she was alive became hers too. I asked Grandma if this was true, that a man could open the path to his own daughter's womb. She admonished me for spreading lies and said that in times of desperation, lions eat grass and sometimes their own cubs. Not out of hate. Not out of depravity. But she also said that these were burdensome stories without the courage to leave one's lips. We all of us, with our ear to history's curved shell, we listened to conflicting sounds from her mouth.

Thabo's father, in his grief, mistook his garden for his wife. He would talk to it, stop and laugh like an injured hyena. All the while calling his wife's name: Sabelo! Sabelo! Grandma said Thabo's father had black ants deep inside the labyrinth of his mind.

At night Grandma visited Grandpa's grave, a mound of earth and rocks lying under a thorn tree, with the headstone facing sunrise. She talked to him about the way things were and what we'd become. First she'd clap her hands together for what seemed an eternity. Then she'd address herself to Grandpa, knees folded at the seam, striking a lonely figure in the dark.

"Since you have been gone," she began, "our land has turned into an empty graveyard full of ghosts and shadows. Our young people are being taken away and the cattle pens are dwindling. Soon we will be boiling river stones for food. It is the only thing we have left. Even the rivers are dead. And is it not loss of pride for those who reside in the mountains to ask for cornerstones from those who live on the grasslands? Our enemies and neighbours are the same people and their ears and eyes are betraying us for food. How else can they afford to eat, when all around us dust prevails? We are dying like flies and war is in everyone's eyes. Worms might fatten on decayed leaves, but the earth devours everything. Now we are people in name only!"

When she came back she'd say, "Grandpa says hello."

She said that she had met him when she was a young girl. He was handsome, she said, and she could always smell lavender in the small of his neck. On Sundays she waited in anticipation for the glimmer of his bicycle light in the dark.

I have vivid memories of Grandpa. I remember the smell of tobacco in the evening just after sunset. His pipe, a miniature chimney in the dark, glowing intermittently like the firefly, in between puffs of smoke. We walked together once. He took me to a secret tree pregnant with wild cherries. Big round cherries, the colour of sunset, with raindrops dangling on the leaves like pearls.

It had rained heavily that day and the snails and the millipedes were out in numbers. He was tall and fragile and each time he picked up a wild cherry, he'd look at it and turn it over before carefully placing it on his tongue. Then he'd spit out the stones carelessly, as if annoyed by the whole thing.

Months later a man arrived with a letter and gave it to Grandma, who passed it on to me, as she couldn't read. It was Ma's handwriting, and in a single sentence, written in big bold black letters, she announced his death: "Father died today." I read it to Grandma and she held her belly with both hands and wailed like she had unbearable pain. She swayed and swayed as if moved by the wind until the pain in her stomach planted itself on her face, and from that day onwards she walked around with an expression like she'd stepped on thorns. Grandma said that my own life was implicated in Grandpa's death. She said that if he'd survived, I wouldn't be alive. I didn't know what she meant by that. But I didn't ask, because Grandma was like that sometimes. She was careless with words and said things that stayed long in your heart. I guess her heart and tongue were in different places, much like one's toes and fingers. But I also knew that she didn't mean it like that.

Grandma said that a hyena does not lick one's wounds out of kindness. Those who fought in the war had predatory hearts of their own. The howl of the hyenas was getting closer and so were the ghosts and moving shadows. Kehinde's sister, Maya, had seen the shadows, and after her visitation she walked like our dog and smelt like the starfish flower. No one played with her. She spent most of the time talking to herself and playing with rag dolls with spiky black hair and beady eyes. Rumour had it she had black ants in her head. Grandma said that she was cursed.

Soon after that the shadows emerged from the dark and entered our home. They were hungry and cold. We had no food to give them, so together with the blankets they took my sister, Thabo's sister and the two daughters of the man who killed the puppies. War had its own demands and unwritten rules. Stories abounded of razor blades, silent cuts, Vaseline and unimaginable cruelty. According to Grandma, one thing was certain: one didn't borrow foreign blood to fight one's war. The forests had eyes and ears and people in villages, memories that span centuries. It was our turn to give blood to appease the shadows.

At sunrise my sister came back dishevelled and disoriented. She walked sideways like a wounded crab. Her movement was timed and unsure, and with each step her face pulled itself together into an unsettled contortion. Her head was a swallow's nest: specks of grass, fragments of leaves and caked reddish-brown mud from the nearby fields. She looked at no one and her small hands clasped into a nervous ball, holding her blood-soaked rag of underwear. Touching her was out of the question. Asking her what had happened – unthinkable.

"Here, drink this. It will do you good." Grandma gave her a glass of milk – all we had – and looked away, as if sheltering from her own rain, now that we had our very own Maya. My sister grabbed the aluminium cup and embraced it with both hands. She drank the milk in small desperate gulps until the bottom of the cup unveiled itself and she peered into it as if looking for answers.

I suddenly remembered school and I seized my satchel, slung it across my back and took off. I hadn't eaten anything, but it didn't matter. There was no food anyway. I ran at full speed, carefully placing my bare feet in between small rocks, pebbles and tree stumps. And all the while it was raining inside me.

When I arrived at school the timetable was in full swing. I was late. The evil stare of the maths teacher followed me across the room. Our classroom was a dilapidated building, half-baked red clay bricks thrown together in a pile. On top of them lay big, broad termite-infested wooden beams supporting the sieve of a corrugated-iron roof. Beams of white light flooded the room through the holes in the ceiling and eggshell cracks in the walls, home to spiders, small lizards, ants, the hesitant chameleon and the occasional black scorpion. Behind a miasma of dust, the blackboard stared back at us with algebraic equations etched in permanent white chalk.

Slightly beyond the school yard, caterpillars had decimated deciduous trees into thin, gaunt-looking orphans. Grandma called caterpillars the ghosts of creation. It was a mystery, she said, how they turned into butterflies. Beyond the green cactus plants, flies were singing a frivolous hymn of praise in the depth of the pit latrine. A human foetus had been found inside its belly the week before, floating in a sea of excrement, bloated like an upturned white-bellied bull frog. Since then, a congregation of blowflies had gathered daily, shouting maddening hallclujahs, drawn by the stench. Each time I went to use the pit latrine, a cloud of flies rose to the sky like a ball of black cotton wool, only to drop rapidly to the ground in a synchronised wild dance when I left.

Grandma said this was a sign of the times. Someone amongst us harboured a dark secret. It had come to this, she said, that we were fighting ourselves both inside and outside and blamed the shadows. Little did she know that she'd one day find my sister, legs wide open, coat hanger in hand, about to dig her way out of war mischief.

I looked out of the window towards the edge of the forest and thought that the trees and tall grass were moving. Mounds of ant heaps morphed into strange formations, heading towards our school like a mirage in the midday sun. The forest was edging closer and closer like a silent wave. Red berets tilted to the right on multiple heads like scarecrows.

"Soldiers!" somebody shouted.

An armed man entered our classroom. He was of short, stocky build and charcoal black, with a bulbous nose that imposed itself between the lower end of his cranium and the thick upper lip of his wound of a mouth. It was as if an angry, harried god had plugged it there maliciously, like a big black mollusc clinging to the face of a gigantic rock. He rolled up the sleeves of his camouflage shirt and in one fell swoop, the textbooks, boxes of chalk, cane, empty bottle of ginger beer and blackboard duster fell to the floor, followed by the maths teacher who crashed backwards like an uprooted tree.

The soldier impaled a hunting knife in the desk. The blade cast a shadow on the dusty cement floor.

"We've come to flush out the dissidents amongst you and we won't stop until you tell us where they are," he yelled, and his piercing eyes were devilishly red with anger and delirious with hate.

His rifle leant against the wall and on his belt hung an upside-down bayonet. On his boots clung the soil of our country, a dusty reddish-brown tinge, the colour of freshly tilled fields.

There was silence in the room. A beam of light focused its

trajectory on the figure of the maths teacher, who was now lying face down on the table in front of the class, trussed up like a trapped crocodile, baring its teeth.

"I am only a teacher, sir. I have never seen any dissidents."

His tight reedy voice quivered and he tried, in vain, to lift his neck and look backwards while he spoke. We all knew there was no right or wrong answer, and whatever he said didn't matter anyhow. It wasn't about the dissidents. It was, as the President had said in his recent broadcast, about the cockroaches and enemies of the people. And that could mean anything.

"Don't insult me!" the man bellowed back, caressing a large wooden stick, freshly cut from the forest. "We will purge until there is no more blood to purge."

The soldier worked the maths teacher's buttocks with a religious determination, sucking up all the air in the room, making it difficult to breathe. We were all sweating profusely and flinching with each blow. In the end all that was left of the man was a big stain on the floor.

When the soldier finally let us go, the main road outside the school perimeter resembled a jungle airstrip. Each convoy that went by generated a cloud of dust, which settled on the trees and flowerbeds and sometimes on us, like brown snow flurries. Female teachers and older schoolgirls were lined up, trucks waiting. No one knew their destination. The belly of the truck opened up and they were pushed inside like cattle. Amidst the wailing and chaos in the school, the trucks left with their bountiful harvest, heading east towards the mountains under the cover of dust.

When I got home, an old stray dog lay under the meagre shade of the cactus tree, scratching its flea-infested ear, indifferent to the world beyond its own wounds. My sister lay under the scarcely more comforting shade of the acacia tree, on her back, her legs tied together by Grandma, sidestreams of tears flowing from the pools of her eyes into the thick mangrove of her hair. She was sifting the soil with her soft fingers like the rosary beads. And she had nothing with which to measure the distance between herself, the sky and heaven. Was it the same distance as the distance between her shoulder and hand? The tip of her fingers? Or was it farther than that?

That night we had food for the first time in many days. Ground millet porridge with sour milk, under the watchful gaze of the kerosene lamp. My sister's eyes drank the light and she made no attempt to get up and eat. There was a determination on her face that said nothing of the pain inside her. And the distance between her, the dull flame and us concealed everything.

The wind blew out the lamp and someone took advantage of the darkness. When the light came back, the plate was empty. This was our condition. We were the shadows.

Like Father

KATE SEFERIAN

On the eve of my retirement party, I talked to my dead wife for the first time in almost twenty years. It was nearly midnight. I had been sitting on the toilet for the better part of a half hour, sweating like a racehorse and suffering from a heinous bout of diarrhoea. Over the past six months, this affliction transitioned from annoying interruption to accepted and expected. I learned early on that I didn't need to try to be quiet when I was hit with the runs in the middle of the night, as my second wife, Serena, could sleep through a jackhammer. She was asleep now, her face covered in green mud to wage the nightly offensive against wrinkles. A giant sleeping mask enshrouded her head from the nose up. These night-time accoutrements did little to spark my sexual appetite, but that didn't matter any more. Come daylight, Serena's breasts poised fake and pert, her lips pink and pumped full, and her ash-blonde hair flicked here and there above her shoulders. Both men and women often swung their eyes up and down her body a few times. She basked in this attention; going under the knife for various tweaks and tugs, each more aggressive than the last, wasn't easy. There were a lot of yellow-stained bandages to change.

A brain aneurysm clipped my first wife's life short. Liberty was an umbilical cord that got tugged away prematurely, leaving our son and me flailing for a lifeline. I was coaching Blake's peewee football game when it happened, when that budding balloon in her brain popped. That was two decades ago. I never attended another of Blake's games.

As I sat on the toilet, the sweat beneath my thighs greasing the porcelain, my mutterings floated out and wafted away with only the bathroom ceiling fan whirring in response. I let out a quiet groan as my colon doggedly continued its cleanse.

"Liberty, come on."

Silence.

"Liberty, please say something. Tell me what the hell I'm doing."

Remember when we visited Ocean City that one summer? How long ago was that? Blake was – what, six years old?

"I remember. I had to reschedule my flight to Tokyo for the annual budget meeting so I could stay at the resort through Sunday with you guys. Blake would've gone ballistic if I missed his Shark Week swimming debut."

That's right. I got that horrific sunburn and ridiculous tan lines. You called me Mama Lobster and Blake dumped aloe vera gel into our bed.

"Yeah." I winced as my stomach cramped and gurgled. I pressed my fingertips down hard over my temples.

And Blake got that eye infection from swimming in the ocean. We had to go to the doctor twice that week. He ended up missing his big show after all.

"He cried for hours when we told him he couldn't swim for Shark Week," I whispered.

He had to wear that black eye patch for a month, remember? And you swiped a second one from the doctor's office so you could wear one, too.

"I remember."

The retirement party wasn't my idea. I didn't want one. Serena insisted we host it as a show of our intent to stay relevant now that I would no longer have much of a presence in the office – and by default, in the office's buzzing social circles. Serena assured me I wouldn't have to do a thing to prepare for our party, and I kept getting awkwardly underfoot while caterers in cummerbunds and bow ties scurried around our backyard. Holly, newly bespectacled – Serena's attempt to bribe the optometrist to jump straight to laser surgery was unsuccessful – hovered behind me while watching the black hole of party planning develop into a clean and billowing white tent with string lights and potted peonies. Liquor bottles gleamed on the bar, and vases filled with shimmering, pointless pebbles decorated the tables.

"Mom is really gearing up for this shindig, huh?" I said to Holly, placing my hand on the top of her warm head. Holly peered at me, her eyes slightly larger due to lens magnification. She looked like Bambi.

"Do you think it'll be OK if maybe I go to my room after dinner?" Holly whispered. She tugged at the sequinned dress Serena had bought for her. "This thing itches."

"Ah, a getaway plan for Dad's party. I see how it is," I replied, winking at her. "Yeah, kiddo, don't worry. I'll distract Mom. Just don't hog all the whisky, all right? I need some comfort during this nightmare, too."

"Daaadddddd," Holly squealed, looking appalled. "I don't want that stuff. And Mom would kill me."

I laughed. This kid was too sweet to be Serena's daughter. "All right, we'll eat our feelings with the cake, then. What'd Mom get? Chocolate? Gluten free?"

"I think it's cheesecake. With strawberries," Holly said. "I saw the caterers carry it in."

"Nice. Artery-clogging. I like it. Now don't tell your mom, but I'm ready for a pre-dinner drink."

What Serena didn't know was that I'd invited Blake. I hadn't seen him since he was arrested the day after Christmas five years ago, hadn't talked to him since he called me from jail. On the phone he sounded stoned and far away, each response delayed just enough to fuel my quickly mounting anger. All I could decipher through the gauze of my own fury was our mutual need for his mother. I was a pathetic replacement.

When Blake was released last month, the prison provided me with his contact information and the name of his parole officer. His phone rang seven times and went to voicemail, Blake huskily telling me to leave a message. My son spoke to me for the first time in years just then, but it wasn't really him – it was static, a one-dimensional recording. Even so, it was enough to nearly unravel me. I stuttered out an invitation. Then I went into my study and poured myself two fingers of Glenlivet. I didn't want to tell Serena. So I never did.

The animosity Serena held tight and hot for Blake wasn't unfounded. She had never liked him and, initially, simply kept whatever interactions they had to a minimum. Holly was her excuse and her distraction. Holly's father had skipped out shortly after she was born, and she was only a year old when her mom and I met. The first time I convinced Serena that Blake was capable of babysitting Holly turned out to be the last time. We came home to find both kids gone, the driveway deserted, and the downstairs lights still on. Blake, in good spirits, pulled in an hour later, Holly safe and sound in her car seat in the back. Serena was livid, and I couldn't quite tell if that was because Blake had stolen her Vicodin or because he had taken Holly with him to sell it.

Halfway through the party, I found myself sitting on the front porch. Lightning bugs blinked on and off and floated above the grass and hedges. My eyes had a hard time trailing the same firefly on its summer flight. I was a little drunk. I had been a little drunk for about three hours now, steadily maintaining my buzz without venturing into the fog of pre-blackout. I could hear Serena's sharp laughter all the way from the side yard. A car pulled into the neighbour's driveway. I squinted and leaned forward a bit, wiping a clammy hand on my thigh. I could just make out the portly figure of my colleague Ed as he emerged from the driver's seat and walked across the street towards me.

"The man of the hour! You look like shit," Ed said as he climbed up my front steps.

"Do I? Once you get your beer goggles on, you might be whistlin' a different tune," I replied, raising my glass in greeting. "Bar's in the side yard. Bring me back one of whatever you're having."

Ed had recently undergone surgery to remove his prostate and, during a networking dinner at our firm's summer conference in Palm Springs, told me that the doctor advised him to regularly try jerking off to see if he would be capable of ever getting an erection again. Ed, his head drooping uncomfortably close to mine and his words punctuated with the sour breath of four martinis, continued to confide over our company-sponsored filet mignon that Viagra was his only way of being able to follow the doctor's orders. Now whenever I saw Ed, it took all I had not to gaze in the general direction of his balls – not out of pity, like a good friend and co-worker might. More out of utter fear.

"Don't punish me for being a little tipsy," I murmured.

You're not tipsy. You're drunk.

"It's my party. I can be drunk if I want. You're being childish with the silent treatment."

I'm talking to you now, aren't I?

"But, Liberty, you're not being nice."

I don't think you're really in a position to pontificate on the tenets of being nice.

"All right. All right. Fair enough. I admit I'm nervous."

What did that one teacher say about Blake's speech skills when he had to memorise those lines for the school production of Beauty and the Beast*?*

"It was *Peter Pan*, not *Beauty and the Beast*. *Peter Pan* was in kindergarten with Miss Felix."

Look at you, Mr Memory. So Miss Felix, what did she say? Something about Blake's charisma getting in the way of delivering the actual lines? He was too creative for his own good.

"I just remember that teacher's startling likeness to a young Sophia Loren."

You would. I think you have those videotapes somewhere, of Blake rehearsing his lines. You told him that someday he could write his own lines to a play, but right now he had to say the lines Miss Felix gave him.

"I told him he was too young to have a damn-the-man mindset. And that he and I could write our own version of *Peter Pan* after he did it the right way for school."

Closing my eyes, I listened to the swelling call of cicadas. The stifling heat kept them awake; their daytime rhythms continued permeating the night-time air.

"And then Blake marched up to Miss Felix during the dress rehearsal and told her to damn the man. Right, Liberty?"

And after the parent-teacher conference the next day, the three of us feasted on ice-cream sundaes.

Ed returned with two gin and tonics. "You talking in your sleep, old timer?" he asked as he handed me a fresh drink. I lifted an eyebrow and took a sip. These bartenders were heavy-handed.

We sat side by side in the rocking chairs on the front porch, stretching our legs out and slouching low. The hot, still air sat on top of us. Sweat dripped down the back of my neck and gathered in the crease above my belly. Ed pulled out his pack of Camels and lit up. He tapped one out and proffered it to me, but I shook my head.

"Serena won't mind if I smoke?" Ed asked, looking around for an ashtray or a discreet place to tap his ash.

"Don't worry about it. Front porch is my territory tonight," I said.

"Speaking of, I'm surprised you aren't out back now, you know, playing hostess," Ed said. "I said hello to Serena, and she asked me if I had seen you around."

"Ah. She must be itching to tell some fresh meat her party story," I said.

Ed chuckled. "Yeah, I'm sure there's someone here who hasn't heard it yet. You could at least give her that much. She likes telling that story. All you have to do is grin like an asshole and stand next to her. Hold her drink. Maybe tickle that tight ass of hers when she's done regaling her guests."

Ed could say stuff like that without getting punched. He had just enough smarm to be entertaining, but not so much that you got offended. He was shady without being off colour. He knew how Serena was, and he appreciated her assets. Plus, he was spot on about the drink. Whenever Serena and I attended any kind of social gathering, her go-to cocktail story was how she and I first met. Once we were standing in a nice bundle of partygoers, she'd hand me her drink, and I knew she was revving up for her little show. She needed both hands to convey how I blustered through changing her flat tyre in the Walmart parking lot. The part she doesn't tell is how I was there on a beer run for Ed's Super Bowl party when I was supposed to be at Blake's parents' weekend at university.

Ed and I had been on the front porch for about a half hour. I heard Serena's heels clacking down the hallway leading to the house's front entrance, and I knew the screen door would swing open. It did. I turned and looked at Serena's body through the mesh, then her face poking out from behind it.

"Ed, we've got some more shrimp put out on the ice if you

want some. And tell Nancy her mustard-greens salad recipe is to die for. I'm so sorry she couldn't make it out tonight," Serena said.

"I will certainly tell her. She'll be delighted to hear it," Ed said. "And I don't mind if I do stick my face in a pile of that shrimp. Harry, you want anything?" Ed turned to me as he pushed his way out of the rocking chair. I declined.

As Ed passed Serena, she kissed his cheek and thanked him for coming. Then she sat down next to me.

"Are you having a good time, dear?" Serena asked. She crossed her tan legs and leaned towards me.

"It's been absolutely wonderful. You put a lot of effort into this," I said, looking out into the darkness of the front yard. No cars had passed by since Ed arrived.

Serena exhaled, humming a single note. She folded her hands in her lap. "You've been sitting out here for almost the entire time. It would be nice if you could mingle with our friends for a little while. They keep asking for you. I'm almost embarrassed to direct them to the porch."

"*Our* friends?"

Serena's eyebrows furrowed into quizzical brackets. "Yes, *our* friends. The people we invited."

"Right."

I swirled the liquid in my almost empty glass. The remaining ice cubes clicked and tinkled. For a minute I listened to artificial exclamations and staccato laughter coming from out back. Cicada chatter would be cotton for my ears. I couldn't bruise from what I couldn't hear.

"Where's Holly?" I asked.

"Oh, who knows. In her room, I think. She ran off right after she scarfed down a chicken kebab. I should go get her. She doesn't need to have her nose stuck in a book when we have people over."

"No, let her be. I don't think this is her idea of a good time."

"It's rude. She's being rude. And you're being rude."

I stayed silent. The sticky air muffled the faint stutter of a car engine down the street.

"Harry. Harry? What, is this not your idea of a good time, either?"

"This wasn't my idea, period. I didn't need this party."

Serena blew a breath out. "Well, I did it for you. I know you didn't ask for it. But I wanted this for you. And people came. So it would be decent – no, *great* – if you could get your ass up off this front porch and show some face."

"I'm waiting for someone."

Serena had stood up to go back inside, and she smoothed out the bottom of her silky sundress. Then she looked at me. "Oh? Who? I think everyone who RSVP'd is here," she said. She brushed a crumb of something off the hem of her dress. The pleasant drowsiness of my now four-hour heavy buzz made me brave. Made me reckless with my words.

"Blake."

"I'm sorry. What?"

"I'm waiting for Blake," I repeated.

"Like hell you are," Serena said. "That's not fucking funny."

"I invited Blake to my retirement party."

"Harry."

"What."

"Harry," Serena hissed. "Look at me."

I looked at my second wife. "He's my son."

"You didn't think this was something you should tell me before the goddamn party?" Serena's voice was a paper cut.

"I haven't seen him in more than five years."

"That's because he's a convicted felon! That boy is to go nowhere – Harry, look at me – *nowhere* near my house, my daughter, or my guests. I will not have a scene here. I will not see his face on this property."

"You mean our house, our daughter, and our guests," I said quietly. I tipped an ice cube from my glass into my mouth and crunched down on it. I held the empty glass out to Serena. "I want another goddamn drink from the goddamn bar at this goddamn party."

Serena walked back inside the house without a word. She didn't take my glass. I had been planted in the rocking chair for the entire evening, and I heaved myself up onto my feet. I could hear caterers puttering around inside, and I went down the front hallway and turned into the bright, yellow kitchen. An acned young waiter, probably a teen working his summer job, smiled at me and continued folding the napkins. I pulled a twenty out of the cookie jar we use for grocery money and handed him the bill.

"Take this. You're doing a great job," I told him. "Are all the liquor bottles outside by the bar?"

"Thank you, sir! No, sir, no, we have backups by your pantry door," the boy said, pointing to the boxes stacked on the other side of the counter.

"Perfect," I crowed. I walked over and opened a new bottle of Jim Beam. After I refilled my glass, I returned to the front porch. Chinese lanterns lined the railing, and they softly bumped into each other as I thudded across the floorboards. I noticed that Ed's car was gone from the neighbour's driveway across the street. Son of a bitch didn't even say goodbye.

I waved to the guests as they walked back to their cars, arms loaded with Tupperwared leftovers. I had no idea where Serena was. She wouldn't be helping with the clean-up. I could hear the caterers dismantling the tent and breaking down the bar. They were done with work for the evening; their hoots and hushed laughter carried through the musky air.

The Chinese lanterns glowed brighter as the headlights and tail lights of departing cars and the catering van disappeared down the road. The house lights downstairs turned off. The buzzing of the cicadas was now deafening and pulsed in my ears. I liked how I couldn't even hear my own thoughts. It was close to 1.00 a.m. There was still time. I unfolded my limbs and pushed myself up – too quickly. My spit turned thick and the porch dipped. I leaned towards the railing and vomited onto a wayward lantern and into the rose bushes. The acidity brought tears to my eyes, and I heaved twice more. A single drop of sweat fell from my nose.

"I'm sorry, Liberty," I rasped.

Don't tell me. Tell Blake.

"Blake," I coughed out.

Yes. Blake. Our son. Your son. Not me.

"But . . ." I said, turning in a circle wildly. I wiped spittle from my chin. I knew how this looked. "Don't pity me, Liberty."

I don't, Harry. Don't you worry about that.

"You're the one that left us. Left me with the mess of myself. I couldn't clean up after Blake, too."

I stumbled back to the rocking chair and eased myself down into its embrace. Keep your eyes open, Harry, I told myself. I stared at the darkness coating the driveway and made sure there was still time.

The moist morning air snaked into my open mouth and across my skin and woke me up. The grey dawn was doing its best to illuminate the sky, but a dismal atmosphere deadened the daylight. A cloud surrounded the house. I felt like something died on my tongue, its rotten taste seeping into my gums and down my throat. I wanted water, but I didn't want to move.

I stayed draped across the rocking chair for some time. I heard Holly's light footsteps approach the front door and a timid squeak of the lock unhitching.

"Dad?" she whispered. "Daddy? Do you want some orange juice? Are you awake?"

I opened my eyes. I could feel the crust of sleep clumped like sand below my lashes. "Yes, sweetie, good morning," I croaked. "Juice or water would be nice."

"OK. I'm going to make pancakes, too. But no chocolate chips. I think we're out," Holly whispered back. She closed the door softly and pattered away down the front hall.

Serena couldn't see me like this. I threw my weight forward and landed on all fours, my knee knocking over an empty glass and my hand landing on top of it. Shattered pieces burst from beneath my palm. A shard lodged itself in the meat of my thumb. I watched little dots of blood grow along the shard's edge, the flesh pink and fuming. Gently, I dabbed my fingertip into the wound and then swiped it across the rough wood beneath me, leaving a weak, dirty-red slash.

Finger-painting now, are we?

"Maybe I'll get a splinter as well," I murmured. My voice snagged on its own words.

And that'll make you feel better? You like leaving these scars? Don't be silly, Harry.

"Last night did me in. I'm feeling a bit empty right now, Liberty. I'm feeling a little hurt. That's allowed."

Moving forward is better. That porch chair is bad news. It's not good for you to sit there, just lingering and wondering.

"Yeah, well, I think it's pretty clear that I don't know what's good for me these days. I sort of like what's bad. And if it ain't broke . . ."

Tell me what's not broken. I'd like to know. Because I know I –

"I'll get you a towel," Serena said loudly. She peered at me through the screen door but didn't open it. I watched her robe swing as she turned away from me and walked back down the hall.

I sat there, cross-legged, and listened. Off in the distance a dog barked, its echoes cracking and bouncing across the neighbourhood.

When Serena returned, she stepped outside and dangled the dish towel in front of my face.

"Well, would you look at that," she remarked, gazing down at our porch steps. "I've never seen one up close."

She bent over and plucked up the dead cicada. "I heard the males die immediately after they mate. God, they make such a racket in this heat."

I reached out and touched the husk of the cicada's body, traced its tissue-paper skin with my bloody fingertip. The wings were transparent, the thread-like veins forming a lifeless map. Two eyes bulged out in a forever stare.

Serena flicked the insect far into our front yard. "You should use some hydrogen peroxide when you clean that cut," she said over her shoulder as she went back inside the house. The screen door slapped back into its frame, the hinges squealing. I could smell Holly's pancakes.

I looked down at my upturned palm and grasped the fragment of glass with my other hand. I pulled the piece out slowly. It didn't feel like anything.

"The ability of writers to imagine what is not the self, to familiarise the strange and mystify the familiar, is the test of their power."

Toni Morrison

Kite

ZOE GILBERT

Firwit wakes with his cheek hot against waxy sheepskin and remembers, as he rubs away the itch of it with his gnarled knuckles, that he is alone. His mind is slower now, it creaks in the mornings as his bones do, and it is only the feel of this sheepskin wad beneath his head that reminds him. He has burned the feather pillows, choking on their scorched smoke. In case of fever lurking there, he told himself. He did not believe, and still does not, Ma Rincepan's words, the day she helped him clear the sickness from the room.

"Look close," Ma Rincepan said, dangling one of the pillows from her stubby fingers. All Firwit saw was a well-used sack of down, blotched brown. "I can know who stuffed this from the jig-jag tacking and all the quills poking through, for want of soaping the inner. One of Guller's, done himself." She tore at a loose corner, and pulled out a fistful of brown and grey down. "He'll put any old flotsam in them. I daresay whatever he sweeps from his own floor. I opened up one I had off him, once, to put into fresh ticking, and found a lark's head amongst the down. My youngest had been talking in his sleep all winter and that were the reason." Ma Rincepan poked about in her fist, sending curling drifts into the air. "Here's one, see?" She picked out a straight grey quill. "A flight feather, that is. Put those in your pillows and even the soundest mind won't rest. No sleep, not even for the blessed, with that under your ear. Guller knows that sure as anyone. Maybe it's carelessness, or meanness with his stuffing, but I see malice in it."

Firwit did not see malice, for he was too weary to see anything at all at that moment. Then he saw only the tales of the village women, his neighbour Ma Rincepan among them; women who will find magic where there is nothing, and prefer gossip to good sense.

He is too old now for fancies, for dreaming. He burned the pillows only because he wanted them gone. But turning against his folded sheepskin at night now, for he will not take a new pillow, he dreams his brother, Murnon, over and over.

A cracked heel bone – a stumble in the sheep field, his first slip in sixty years – was all that kept Murnon in his bed at first. He was rueful. The sheep would keep, he said. But Murnon, his foot nestled in a pile of fleece, could not keep his nightly habit of walking out at the deepest hour. He lay awake, a fidgeting, twitching heap against the pillow. Even though he'd never wanted more than a few hours' rest before the dawn, after he came home from his nightly ramble, sleep was stolen from him now that he must lie in bed. A sickness only, a strange fever that would pass, Firwit thought, brought on by a split bone. So, he let in the night wind off the hill, hoping the brackeny air would bring Murnon peace. He warmed the hardened honey and sweetened the last of the barley bread his brother had made, but Murnon would not take it. You eat, he said, and rubbed his reddened eyes. In the dark, Murnon whimpered, but when Firwit lit a candle for the comfort of light his brother snuffed it out, as if he knew, even then, it must not be used up.

After four days and nights of wakefulness, Firwit could no longer get sense from Murnon. After six, he barely recognised his brother. His haggard face became a wraith of its original, eyes shrunk deep in hollows dark as bruises. The voice that rasped from his parched mouth spoke in riddles, only halting now and then to beg for a sight of stars.

Firwit used strips from his own workshop, edge cuttings of sheepskin, to bind the mittens tight on his brother's hands, for after Murnon had plucked the lashes Firwit feared he'd tatter his very eyelids away. Still, his brother chewed through the leather, every night when Firwit gave in to sleep for an hour or two. Sleep, the gift he could not give his brother.

A fortnight it is now since Murnon took those chewed strips, hoarded for the purpose, and made one long cord. Plaited neatly, it had been, as if his fingers found calm at the end, as if his mind regained judgement and his wrecked body some unworldly strength. Firwit, waking to a chilly dawn, a cold and empty bed beside him, stumbled senselessly out along the lane, calling softly. The tree his brother had chosen was not far away, but it was high. The cord that held him there below the branch shadows was tough, too tough for Firwit's pocket knife, so Firwit hacked in panic at the leather and was not ready when the weight of the body dropped hard and threw him against the knotted tree roots. The criss-cross pattern of the plaited leather stayed in the loose skin of Murnon's throat. Firwit covered the mark with his own best kerchief for the burying, in pity, in penance.

It is that moment, the struggle of his knife against the cord and the joined tumble of two old men against ground that hurt only one of them, which tosses Firwit from his sheepskin sleep each night. He bears the terror without the comfort of light, for he wants his share of darkness. It was Murnon made the candles from their own sheep's tallow, never Firwit. There are two left, pale guardians standing on the mantel, silent on the matter of how they came into being. In the midnight black Firwit listens to his own fast breath like the ghost of his brother's in this room. Then he listens to the parchment in the windloft above his bed, the smooth, creamy skins of Murnon's sheep splayed in their frames, which shift and jolt against the beams in the night breeze. So unlike the sheep they came from, those thinned skins. They are like row upon row of ships' sails, catching the breeze through the latticed walls, longing to cut across water in full sun. The gentle clacks of the frames in the rush of air used to call him to a calm day's work of soaking, scraping, cutting. They sound to him like awkward wingbeats now. Is this what Murnon heard, a roof full of flapping birds above his sleepless head? Was it this, over a pillow stuffed with Guller's feathers, that made him walk out every night?

Firwit rubs his knuckles, stiff as untended hinges. When his fingers will bend he pulls on boots, fleece and cap, pushes the door and steps out into the quiet night. Its air is a sweet-salt draught of grass and sap and seaweed. Bones aching, he lets the slope lead him further up the hillside, treading his path from the night before, the night before that. The sea hushes far below; it must be calm at the shore. The forest whispers back. He is the only restless one, out in the night.

Before the turn, before sleep left him altogether, Murnon was the night walker, out for hours, watching the sheep, watching what else? Firwit has not dwelt on it till now, now he is taking his turn in the night. He has come to think that this is where his brother left his spirit, in the dark on the hill, for he is sure it was not in his body that last week. The raging, weeping thing that half-resembled Murnon, writhing in its feather bed, did not know him, and he did not know it.

He climbs higher with the path, hearing scurries in the undergrowth, until in the moonlight he can see the stone wall of the sheep field above. The smell of their dung comes to him and is a comfort and a worry at once. He only understands these creatures as carcasses, can handle a flayed sheepskin with his eyes shut, but living, breathing in this field, they are Murnon's domain. Reaching the wall he scans for the huddle of bodies, imagines them warm in their waxy coats. He would like to grasp those curls, like a human head, like his own before it withered to the whiskered scalp beneath his cap. Murnon's curls were white as sea foam by the end.

The sheep are at the high end of the field, where the earth is driest, he supposes. Perhaps he can get to know their ways, get to grips with the work his brother did. He skirts the field outside the low stone wall, creeping towards them. His toes are dampening with the dew soaking his boots, the wind rushing louder on the hill, filling his ears with its low chords. He stops when he hears a high, mournful whistle floating in the currents above him. A shape circles against the ghostly cloud, then sweeps down to land on the top wall of the sheep field. Crows will peck the eyes from new lambs, Murnon has told him. But there are no lambs yet, and he knows that whistling song. It is no crow.

He walks towards the shape. When he raises a hand to pull his cap down tighter against the wind it rises and swoops close over him, its piping wail threading through his head before it turns and flies off towards the forest. Firwit stares after it. That whistle is the call of a kite. Never has he heard one at night, but when has he listened? He knows from the hunters that kites sleep through the dark. The younger ones even lie down, like people in their beds.

There are still many hours before dawn will come and the night is chill, as if the moon's icy eye made cold where it spread its light. The sheep are quiet. Firwit unbends his creaking knees and begins to tramp again, along the ridge of the hill towards the wood. The ground drops down to the trees, where the wind cannot reach to whip at him. He steps between two trunks, into the wood's held breath, and stands. The quiet is like a new blanket about his head. It is darker, the wood is fuzzed grey where moonlight reaches down between branches, and Firwit stalks slowly on his hidden feet, placing palms on trunks, soothed by the scent of bracken as he treads it down.

From deep in the wood, he hears the long, piping cry. He shakes his head, to shake out the sound, but it comes again. He is careless of the brambles that tear at his legs, of the cracks of snapping deadwood as he pushes through the tangle, holding twigs from his eyes with his bent elbow. Moonlight pours into the clearing and he can see, in a wide patch that has been swept clean of leaf mulch, a dark thing, lying like a dropped shawl. He looks around at the still trees. Bending down close, he makes out that the thing is a large bird. It looks dead. He nudges it with a knuckle, then grasps a wing, the feathers seeming to thrust against his palm. He turns it over. It is not whole. There is no mound of chest, or soft belly feathers. Rather, it is the husk of a kite, no bones within, the inside of the skin rough but dry, hardened. Someone has made it, carefully peeled the skin from bird flesh, cleaned it, kept the feathers good. He thinks of Guller, the bird man, for who else would know, or want, to make such a thing. Firwit picks it up by the head and finds twists of wool stuffed inside. It is wool from Murnon's sheep. He knows by the feel of its waxy warmth, the spring of the curl.

All the walk home, the world is silent. Firwit carries the kite skin, the wind giving life to its wings even in his grasp. His thoughts drift with the whistle in the woods, the looping calls of kites woven together with his brother's cries. Murnon, Guller, birds where they should not be; there's no sense to it, and he feels the place where keeps his brother in his mind grow dark. He cuts Murnon down from the tree three, four, five times before he reaches home, where he tucks the bird husk under the rosemary bush in the yard before he opens the door. It does not belong in the house.

The parchment is silent in the windloft. It will soon be day.

After dozing through dawn's rustlings, Firwit wakes as he often does now, to a rap at the door and his name called, loud and cheery. Ma Rincepan has taken to bringing him milk, and lately adding a loaf or a cake, of a morning. He watches her gaze flit around the smirched room when she sidles in.

Ma Rincepan frowns. "Don't you get worn, Firwit," she says, as she clatters about. "You get back to your habits, that'll set you right." When she passes him a cup of milk he sits up, heavy, in his bed, and watches her. She is fishing now into the cold pot where yesterday he tried to boil the salt out of some cured mutton for supper, as Murnon used to do, but instead turned the meat to shoe leather.

"Three soaks, and change the water," she says briskly, the grey strip dripping between her fingers. "I'll give this to the hound."

Firwit's only skill with food is turning the sheep's soured milk into cheese, but the season is long over, and he's none left to trade. Bread and meat were Murnon's gifts, another thing he will have to learn. As if she sees his thought, Ma Rincepan goes on, "I'm needing some good raw wool, myself. Enough for a dozen skeins or so. I know Murnon had a few sacks left to trade." She is glancing at the stack of sacks, dry in the hearth corner. "Keep you in milk and meat a good while on that. Eggs too, if you want, from the ducks. Better than those nest-robbed nothings Guller used to give your brother – barely a mouthful each one, and beaks sticking between your teeth."

Firwit is grateful for the kindness. He nods and Ma Rincepan opens up a sack and begins pulling out handfuls of waxy curls, filling her basket. As it reaches brimful, Firwit again reaches the edge of his knowledge, which used to match so neatly with Murnon's that neither took any notice of where one stopped knowing and the other started. How much wool is a good trade, he cannot guess. How many eggs, how much meat, is a brimming basket worth?

Ma Rincepan closes up the sack, and rubbing her hands on her skirts, peers into the empty grate. "I'll send Pud up with some wood if you're lacking. Keep your bones warm. This spring's chilly yet."

Firwit is still clutching the cup of milk, not drinking though he is thirsty. He is thinking of the bird husk in the yard, the kite whistling in the forest. Ma Rincepan is staring at him, hands on hips. "Must keep body and soul together, Firwit," she says, stern as to a child, "and the best way to keep whole is to keep at your work." She nods up at the windloft, from where the faint tap of the parchment frames echoes.

As she bends to poke at the dead ashes, a feather slips from between the ceiling planks and drifts down to stroke Ma Rincepan's neck. She shrieks and bats blindly at it, but when she sees it is not a spider, or a moth wagging frantic wings, she is solemn.

"What's one like this doing here?" she asks Firwit. The feather is as long as her forearm, striped red. He can't answer. He works at keeping birds from the windloft, hooking down nests that sometimes sprout in the rafters. "Not one as belongs in a house. You mark this, Firwit. The only man likely to have feathers like this about him is Guller, and you know where I believe he stands in all of this."

Firwit's neck is hot against the sheepskin wad. Old Ma's tales, he reminds himself, but the feather has irked him. It looks to be a kite's. He left the bird husk in the yard.

He climbs the ladder to the windloft, when she has gone. The wind flicks the parchment skins in their frames, taut white sails, and he walks between the rows, letting the breeze that has dried them cool the sweat on his neck. The wind is soft today through the loft's open sides, the lattice of beams there casting stripes of shadow across the skins. They are sleek, unblemished, every one scalded and scraped in the good calm of work that Firwit used to find so easily. He crouches in the shady space between the frames, and picks up a long feather, reddish brown. Another lies in the next row, turning in the draught. He looks up for nests, even though he knows Ma Rincepan was right. These are no eave-birds. The long whistle of the kite on the hill, and its reply caught in the deep net of the forest, echo in his head.

It is Murnon's flock that gave the hides, Murnon's skill with a knife that split them, so cleanly, that each hide yielded two faultless sheets. At the loft's far end is the last skin, the one he's yet to work at. When it is finished, there will be nothing to do but take up Murnon's knife and begin learning how to slaughter, how to bleed, and finally, how to flay. Murnon's blade is long, heavy, petering to a fine point. Firwit picks up his own blade, a dull crescent moon; feels the sweep and arch of the scraping work in his shoulder. He tests the curved metal edge with his thumb. He has done half of everything, more than forty years.

He puts the blade back up on its hook and carries the two feathers down from the windloft and out into the yard. He cannot remember which of them, himself or Murnon, hammered down the stones that shine now in the places they've trodden most. He scans the lane below and then ducks to look beneath the rosemary bush. The bird skin has gone. Carried away by a fox, of course, or one of the village dogs. But it is Ma Rincepan's warning he cannot shake from his mind as he lies back down on his bed. He's not spoken to Guller for many years. It was Murnon did any trades they might need with him. Firwit, ever hearing the man's shrill laugh in the ale room or on the lane, would turn away. There was something in Guller's childlike face, some darkness behind it, that he could not abide.

Firwit sleeps, deep and dreamless against his sheepskin, until dusk. Later, when the bats begin to sweep the insects from the gloom, he sets off again, up the hill, letting the wind fill his ears.

At the sheep field he sits in the nook Murnon built into the wall for the purpose, the stone pressing into his spine, and waits. When the piping call of the kites begins, he follows the sound in his mind, its threads spooling over and round and down to the wood. But pushing once more through the wood's spindles and sweet bracken, he finds the clearing empty. They are leaves, not feathers, that rustle and rise around his boots. Only as he is tramping home in the rug-thick dark before dawn does he hear the faintest wheeling cry behind him.

It is up to the windloft he goes in the first morning light. Long feathers litter the floor, turning, red and silver grey. He gathers them up, feels them resist his clutch as they pulse in the breeze.

His head is furred with lack of sleep. His bones feel weak. Ma

Rincepan will not come knocking yet, and it is for the comfort of the familiar arch and sweep that he takes his crescent blade from its hook and begins to work at the last skin. The long rasps as he scrapes are like breaths. He sees Murnon lying in his feather bed, his eyes red raw, his skin faded to ash. Still he scrapes, long slow sweeps across the skin. When his arm is tired he changes hands and scrapes the other way, but still no calm. He drops the blade, picks up the bag where he has stuffed the feathers and climbs back down, his hands shaky on the ladder.

Firwit's knuckles are hardened wax again when he raps at Guller's door, which is streaked in green-grey ridges. Above the door, a frame the shape of a small crooked house is built into the wall in place of a lintel. Inside the crooked house, caged by iron spindles, a magpie rattles back and forth. He's seen this before, as a child, when the first fowlmonger lived here. The magpie hunts for the way out, not understanding what it is to be caught, no notion of a trap.

As the door swings open a rancid stink hits him, of bird grease and feathers scorched in the grate.

Guller's black eyes stare up at him. He is no taller than a child, and his smile is childish, gap-toothed.

"Ah! Fine to see you, Firwit the parchment man. Come in, come in." His voice is wheedling.

"Let that sorry prisoner out," Firwit replies, nodding up at the scuttling magpie, and waits for Guller's shrill laugh to be over before following him inside.

A string of songbirds, tied like onions, hangs drying above the hearth. There are feathers everywhere, stuck in cobwebs, drifting like thistledown on the floor. A white goose lies on the table, each wing severed and fanned, held outspread by a peeled branch tied along its length. The goose's eyes follow Firwit as he steps around the room.

"What use would a bird skin be?" Firwit asks. He does not want to breathe this foul air long.

"Where shall I begin, parchment man? A wren skin for luck at sea. A rook skin for stealth. A swallow skin to dry a drunk."

"A kite skin."

"Ah! Those high-sky spirits." Guller's eyes dart and flash. His grin reveals sharp yellow teeth. "You hear them, up on the hill?"

"I believe that's where they belong," Firwit says.

"And that's where you found those, eh?" Guller is looking at the reddish spears that poke from Firwit's sack.

"These I found in the house."

"What luck you have. Brought them for me, have you? I'll do you a good trade for those." Guller scoops from a pocket a fistful of tiny eggs, blue, brown and white, some speckled, not two the same among them, and holds them up to Firwit. "Shouldn't find beak nor bone in there," he says, "but they'll make breakfast either way."

"A kite skin," Firwit repeats. His jaw is tight.

"Good for flying, I'd say." Guller laughs, looking sidelong at Firwit. "So high they fly, those sky spirits. You hear them, even when you can't see them." He begins to whistle, that same looping, wavering note that spins in the darkness above the sheep field and into the wood. Guller's eyes are closed. He begins to sway and drift around the room, singing, whistling, as if the spirit of a kite were in his mouth.

The smog of the room is caught in Firwit's throat. He grips his bag of feathers and stares at the goose on the table, its wings outstretched beside it. The dark red spots on its sides have spread.

"A kite skin, Guller, with my brother's wool tucked inside." Firwit's voice croaks. "I had it. Now it's gone."

The whistle has carried Guller in his dance to a dark corner. He shakes something out, making dust rise, and brings to Firwit the hollow bird he carried from the hill.

"Yours now, then, parchment man," he says, and holds it out. "It was Murnon's. I made it for him myself, when he asked."

"What for?" Firwit grasps the wings, feels again the strength in them, the force of taut feathers.

Guller grins and lets out a curling note between his teeth.

"Good for flying, like I said. Lifting the spirits. You put your mind to it – and Murnon could – or, you put your mind in it." Guller nods at the skin. "Only takes this, and a little wanting, a little bite of a red-top agaric, chewed up. See the stars from up there, kite-wise."

Firwit turns the bird skin and pokes his finger into the pinch of Murnon's wool beneath the scalp.

"Sky spirit, your brother. Lover of stars." Guller's eyes no longer flash. "Come yourself, to the woods one night," he calls, as Firwit opens the door and leaves the rattle of magpie in its cage behind him.

Firwit lies down on his bed with the bag of feathers stuffed beneath his head. Flying, Guller said. A sky spirit, your brother. He knew Murnon by day, sheep-tender, bread-maker. He did not know him by night. He twists and turns, searching for Murnon in the reddish dark behind his eyelids. Flight feathers, they are, inside the sacking, but it is only the quills poking through that keep him from sleep. Perhaps it does not matter, the dark space in his mind where Murnon sits. Perhaps his brother felt this too, and that is why he walked out at night. The wind rises and the parchment frames clatter in the windloft, until he rises and climbs the ladder, squinting in the bright stripes of light.

The skin he meant to finish leans up against the lattice, lit from behind, and he sees that with his scraping, the sweep of one hand and then the other, he has thinned out shapes like two curving wings. With his short cutting knife, he slices through the parchment skin. He needs only a length of twine then; a few stitches. As he works, the last dots of down that have followed him from Guller's house lift from his shirt and are carried out through the open eaves and lost.

He climbs the hill in the light. The sheep look up from grazing when he reaches the wall. He does not know whether they sleep at night, or only rest sometimes, when the world wearies them. He tucks the kite skin between the stones around the flat seat of the wall nook, and then in the white daylight he sits, the waxen white curls of the sheep below him, the deep white ruffs of cloud above, the cut parchment pale in his hands. When a kite's whistle streams from far above, it is as it should be: the sound of the hill, with the chit of the birds in the undergrowth and the hiss of the insects in the grass.

Firwit lets the evening lull him, but when the first bats come to cut through the dark he is alert. With the night the wind grows stronger, the sounds of the hill are washed away, and he unwinds the twine across his lap, his fingers slow from stillness. There are no stars to be seen, but a smudge of cloud is brightened by the moon buried deep behind it. His brother's night sky to fly in, but he will learn this, too. He clambers up to stand on the seat, the twine end between his teeth. Then he hurls the parchment up and the wind takes it, flies it fast and spreads its wings white and high above Firwit's head. It wheels and settles into a rising, falling flight, the tug of the twine sending throbs into his hands. When, soon, the eerie whistle of the kites pours up from the wood, Firwit listens as the parchment bird, with no need of feathers, is woven in the silver threads of their sound.

A Matter of Taste

NATASHA SUTTON-WILLIAMS

New York Times *Culinary Insert*
Edgar Jacobsberg's weekly column
13 February 1994
Spicy, succulent braised pork belly delights the senses in an intoxicating wonderland of complexity. Blood orange, mustard, white wine vinegar and extravecchio Modena balsamic marinade with just a hint of aniseed and green onion makes a pleasurable exception to Mumtaz's otherwise mundane menu.

Washington Post *Culinary Review*
Janise Lebovitz's monthly feature
27 February 1994
Suka Suka's green jelly dessert "ais kacang" is made from shaved ice mixed with red beans, lychee fruit and green grass jelly, topped with evaporated milk. It looks more like a colony of green slugs than your typical dessert, but the more adventurous diners among you will agree this green jelly delicacy slowly releases a delicate blend of freshness and flavour that excites and refreshes the palate.

Janise Lebovitz and I had always had an interesting relationship. How could we not? We were rivals. We were lovers. We were foodies. We were almost friends. I write for the *New York Times*. She writes for the *Washington Post*. We didn't meet through food. We met through drink. It was one of Lucille's soirées. She thought it would be amusing to pair us up, though we had no idea who the other was. Like myself, Janise never had a photo for her byline so she could retain anonymity while dining. Lucille intentionally did not mention Janise's second name when we were introduced, and I was too wrecked on Dalmore to deduce that Lucille might be acquainted with more than one top food critic. Janise was juiced up as well. She was hot and slim, had a lion's mane of blue-black hair, wore slinkily cut little black numbers. We were Jews. We fucked immediately. It was during our post-coital brunch at Leonardo's when we suddenly clocked who the other was. The revelation occurred when I was noting down on a cloth napkin the type of oil used for my Dungeness crab eggs benedict.

"What are you doing?"

"Noting down a note."

"What for?"

"For my work."

"Why would you need to write down the incorrect oil used on your eggs for your work?"

"I can tell they used Lambda olive oil. It's splitting the hollandaise sauce."

"You'll find that it's in fact Casas de Hualdo olive oil."

"How can you tell it's Casas when you haven't even tried my benedict?"

"From the slight sheen it's left on your plate. And I can smell it."

This impressed me. She carried on.

"That smell is not Lambda premium extra virgin olive oil. Doesn't even smell Greek. It's Casas."

We stared each other down, seeking to find the true identity of the other.

"You're Edgar Jacobsberg, aren't you?"

"You're Janise Lebovitz, aren't you?"

"New York Slimes."

"Washington Ghosts."

"You over-write."

"You under-write."

"You're overpaid."

"You're underworked."

"You're an arrogant prick."

"You're a prissy bitch."

"You've no sense of style."

"You have no vocabulary."

"That's Casas oil on your eggs."

I pressed my fingertip to the plate, smeared some residue oil onto my skin and dipped it into my mouth.

"You're right."

For a moment I was dumbstruck. I leaned over the table and slithered my oiled tongue down Janise's throat. She tasted like oak-smoked bacon, because she'd just eaten some, but still, she tasted glorious. We were kicked out of Leo's after we ended up on the floor, pulling the table setting with us. We would never be allowed in again, but what did we care? We were top food critics. We owned this town. An article came out in the *Pan-American Food Review* that month about our mutual masturbation under the table. I didn't give a shit. Neither did Janise. The thing I love about that woman: she has balls.

Now Janise knows me, and she knows what a delicate palate I have. There are certain things I can and cannot put in my mouth. Anything bitter was out of the question. I couldn't be in the company of people wearing strong perfumes as it would affect my nasal cavity, poisoning the scent and therefore flavour of the food. And I couldn't go near a vagina. It wasn't the smell. The smell didn't bother me. That's what gets most guys (and girls, I presume): the smell. But for me it was always the taste. I just couldn't hack it. They always tasted like sweat. Fresh, but bitter. I hate sweat. Some of my lady friends over the years got uppity about it (feminists mostly). I wanted to give it a go each time, I really did, but when it came to it, I just – couldn't. It hadn't seemed to bother Janise, which was why I was surprised when during one of our fortnightly sessions she was so put out about my unwillingness.

"Now that my sourdough layabout of a husband is divorcing me, he's severed all ties between me and his tongue, so you're going to have to make up for the shortfall."

"Sourdough husband? Divorce? What the hell are you talking about?"

"He read the review. He found out about us."

"*Us*? I've just found out about *him*."

"I didn't think he was relevant."

"You might have mentioned in passing you were married. Is there anything else I should know?"

"We have three little brats. He's a stay-at-home daddy. I'm a go-to-work mummy. Thank God it's that way round, but now he's suing me for alimony."

"Because of the review? It wasn't that bad."

"He's conventional. He thinks I should commit to committing. It's a shame. He was a great pussy-eater. Great stamina, really thorough. No stone left unlicked. But his tongue is dead in the water now. You're going to have to cough up. Let's go."

But I couldn't. And it infuriated her. It wasn't worth risking my work tool for her pleasure. I couldn't imagine what I would do without my refined palate.

So when the problem struck I turned to Dr Iva Hepotitus: renowned English ear, nose and throat doctor. He shoved a large cotton-bud-like-thing in my nose and throat to take swabs. He did the scans and fucked my facial orifices with his massive camera.

"Mr Jacobsberg, first of all it is a great honour to meet you in the flesh. I never thought you would be so thin!"

"Thank you."

"As a long-standing foodie myself I always read your column and have taken your referrals very seriously. Although I must admit my wife and I very much enjoyed the spicy guacamole in the Falange Tapas Bar and were rather dumbfounded that you only gave it one star."

"The guacamole was unmashed, the courgettes limply wet, and though I enjoy the texture of my girlfriend's nipples I do not appreciate that texture in the form of a meatball."

"Touché, my good man, touché! Have you been to that new French place, Bataille's Egg, on 55th?"

"Have you got my results?"

"Of course, Edgar! You don't mind me calling you Edgar, do you? I feel we have an intimacy. Must be due to the column, no doubt. It feels like you're writing for my eyes alone. I have a familiarity with you I can't quite describe. If only I had your skills at description, for I am only a humble Cambridge-bred ENT doctor. I know we've only just met but I have this dinner reservation on Thursday at the Flamingo and it would be heaven, absolute heaven, if you were able to –"

"Can I have my results?"

"Certainly. Now, I'm afraid to say, Eddie, I am the bringer of bad news. Bad news, to the world of culinary delights and its critiquing."

"What is it?"

"You've lost your sense of taste."

"I'm aware of that. How can I get it back? What can you do?"

"Nothing, my talented culinary-critiquing wizard, nothing. That's the tragedy for you, for me and for the gastronomy advocates of the world."

"Can't you do anything?"

"Once you burn your taste buds off, they don't come back."

"But . . . but . . . but you're the best! I've been told! That's what I'm paying for! You save people's mouths! You save people's tongues!"

"I'm an ear, nose and throat specialist. I have to have expertise in all three disciplines. Like you, Edgar, I take my job very seriously. I am not just a mouth man. I am an artiste. Now, if you had something I could work with, if half your tongue wasn't deadened, or even a quarter, even an eighth, I could help you. You could taste again. But you don't have *any* taste buds left, Edgar. You must have eaten something excessively spicy. Do you know when this occurred?"

In my mind I pinpointed the exact moment. It was the opening night of Cardamom, the new Indian restaurant boasting the most exquisite food from Bengal. They'd converted one of the massive meatpacking warehouses on the Lower West Side into this huge gaudy place: overdone decor, overcooked meat and overegged waiters. They invited me, of course; who wouldn't? I was game as I had tasted the skills of Navnit, their head chef, while on holiday in Bengal several years ago. I was curious whether he'd learnt anything about presentation over the years. He hadn't. They were boasting the hottest spices in the city; I knew I had to take up the challenge, that's what my readership expects of me, and that's what I deliver. So I ordered the aubergine phall and chomped down on a couple of turgid poppadoms and overripe mango chutney. Only the raw onions were satisfactory.

It happened in a moment.

The phall arrived. I scooped a delicate forkful from the brazenly designed plate and put it in my mouth. I felt a slight burning sensation. I was dizzy and light-headed. I started to sweat profusely. A giraffe, typing Arabic on a typewriter, asked me if I wanted a plastic bag with that. I realised I was hallucinating. Suddenly I felt like crying. Then it was all over. I was back in the room. And I just – couldn't taste anything. Nothing. Obviously you can see the problem this posed. The ability to taste was my livelihood. If I couldn't taste – well, I couldn't pay my rent. I wasn't good at anything else. I may be an arrogant prick but I know what I'm good at, and it's not a lot.

After the phall, I didn't know what was going on. I left Cardamom without dessert and went down to Leland's for my usual post-meal cognac, but I couldn't *taste* it. I thought maybe the phall had just fried my mouth out. So I went back home and started sampling small amounts of everything in my cupboards and fridge. But no taste. No taste at all. I thought I might have tasted some of a gone-off sardine, but I realised I was most likely just smelling its rot as opposed to actually tasting it. Thing was, the phall affected my sense of smell as well! I could smell, just not that well. I had perhaps 9 per cent smell capacity left. As you can imagine, these new revelations disturbed me. I felt sick, but that might have been the sardine. I am the food critic for the *New York Times*, for Christ's sake! I am the man! The man that people of stature, intellect and refinement come to to be told where to eat, when to eat, and most importantly what to eat.

Dr Hepotitus interrupted my train of thought.

"Eddie, are you listening? Your tongue, for want of a better phrase, is a dead duck. But unfortunately you won't ever be able to taste a dead duck AGAIN!"

At this point Dr Iva Hepotitus promptly burst into tears. This is how much my column means to people. And though I felt embarrassed for the doctor, I had bigger problems than comforting a sycophant. I knew this wouldn't do. My livelihood was at stake. I had to keep writing, even if I was profoundly disabled. People needed to read my column. I am a national treasure. And this national treasure needed help; someone who would help without realising they were helping. So I turned to Janise.

This was a risky manoeuvre as I am infamous for dining alone, but now I needed someone with insight into food in order to glean taste information. Janise's palate is nowhere near as refined as mine was, but I have to give credit where credit is due; I knew she would do for the job. I just had to be smart about it. I'm not going to deny she was suspicious the first time I asked her to join me. In fact, I recall her exact words being: "What the fuck?"

I stroked her metaphorical clitoris a little and made some excuse about missing her and wanting to spend more time as a couple.

"But we aren't a couple."

She was sceptical, but acquiesced.

Janise specialises in desserts, which was of less use to me as she had a palate defined by sweetness, as opposed to mine, which had focused on spice. She literally used different parts of her tongue to taste than I did. But she would have to do.

When we went to the Clove Garden in the Meatpacking District I tried my subtle best to understand and memorise what she was tasting for my upcoming column. I made sure I ordered the exact same dishes as her, which I cannot deny was out of the ordinary. We would always order different dishes, just to defy one another and underline our independence as professional foodies.

"Mmm. I love this. This tastes great."

"I totally agree. What do you think that . . . that *je ne sais quoi* is?"

"It's just coriander, isn't it?"

"Just coriander. Just simple coriander, yes. What about the biryani? It's so . . . Mmm, I can't describe it."

"The beetroot has been roasted too long."

"Overcooked beetroot biryani, overcooked beetroot biryani, simple coriander. Yes, I agree, that's it. What do you think of that chocolate-covered onion bhaji?"

"Haven't tried it yet."

"Haven't tried it yet, haven't tried it yet. I mean, you haven't tried it yet! Oh, you must, you must! The texture is divine."

After a tense moment she slowly bit into the outer chocolate coating of her onion bhaji. I timed my own bite so the "taste" would occur simultaneously with hers.

"Mmm . . . So . . . So . . ."

"So what, Edgar?"

"So . . . oniony."

"Really? I feel the deep-fried batter mixed with the chocolate top coat overpowers the taste of the underdone onions."

"Yes . . . Well, on second thoughts . . . Deep-fried batter chocolate top overpowers taste of onions. Deep-fried batter chocolate top overpowers taste of onions."

"Edgar, are you all right?"

"I'm fine."

"Are you sure?"

"For sure I'm sure."

I'll admit, looking back, I didn't have my suave cap on that night, but luckily she didn't cotton on. She's too self-involved.

A refined palate thrives on the balance and combination of flavours. Something as simple as too much or too little salt can spoil a dish. Unfortunately, due to my disability, all subtlety and balance of flavours were lost on me. What I did have on my side was the cooking process. Without tasting a morsel I could confidently glean what a dish would taste like based purely on the cooking techniques used. How long and how hard had the egg whites been whipped? At what temperature had the naan bread been baked? Had the fish been caught fresh that day? All these vital pieces of information were golden threads to weave a glittering masterpiece of an article. This meant I needed access to the kitchen. But a critic can't go into the kitchen. It's simply not the done thing. I needed eyes and ears in that workhouse. I needed sous-chefs and garbage cans.

The sous-chefs were easy enough. All I had to do was bribe them and say I was a struggling restaurateur looking to steal successful recipes to boost my business. Most of them were obliging and dished the dirt on the food prep and cooking processes. The more difficult challenge was the trash cans. If I couldn't get to a sous-chef or I hadn't asked the right questions I'd have to find answers from the garbage. But imagine how that would look. Me, Edgar Jacobsberg, legendary *New York Times* culinary critic, found rooting round the debris in back alleys of world-class Indian restaurants. Seems somewhat suspect. But there wasn't any choice. I had to time it just right because too soon and they wouldn't have thrown the right remnants away for me to gather the extra ingredients that weren't listed on the menu. Too late, and the dish monkeys would have hauled the garbage out into the main street for collection. The bags would get mixed up and it was too public an area for me to get caught stealing stems of fruit or bones of animals. Just too risky. So I had to time my garbage hunts accordingly. I got quite good at it. Only once did I get caught. Luckily it was by a tramp who'd come down this alley to do the same as me. I was all suited up, my sleeves totally covered in crap from the can. He didn't seem surprised at my behaviour. Instead he said, "Nice night for it."

He was a sweet guy, for a hobo. He even recommended a couple of hot spots to get some good garbage grub. I realised this bum could come in useful, what with the knowledge he had on the restaurant-garbage circuit.

"Listen, I'm looking for specific items in these trash cans. If you can find them for me, and save me the trouble, I will pay you dividends in cigarettes."

"You want me to be your own personal dumpster diver?"

"For want of a better title, yes."

"Agreed."

The deal was sealed. Eventually we found the fruit stem I was looking for, plastic-bagged it, then ran for the 5 a.m. food market in Queens, moving from stall to stall, interrogating each fruit seller as to whether they sold a fruit with that particular stem. After three hours and an increasingly high blood pressure the tramp saw the stem on a stall across the way. It wasn't even a goddamn piece of fruit, it was a vegetable! Turns out it was a rare type of okra plant that has a saccharine taste. These were the lengths I had to go to in order to stay on top of my game and fool the world I could still taste.

I got good at it, you know. I still had the memory of taste. I liken myself to Beethoven and his loss of hearing: I'm still an artist, I just don't have the finesse I once had. But I've developed in other areas. My ability to bullshit has gone right up. My sense of smell, although massively deteriorated, is still vaguely there, all 9 per cent of it. And so much of experiencing food is experiencing it through smell. The texture of food also gives a good indication whether or not an expert has cooked it. You'll notice how the focus changes in my later articles after the Cardamom debacle.

> **New York Times *Culinary Insert***
> **Edgar Jacobsberg's weekly column**
> **26 June 1994**
> *Meat of an unknown origin (who knows when this animal died and what of) is beaten and batch-cooked in sauces of a colour that only a tanning salon in New Jersey could love. Deep-fried doughy balls fill the air with a pungency of violent garlic. The saving grace is a sweet goat-mince curry textured with fenugreek nuttiness. For an extra ten bucks they will make it with pearls of brain. Ever the adventurer I tried it and needless to say, I should have spent that $10 on mouth gargle.*

See? And no one seemed to notice I only vaguely mention taste. I was having my cake and eating it, except I couldn't taste it. I'm not going to lie; I was getting a little big for my boots. Once I lost my taste, I could do things that were humanly impossible. I got off on that, this new streak of attention. The favourite party trick was eating the hottest chillies anyone provided me with at dinner parties. People loved it. They were shocked, amazed, flabbergasted, but always impressed. A tiny bit of one of those chillies is enough to blow the roof off any normal human's mouth. It must have been affecting my high and low palates, but my mouth was totally numb. It didn't help my disposition for the squits, but I felt it was worth the accolade I was receiving. Eating super-hot chillies like the Trinidad Scorpion or the Naga Viper as a party trick isn't of the highest integrity for a food critic so I tended to pull these tricks out of the bag only when I was really hammered. One of the only things I really miss the taste of is alcohol. But I still enjoy getting laced up on it. I have to be careful, though, 'cause I can glug it down like water, especially the hard cheap stuff. Makes no difference to me what the quality is like, so I have to pace myself, unless I'm too tanked to notice.

Another advantage was that with my new no-taste tongue I was suddenly able to pleasure Janise. Of course she was desperately grateful. Now don't get me wrong, I've always used my cock and she's had a great time with that bad boy (and why wouldn't she? I know what I'm doing), but now I'm tasteless, she's having a ball! With my cock, balls and tongue. It's like licking out pieces of unflavoured flesh. I'm totally immune. I almost enjoy it. She certainly does.

One evening Janise invited me to her Alphabet City loft apartment. This was unusual behaviour in itself as we always go to my place to screw. She was secretive, and I thought being Washingtonian she probably didn't have her own place in New York, or perhaps her ex and kids were squatting there, but I realised when I was allowed entry after a year of knowing her that the apartment was merely a shithole: damp, cramped and hadn't seen a refurb since the 70s. She had culinary reviews and ideas for features pasted all over the walls of that dive. She was visual and needed these aids to improve her writing. I never had to make such a mess, but people work in different ways.

That night she invited me to pickled anchovies and white wine. I'd never been a big fish lover when I had taste, I assumed she knew that, but I didn't really care so long as I got some nutrients in. I was up for getting glazed and having a long session with her, so I took to the booze quickly. She seemed surprised but did not comment. I glugged down several glasses and wasn't feeling any real effect. She seemed to be staying off the drink herself.

"Is something wrong?"

"No, I'm just not really into drinking this evening. But you go right ahead."

So I did. I don't really give a crap whether I'm on a different mental plane from my partner. Kind of makes me enjoy it more, if I'm totally honest. I drank the whole bottle solo, with little effect. Janise seemed mesmerised, watching me take sip after sip. I got bored so grabbed a bottle of Hendrick's and pulled Janise into her ramshackle bedroom. She suddenly seemed very much in the mood. I started licking her out. Getting her all sauced up for the entrance of my pillar of salt. I felt proud I was finally able to moisten vaginas properly with my mouth before I entered them.

Previously I would have to go with whatever juice was already there, or use lubricant, which I always felt was for pussies. I was really going for it that night, really getting into it: sucking on her clitoris, jabbing my tongue deep into her opening, licking out her anus. It was great, I couldn't taste a thing! I could feel her orgasm rising, so I increased my speed. She came violently, and as she did she screamed: "You have no taste, do you?"

"WHAT?"

"You can't taste anything, can you? That's why you can suck on my pussy. You used to have such a delicate palate, remember? You'd never go there. But now your palate's gone."

"No, that's not true."

"You drank an entire bottle of vinegar this evening without even realising. Explain that. You've been like this for months – since 6 March."

"How can you be so accurate?"

"That's when you first went down on me. You've got no taste, yet you've still been writing."

I knew I was cornered. I had to come clean. So I told her the whole story. She seemed particularly interested that the burning-out of my mouth had occurred at Cardamom.

"Janise, you can't tell anyone about this."

"Oh, really? Why not?"

"You'll ruin me."

"Exactly."

"But . . . but . . . but . . . no! Don't you have any empathy for a fellow critic?"

"Do you?"

She had me cornered again.

"What do you want? I'll give you anything, *anything* for your silence."

She paused for a moment, then smiled.

"I want your apartment."

"What?"

"You said *anything.*"

"But . . . that's my home."

"And what about your livelihood? You can afford another place, for now, but who knows what will happen if this information were to leak?"

"God damn it! Take the apartment! See if I care."

"Excellent. That place is a muff-dive magnet."

"Yes, well, all the best with your future plans."

"And another thing, Edgar. I'm going to need 25 per cent of any revenue made on your articles from this point onwards."

"Are you insane?"

"I'm completely rational. That should more than cover my alimony. The alimony I have to pay because of you."

"That wasn't my fault. I didn't even know you were married."

"This is non-negotiable. I want 25 per cent profit from everything you write, or I'm outing you."

She slipped into her dressing gown and got off the bed.

"You've got my balls in a vice grip, Janise."

"Just the way you like it. Now get out. I'm tired."

I pushed the duvet away and hoisted myself up.

"On second thoughts, Edgar, you stay. I'll head home to your apartment. Are the keys in your pants?"

And like a lamb to slaughter I went along with it. What else could I do? I was seething, especially when I found out she was banging the chief travel editor of the *Wall Street Journal* in *my* apartment. They even went to Honolulu together, where she reviewed not only the coconut haupia dessert but the savouries as well! She mused on the lau-lau, kalua pork and lomi-lomi salmon all the while getting blitzed on Blue Hawaiis. I was more than pissed. I love Hawaiian cuisine. At least, I did.

Even as a food critic with no taste I'm *still* a better culinary reviewer than her. But the bile was starting to seep through.

> **New York Times** *Culinary Insert*
> *Edgar Jacobsberg's weekly column*
> *18 September 1994*
> *The dhansak filet mignon was as overdone as the culinary critiquing at the* Washington Post.

When she found out this had been published she called me to let off what I can only imagine to be premenstrual steam.

"Edgar, I know you're resentful, especially after my dining-editor promotion at the *Post*, but insulting me publically is going to cost you. Any potshots cost 10 per cent extra and your old apartment needs a major refurb. I'm putting in skylights and a Jacuzzi. Nothing like a tub of simmering hot water to get the male saliva juices flowing, eh? You have been warned."

I was outraged. She couldn't control me like this. She may have had my balls on a plate but she wasn't going to eat them too. In response to her threats I wrote this:

New York Times *Culinary Insert*
Edgar Jacobsberg's weekly column
16 October 1994
Tamarind Tribeca's five-month-smoked haddock marinated in Reshampatti chilli with turnip-glazed compote was as limp and lifeless as taking Janise Lebovitz to bed after she's guzzled her body weight in cheap bodega cava.

But what difference did it make? I was falling in slow motion; the floor had literally been ripped from beneath me. I didn't know what to do. Filled with desperation I went back to Dr Hepotitus with the hope that in the last eight months there had been some medical developments in treating tastelessness.

"I'm devastated! Utterly devastated! I'm so sorry! I didn't tell anyone, I swear!"

"What?"

"I am a man of stature – a rule-abider. I would never break doctor-patient confidentiality, especially when dealing with such breathtaking talent as your own – or at least, the talent you used to have."

"What are you talking about?"

"Yesterday's column in the *New York Times*."

"What about my column?"

"I don't think it was the one you submitted."

Breathless, I ran into the waiting room and snatched the newspaper out of the weak hands of a coffin-dodger. To my horror, on the front page of the culinary insert, Janise was pictured outside Cardamom with a small crinkled red chilli in her hand, dangling it above her open smiling mouth, a demonic twinkle in her eye directed at me and me alone. I realised it was a Bhut Jolokia pepper, otherwise known as the ghost pepper because of what it does to you; it's the hottest chilli in the world.

My eyes darted back and forth to read the headline:

Edgar Jacobsberg: Culinary Fraudster

Our new NYT food critic-turned-investigator, Janise Lebovitz, initiates the unadulterated outing of Edgar Jacobsberg: the multi-award-winning culinary critic who unfortunately has no taste.

"I love the swift leap of a good story, the excitement that often commences in the first sentence, the sense of beauty and mystery found in the best of them"

Raymond Carver

Anna

MADELINE CROSS

Anna Grey is dead. She's walking towards me carrying a jug of water and is as solid as the bed I'm in, but that doesn't change anything. The other nurse laughed at me when I told her, but that might not even be the nurse I'm thinking of because they all keep changing, except for Anna. Death seems consistent like that.

The more I watch her, the more I believe she knows about all of us and who we are and how we will die. I want to climb inside her head and get to the truth, too. There's no other truth in these rooms, except when they take one of us away. If she is dead, then it's a tragedy because she died young, hair still milk-tea brown and eyes bright as violets, barely passing twenty and with everything still in place and more ahead. She wears it gently, though, like a cloak, and it comforts me to think that death might be a weightless thing I can carry like she does.

She fills the cup on the table over my lap and then slips a straw in because the arthritis in my hands means there's no point in me even attempting to pick it up. I lean forward and drink, but I pull my mouth back too soon and a bead of water tips out from the top of the straw and dribbles down my chest. I remember picnics in the garden as a child, with straws that curl up and around like rollercoasters from cups of pink lemonade. Anna mops up the trickle of water with a paper towel before it can disappear down my nightdress. She rearranges the scattered bedsheets and her movements are slow and overly careful. She's pushed up her sleeves and I can see her slight wrists as she folds the top of the blanket down over my knees. Pathways of blue veins disappear under the cuffs of her blouse.

Stephanie and James came to visit me yesterday and I told them that Anna was dead. Stephanie, bless her, asked how I could tell, but James ignored me and looked out of the window, his square chin lifted up, something he's been doing since he was a boy and realised he'd never be tall. I could have told him there's nothing out there except a vast grey sky and a flat stretch of nothing-land. Sometimes that big sky is blue, I could have added. But it isn't today so look at me while I'm talking to you! I told Stephanie, because she was willing to listen, that I can tell Anna is dead because every time someone dies within these walls Anna seems to be the very last person they speak to. "What does she say to them?" Stephanie asked.

I can't possibly know this because they die and take that secret with them. Of course, I told Stephanie, this is confusing because it leaves me wondering whether she is in fact dead, or if she is Death itself. Stephanie thought about this, and then she asked me if the food was getting any better.

I slipped in the snow two years ago and have been here ever since. I hit my head on the kerb and there was a reasonable amount of blood to go with my broken wrist but I forget very little on a day-to-day basis and can walk fairly well with some small effort. Everything else is just natural deterioration and I like to think about how many rings they'd find inside me if they cut through my trunk with an axe. My hands cause me the most trouble. I never imagined they'd be the first thing to become completely bloody useless. I look at them now like they're not attached to me, as if they are lumps of gnarled, splintered wood with no purpose left. I'd like to tell James that my brain has always worked this way and that nothing has changed. But it must be my fault for keeping such thoughts bottled and stored away from him so that he would have the faith in me he should have. Then the parent gets old and falls over and the cork comes out.

At least I'm not imagining Anna. I know she's a real person because everyone else can see her too and that says a lot about my state of mind. James is still not convinced. When he held my hand yesterday he looked into my eyes for slightly too long, as if he might find something hiding there. I am not hiding anything from him. If anything, I'm trying to make him see what isn't hidden at all.

"I didn't want to bring the kids too often. I don't want them to get upset. You understand that, right, Mum?" he said.

"Of course, James," I said, because he is my son and I'm supposed to understand him. It had been over a month. But that's all right – better for them not to get too attached. At least Stephanie's two were older and had gone off to university and didn't visit at all except Christmas and maybe once in the summer. There was no risk of upsetting them. It's only death, after all, and isn't death just another big adventure?

Anna came into the room, signalling that it was time for me to eat something so everyone had better leave for the day. James was relieved. He got up from the armchair and placed the Rubik's cube he'd been fiddling with back on the chest. Stephanie had brought it once to help me test my mind, but she'd forgotten it was too late for my fingers.

"How are you, Anna?" Stephanie asked.

I flashed her a warning look, but all I got in return was James glaring at me from the corner of the room.

"Very well, Stephanie, thanks."

"How's John? Mum told me they've been spending a bit of time together."

Anna pulled the curtains closed and blocked out the final dregs of sunlight that had at last leaked through the grey and were slowly journeying across the bottom of my bed. "He's the same as ever," she said.

"How long has he been here now?" James joined in with a sideways look at me.

"Six years."

I had forgotten it was six years. It seemed a phenomenal length of time. Anna left the room again. James gave me a rough kiss on the cheek.

"You need to shave," I said.

"Yes, I do."

"Back soon, Mum," Stephanie said, her face lingering against mine.

And then they left. It was swift and soundless, but James still had time to leave a new photo of my youngest grandchild on my lap and smile crookedly before he was gone.

I finish the water and Anna helps me out of the bed so I can visit John. John is bedridden. He had a brain haemorrhage when he slipped in the snow like I did. This is just one of the many things we have in common. He still lives a vibrant life from the confines of his rectangular bed. He likes to kick the blanket off his feet and wiggle his toes and tell everyone how exhausted he is from walking all night. He has a family to make anyone envious, including three grown-up grandsons who keep bringing him hats for different occasions. They take pictures of him in the different hats and stick them to the magnolia walls. I'm not always sure John can tell the grandsons apart but they all have floppy blond hair and they probably can't tell the difference themselves.

"How are we going to prove to everyone that Anna is dead?" I ask him.

"It's tough when we live in a ship."

"Yes – it's not easy, but we have to try," I say. "If we poisoned her and she didn't die, surely that would do it?" But then if she doesn't die, how do we prove to anyone that we poisoned her in the first place?

"A long secret," John says.

"Yes, maybe the secret is too important to her."

"I can't tell you."

"Don't worry, John, you don't have to."

"I can't even tell my own family."

"Is this the same secret or a different one?"

"I'll tell you when the time's right."

"I don't know if we're talking about the same thing. Are you talking about Anna?"

"Anna?"

Anna comes in with a plate of biscuits and I watch her move across the floor with her feet barely touching the lino. John starts to sing, "*Drunk last night, drunk the night before.*" His voice comes right from the bottom of his chest and sometimes I wake up to it in the morning and I remember where I am and am relieved that it's John who's brought me back into the world.

The three of us eat custard creams together and I briefly forget what Anna is.

In my room I check the calendar where Stephanie and James have kindly marked their routines, as much for themselves as for me, so they can be sure their lives really are that busy and they're not just making excuses. But I remember what it was like, and if we had the time then maybe I could tell them this: "It's all right," I'd say. "I remember the beginning just as much as the end." They don't want to hear it, though. I do remember things. My own mother died when she seemed much too young and it was as though she died in my very hands with my fingertips joined to hers. I kissed her dead face and tried to imagine where she'd gone to. I was nineteen. I am still nineteen. I am not any age at all.

My heart beats irregularly.

Death is solid and cannot walk through walls. Anna comes into the room and by this point I'm feeling so ill that I really don't want her near me because my train of thought is still trudging along and she is too much of a risk to it; I'd like to reach its end. I know that I'm overtired because when she touches my forehead softly with her milky fingers (piano fingers, my mother would have said) I flinch. We are still looking at each other and for a brief moment she seems confused; a creasing around her eyes changes her face and makes her look more human, anxious even, and then the creases are gone and her face is moon-like again.

"What is it?" I say.

"We're getting the doctor in," she says.

"What's it like?" I ask her.

"What's what like?"

Being dead – not being alive – not existing.

I just want her to tell me the truth. Another nurse brings me dinner after the doctor's been and gone and I've already forgotten his face. "Where is Anna?" Nothing, no answer, maybe they don't hear me. Maybe I didn't actually say it out loud. I try again. My mouth is hard to move and again I'm not sure any noise comes out. I open my eyes and the flashing numbers tell me it's the middle of the night and I've been asleep. There's no one with me.

John's voice warbles bird-like in my dreams. At first the song is wordless, just notes flapping closer through the empty corridors and half-empty rooms, and then I wake and the words find me. *"Drunk last night, drunk the night before."*

When I'm dressed and feeling better, I go and see him. His family are leaving and the grandsons pass me in the corridor. They all remember my name and John's son asks me how I am. I mutter something non-committal in case I blurt out to them that I'm dying. Apparently I've done that before. They queue up to use the sanitizer by the back door. I watch them wash us off their long and fully functional fingers and walk out into the cold air with a squeak of glass door and the faint cry of a crow slipping through the gap before it closes.

"I told them the secret," John says, as I sit in the armchair beside his bed.

I look at the bunch of daffodils his family left him on the windowsill between the copper model of a bicycle and a wooden elephant. "You told them? Did they believe you?"

"Why wouldn't they?"

"Have they met Anna?" I think of James attacking the Rubik's cube.

"I was part of the Great Train Robbery."

"What?"

"That's right."

He is watching something through the window, a sparrow on the hedgerow.

"The one in the paper last month?"

"In the paper? Don't recall that."

"What about Anna, though, John?"

"What about her?"

"I want to know the truth," I say.

He looks down at the watch on his swollen wrist.

Outside it seems greyer than I've ever known. I don't remember when I last saw a blue sky. I don't know when I will see one again. I don't know if people can go colour-blind in old age. I don't know what hands feel like any more. John?

Anna has a hand against my cheek. I fell asleep in John's armchair and there John is beside me still, also asleep, his chin resting against his chest, his fingers curled stiffly round the edges of the blanket.

"Not yet."

"What?" I look up suddenly. "What did you say?"

Anna looks back at me without a clue.

"You just said, 'Not yet.' Why did you say 'Not yet'?"

"I didn't know I did."

Pathetic answer. Pathetic. Pathetic.

"Help me up, Anna."

Anna is close beside me, following me into the lounge where bodies sit about and talk about life. Nobody talks about death. Nobody looks Anna in the eye. They don't look me in the eye, either, but I expect that's because of her beside me.

"Go away," I tell her, and walk back to my room.

But it isn't as easy as that.

"Will it hurt?" I say to the darkness.

Someone turns a light on and helps me put on my night clothes. My bed is warm and soft and I sink into the pillows and relief fills my veins and wraps around my bones. The light that shines through the peach lampshade is reflected in the clear, emptying bag that hangs and sways with the movement of me. A car pulls into the car park. The beams from the headlamps swing through the gap in the curtains and split my ceiling into slanting trails of light and shadow. I follow them with my eyes until the car stops and the lights turn off and the ceiling is still again.

I remember car journeys, how I insisted on wearing my dressing gown because it made me feel safe, driving through the dark and watching the steep hedgerows light up as we passed, eating sweets from the glove compartment, watching the raindrops race each other down the windows, falling asleep to the smell of petrol fumes and the sound of my mother's voice as she tried to play along to the quiz on the radio.

I remember my mother's voice.

Anna slips into the room and I turn and smile apologetically because a part of me can recall being rude to her. But she doesn't look as though she remembers. In fact she looks empty of all memories, as if they have all slipped out through her skin and melted like candle wax in the air. She checks the swaying bag and puts her fingers to my skin, then she sits beside me and with her voice trembling, she talks to me about her cat.

Is this happening? Is she really talking to me about her cat? A tabby named Romeo? I look more closely and I can see how young she is. She is nervously fiddling with the hem of her dress. Her eyes are slightly red and there is the beginning of a rash creeping up the side of her swan-like neck. She didn't leave home that long ago, she tells me. The first thing she did was get a cat. Cats. Rashes. Tiny, girl-like wrists. Eyes recently cried. A ladder in her tights.

"You're not dead, are you?" I say.

"What?" She tilts her head and a white ear pokes through her hair.

"I thought . . . I can't remember why I thought. It was the things you said to them. I don't know what it was you said to them."

"It's this place," she says.

But I can't see her mouth move and I'm in a car on the way back home and my mother is singing.

"Anna, please," I hear myself say. But I know now she doesn't know either and she can't tell me anything at all. She gets up and looks straight at me and I see my face reflecting out from her purple irises. She leans forward and speaks into my ear.

It is the morning and someone has opened the window. I can hear children in the hallway. The sound of them gets closer, and two of them burst into my room, barely taller than the chairs. They are followed by Stephanie and James. Anna is in the room already and is rearranging the furniture so that everyone can fit in. She places some custard creams on a paper plate.

The little girl – I can't remember her name – climbs fearlessly onto my bed and studies my face. She resembles me somehow. She slips her hand into mine and her pink palm is as small as an apricot.

Hardscrabble
MICHAEL BUTTON

Malady
February 1857

Frost has slain the peach tree in the orchard, and from her neighbours Julia Grant hears that the winter is as bad as any living soul in Missouri can recall. Most of the folk round here are old friends or wayback cousins; they visit with each other when they can, the hooves of their horses clacking up the frozen roads. Lately, the visiting has been going one way only: Ulysses is sick in bed, again, suffering from a malady he calls Tyler's grip, though Julia thinks that one of the doctors in St Louis would call it influenza. Ulysses coughs and sweats, his forehead as hot as the winter is bitter. He asks William to let the fire in their bedroom run down a little, but Julia won't hear a word of it.

When the baby is down, she comes to watch over him, sits in the chair by his cot and tells him of the boys' latest mischief, or news from White Haven. Her mother is sick, too, and her father fears that she won't rise from her bed again. Julia does not fear for Ulysses, and she tells him tenderly, if he is awake, that he is strong, and still a young man, and that the sickness will pass. If he's sleeping, she works on her cross-stitch.

With her husband incapacitated, she tries to help out with the farm by churning butter, and despite Ulysses saying he does not wish it for her, she thinks he may be secretly proud. She even keeps the chickens, though she lost three to pox in the New Year. But she does not fret. She will get more in the spring, if they are still living here.

Horse
September 1856

He never looks so fine to her but when he is a-horse, back straight and high-crowned hat square on his head. Then, his jaw stern and his gaze determined, she can forget the farmer's grime around his sleeves, the raggedness of his collar, the way a jacket never hangs right on his shoulders.

"There's not a nag in the county your daddy couldn't master," she says, from the porch of the cabin. Fred and Ulysses Jr clutch her skirts, whilst she rocks Nellie in a practised swing from her hips. Fred is awestruck and stares up at his father on the back of the horse. "As I've no doubt he'll tell you one day, he won the prize for horsemanship when he was at the Academy."

"Only prize I ever won," he says, grinning back at her, and then gees the horse onward, pulling a cart stacked high with corded wood in the direction of St Louis. She expects him back late afternoon, but is not troubled when he does not at first appear. She busies herself with floor-scrubbing and child-tending. This is her country, and she knows it well; she takes comfort in the overhead flight of a blue crane, the faraway cackle of wild turkeys in the forest.

Still, it is some three hours after sunset when she hears the wheels of the cart on the road, and when she goes outside to greet her husband, an old fear troubles her. A lantern swings from his hand, and he sits slumped in the saddle, the reins slack. He smiles dimly when he sees her. Scarlet spiders his eyes, and there is a looseness to his face that she remembers all too well.

"I am sorry, my beloved. To be home so late. I chanced upon some fellows who served down in Mexico, and we got to talking. I am gravely sorry," he says, and his voice stumbles with the shame of his weakness. But she understands. She helps him down, ties up the horse, then brings him a plate of salt meat and crackers, and watches him eat.

Departure
April 1858

Evil tidings from White Haven: Julia's mother, weakened by ague, has passed. Though she has long expected it, often imagined it, Julia is rent by a grief that takes her by surprise with its vehemence.

"She will never see a summer again," she says, aware of the banality of her comment, the overwhelming ordinariness of her pain. She presses her face to the faded brown fabric of her husband's coat. It smells of sweat and mud, but its familiarity is all she has to cling onto, the only thing that can stop her giving in to misery.

"You must leave at once, Julia, today or tomorrow. Your father will need your assistance." They separate. His dulled brass buttons have left round indentations in her cheek. "It is a small mercy, but it settles my decision," he says. "I know you have longed to leave here." She looks at him and sees his eyes gleam. She has never seen him cry. "Take the children and the cart. I will follow behind once I have shut up the cabin."

The next morning, outside the cabin, grey rain spits as she takes her seat in the cart. The children are behind her, swaddled in old blankets. Ulysses Jr sits on a chest she has filled with sundries, while Fred keeps ahold of uncomprehending Nellie, whose fingers play with his lank, girlish hair. By the side of the cabin, Ulysses is piling tools to take to auction in St Louis.

"Snakeslayer," says Ulysses as he puts the old hoe on the stack, but she cannot force a smile. Her stomach is raw from weeping.

Julia flicks the reins, and, slowly, the cart's wheels pull through the mud towards the northern road. After she has travelled twenty yards or so, the horse settling into an easy rhythm, she turns to look back at her husband. But he is not looking at her. Instead, he faces the cabin. Its door swings open in the chill spring breeze. His head is cocked and his hands hang limp at his side.

As the horse pulls her towards her father, she keeps glancing backwards. With every look, the cabin gets smaller and smaller. Her husband does not move.

Cabin
March - August 1856

Julia and the children stay in the guest room at White Haven whilst

Ulysses constructs the cabin, all spring and most of the summer. No matter the weather, merciless Missouri sun or shrieking gale, he rises at dawn, emerging from his canvas tent to work. By April, he has dug out a cellar, and in June, the neighbours send their older sons to help him raise walls of cypress wood around the brickwork chimneys. He lays the floorboards, builds the stairs, shingles the roof.

He visits with his family on Sundays, and Julia thinks he looks well, sunburnt and even-tempered. The work suits him. It gives him focus and little opportunity, nor, indeed, income, to indulge his intemperance. When they can find an hour, they saddle up and ride out through the dry country, the mossy woods and the gentle hills, just like when they were courting. Ulysses was never one for fine words, but she believes he loves her well.

By August, the work is finished, and he brings Julia and the children down to their new home. She can see how proud he is of his handiwork, and she conceals her disappointment. The four rooms are small and bare, and what furniture they own is rickety and hand-me-down. But that night as she lies in bed, Ulysses' snoring competing with the chirrups of katydids, the bellows of bullfrogs, she is not unhappy.

The next day she marshals the belongings she has brought, not many, but some. She places baskets and books about the room, hangs doilies on the plain walls, drapes the windows with coloured cotton. Ulysses writes his brother to tell of his venture: *When next you see me, I will be a fine merchant farmer.*

Step
January 1857

Ulysses Jr wriggles with excitement as his little sister clutches the seat of a chair and wobbles unsteadily. "Come on, Nellie! Show us, Nellie!" he hollers, like he is cheering a beetle in a race.

Somehow the room, hot from the blazing stove, has become tense. All of the family are watching Nellie. She wears a long white baby's gown, its hem rimmed with an inch of dirt. Her face is framed by a frilly bonnet, secured with a bow under her chin, and Julia realises that its fussiness doesn't suit her; or that maybe the fussiness doesn't suit *here*.

Nellie gains her balance and gazes warily about, her eyes half-lidded. As if she was drunk, Julia thinks and almost says, before she reins her tongue in, and lets the notion dissipate.

"Calm down now, Junior – she'll show us in her own time," says Ulysses, his beard split by an enormous grin. Even William, a dark spectre hovering at the back of the room, has cracked a smile. His teeth are huge and white. Julia crouches in the dust, a yard away from Nellie.

Nellie sticks her tongue out, folds it over her upper lip. She screws up her pudgy face in concentration. A full minute passes. "She's as stubborn as you are, Ulys," says Julia, and the ripple of humour throughout the room momentarily distracts Nellie.

They wait some more, in silence, and just when Julia thinks she won't do it, Nellie takes a short step away from the chair. For a second, she staggers, and Julia moves to catch her fall, but then Nellie rushes her other foot forward, and lands in her mother's arms, and the room erupts in jubilation.

William Jones
October 1856

"My father has brung us a present!" cries Julia as she enters the front room of the cabin, gay as a girl. Ulysses sits by the kitchen table, his face damp with a sheen of perspiration. Julia's father, Frederick Dent, follows in behind her, and in turn behind him, the black slave William Jones.

Ulysses makes brief eye contact with William, then nods at Frederick Dent. "You are generous, sir," he says, frowning and struggling to sit up straighter.

Frederick fixes Ulysses with eyes sharp under thick white brows, and says, coldly, "How is your fever, son?" Julia sees him unsubtly scan the pine shelves, but she knows he won't find bottles here, for (she believes, she hopes) family life is a charm against her husband's love of liquor.

"Much the same since last you saw me, sir, but pray another week's rest and I'll be back at my labours."

Frederick scowls. "This here William has been with me for the past seven years. He's a hard worker, a quiet worker. I'll trust he'll do you well on Julia's farm."

"The farm is Ulysses' also," interrupts Julia. In the presence of her father, she forces her voice higher and brighter. She turns to William and smiles. "You may be certain that we will not use you too hard." William grunts a vague, surly gratitude.

"Did you decide on what crop to plant in the fields by Prairie Spring Creek?" asks Frederick. Across the table are pencil sketches of the surrounding acreage that Ulysses has been working on fitfully.

"Red wheat, I think. I have ordered red wheat for next season."

"With the market as it is? Well, as Julia says, it is your farm now."

From the doorway, William Jones watches this exchange.

Copperhead
October 1857

Fred and Ulysses Jr are trying to build a snare for rabbits outside the cabin when Ulysses Jr spies a copperhead sliding through the long, yellow grass towards them. It moves with an autumnal sluggishness. Five feet away it stops, and coils in a sinister S, fat, diamond head atop brown-and-tan motley. "We should get Mother," says Ulysses Jr, but Fred is seven now, and older than him, so he is the man here, as he reminds his brother, and he decides he will deal with it himself.

Without turning his back on the creature, Fred edges towards the cabin where a rust-flecked hoe leans against the wall. The implement is longer than he is tall, and the weight of the iron unbalances him as he takes it. He shoos his fearful brother back, and moves cautiously towards the copperhead. Fred can hear the distant voice of his father across the way, calling to William as they gather in the harvest, and he can smell the burning stubble from the fields. He summons his mettle, holds his makeshift weapon overhead, and swipes down, but his aim is off, and the hoe thumps against the grass. Earth sprays over the snake, and it suddenly coils tighter, and slithers towards the boy. Fred yelps in fear, fumbles his grip on the hoe, and scurries backwards.

Fred's cry is joined by a scream from his brother. Inside the cabin, Julia sits Nellie on the floor by the stove, and rushes out into the daylight, her smock unbuttoned. The snake now lies across the hoe, the boys cornered by the wall. They point at it in terror. Without thought she moves, grabs the tool and shakes the serpent onto the ground, where it falls in a slovenly tangle. She swings, and crushes its head into the dirt.

Newspaper
November 1856

At first she thinks it's his usual morning fog, but after two days in bed his temperature soars. She places a damp rag across his brow, and waits for the fever to break. The timing of his sickness is poor, as it leaves only William to reap the few crops Ulysses managed to sow this year. There is not much to sell, and the quality has suffered with the drought, so she offers to ask her sister for a loan.

"Do not worry," she says. "I will keep the chickens. I will churn butter. I will be a good farmer's wife, you'll see, and next year the harvest will be better."

Once he begins to recover, she spends her mornings rooting out potatoes and onions from the vegetable garden, her bonnet fixed to shade her eyes from the long sun. Afterwards, she scrubs the ochre earth from her fingernails in the dishwater.

A cousin brings last week's edition of the *St Louis Dispatch* for Ulysses to read as he convalesces. The newspaper is ablaze with stories of slaves fleeing north and violent skirmishes at state conventions, but it is the wrangling of the Supreme Court that dominates the editorials. He calls William in and speaks to him while Júlia beats a buckwheat batter for griddle cakes.

"You are not to let this news trouble you, William. There may be setbacks, but your race will be emancipated within a ten-year. I believe it firmly."

"As you say, sir," says William.

Something about William Jones' cool stillness unnerves Julia. After he's gone, she turns to speak to Ulysses. "Do not unsettle him," she says. "It is hard for him to understand these matters. I know you would wish to give him freedom papers, but remember we are not rich, Ulys."

He nods his assent, but she can tell he does not agree.

Galena
February 1858

The door to the cabin flies open and a swirl of snow flutters in. It is William, his dark cheeks crimsoned by the cold. He has returned from the Post Office with a letter for Ulysses. An owlish Thomas Jefferson stares from the five-cent stamp, postmarked Galena, Illinois. Ulysses opens the letter.

"My father has need of a clerk for his tannery store," he says, when he is alone with Julia. "He has offered me the position." For a brief moment, she sees his face crinkle with shame.

"Will you take it?" she says.

Inside the cabin, lifeless winter sunlight illumines their worn possessions, the rough table, the tarnished oil lamps. Upstairs, the gentle chatter of children filters down, and the floorboards creak with their small steps. A log fizzes and pops in the heart of the blackened stove.

"I will think on it," he replies, then adds, wryly, quietly, "A clerk in a tannery store! Doggone it, what would your father think on that, Julia?"

"It is no matter what he thinks. _I_ will think it a fine position, should you choose to accept it. Perhaps the leather business will suit you. And Lord willing, the society of Galena may be good for your prospects, or our children's prospects."

Sister
November 1857

Julia reads of an election announcement in the paper, triggered by the death of the incumbent county engineer, and it ignites the aspirations of her husband, long buried by illness. He pens a note to the county clerk declaring his intention to stand for the position. He scratches his name, _Ulysses S. Grant_, with a grim flourish. He writes letters of petition to the local folk they know, and traipses the land to meet those he knows not, and thus he is frequently away for the night, sometimes two. His rival in the election is a Missouri man, with three generations of state senators behind him, and Ulysses tells Julia he must work hard if he is to stand a chance.

The afternoon of the election, outside the cabin, Ulysses prepares to head to county hall, for the ballot, when Julia decides that she must speak with him. She determines to be forthright, as forthright as she has ever been, but despite her boldness, her tongue still trips on the words.

"I have . . . I have received word from my sister. She says that there is . . . talk of you." In truth, the dark hints in her sister's letters implied more, that the gossip about Ulysses was unkind, but she feels she must judge her opening sally with care. She half expects him to explode with fury, though he has never raised his voice to her before. Instead, he is silent, stony-faced, and she softens her tone, and the words flow more freely.

"Your ambition befits you, husband. Your vice does not. Though we have not spoke of it often, there was a time before when the two did not mix well."

He does not acknowledge her comments with verbal reply, and for a moment she regrets her final statement, but she must try what she can. He turns to mount their horse, but, left foot in the stirrup, something stops him and he turns back to her.

"Do you regret marrying me, Julia?" His face is bloodless, his mouth set firm.

She wants to weep, but she wisecracks instead. "Not for an instant, County Engineer Grant. Not for an instant."

He returns in the early evening. She is in bed, but not asleep. She can tell from the tone of his footsteps, his weary shuffle through the cabin door, that he has not won, and her heart breaks for him. But when he comes to their room, there is no smell of whisky.

Signature
March 1858

The loans have been spent and the bank account emptied. They won't starve, she knows; their children won't go unshod, for they can always rely on her father, or his father, and for this she is grateful, truly. And they have the farm, the horse. Ulysses has talked of striking up a tenancy agreement, spoken to several interested parties. Perhaps someone else will have better luck with the unkempt fields that he cannot coax into fruitfulness.

But, despite their penury, Ulysses is adamant. There is a vigour in his voice that she has not heard since they moved to this accursed shack. His recovery is robust – he has no lingering cough, and his face is ruddy.

"My father . . ." she says.

"I have always appreciated his kindness to us. To me. But once the gift is given, it is not the giver's to dispose of. And the nation is changing, no matter what he believes."

"He will believe you unwise," she says, then hazards a continuation: "We could be sure that William's new owners were a good family, a kind family, after all." But even as she says it, she feels herself weaken, and she knows he has the right of it.

Without cruelty, he replies, "Then I will speak to him as I have spoken to you." And he bends to the papers, and he signs his name.

Promise
September 1856

Rays of darkening amethyst scatter across the floorboards of the cabin. Julia thinks that Ulysses is finally asleep, slumped in his chair by the window. She has been sewing a patchwork blanket, and as she drapes the half-finished article across him, to her surprise, his blue eyes flick open, and look at her with mirth.

"I have a name for our cabin, Julia." His voice is soft and the slur has gone. "Hardscrabble," he says, with a strangled laugh. "Do you like it, dearest Julia?"

She likes it not, but she joins him in laughter anyway, for she is his wife, and she will honour the promises she made him.

Sisters

DAVE WAKELY

Since I lifted it out of its fancy satin box a month ago and hung it delicately on the office coat rack in its protective plastic sleeve, the emerald-green ball gown hasn't attracted a single raised eyebrow. I'd explained who it was for – although they must have been able to see it wasn't my size, even before the alterations. And God knows, green would never work with my complexion.

The girls have spoken admiringly of the colour, and cooed about the way the peacock-feather designs had been so dexterously picked out on each sleeve in tiny sapphire and aquamarine sequins and rhinestones. Fussy to the last, Brenda got out her reading glasses and inspected its cuffs and hem. "Brussels lace?" she asked, approvingly.

"Limerick," I corrected her. "It's for Betty. For his curtain call. It'd be wrong if it wasn't Irish."

That, it seemed, explained everything.

The only question was Maddy's. "Sorry, Lionel, but do you mean Mr Wood? In Room 4?" she said. She didn't mean anything funny by it. She was new here then, that's all. But she's settled in fine now, realised that we have our own "normal" here. I only have three rules: hygiene, hope and happiness. It's for *them*, not us. The hospice is the last home they're going to have, so we do what we can to make it theirs, whatever that takes. Emerald-green ball gowns included.

It was Maddy who helped me with the first fitting. Very practical, she was. If she ever gives up nursing care, she'll make someone a wonderful wardrobe mistress. "It's a very hot day and this *is* silk, isn't it?" she said. "We don't want to go getting water marks on it, do we, the amount Mr Wood's been sweating? Why don't we wait till this evening – I can give him a bed bath first, make sure he's clean and dry."

That evening, I threw his windows open to get a breeze going while Maddy expertly towelled him, taking extra care where the leukaemia had left his lymph glands tender. I'd seen Bet with bruises before, but only ones he'd gone out of his way to acquire. More than one evening, walking the dog along the seafront and collecting fossils for the office shelf, I've heard his voice from behind a well-weathered groyne. As I took his measurements, being careful to be gentle with the tape measure, he muttered at Maddy about how unladylike it was to wear such a beautiful dress over grey cotton boxer shorts.

He'd insisted on wriggling into them without her help. "Plums the size of croquet balls, my dear. It's this wretched illness, you see," he said. "No sight for an innocent young lady." I tried to humour him, make some quip about Maddy being a *real* lady, but that only got him upset. "No, Lil. I mean properly *innocent*. Something you and I haven't been in a long, long time."

I just shushed him as I fished his falsies out of his bedside drawer and hooked him into his favourite bra.

He's always known me as Lil, ever since we first met in the Feathers. Betty Wood and Lil Woodant, that was the joke, though it was true enough. Sung together for ten years, we have – the two of us and Davina. Or Dr Mitchell, as the urology ward prefers him to answer the phone. Beverley's Sisters, we are. Or rather, *were*. Bet's solo number was always *Love Hurts*. I preferred *Someone To Watch Over Me*. Eighty-seven grand we'd raised for the hospice before Bet took ill, belting out Abba in our finery on a Friday night and Davina walking through the crowd afterwards with a big hat. "Pension contributions, girls," he'd always tell them. "Drugs don't grow on trees." No one ever argued. Who would, with a surgeon who's seven foot in heels and a nurse's uniform? Especially when he's extending one rubber-gloved hand just below belt level and hissing a single word in your ear. "Cough," he told them. They always did.

Coughing was what Bet was doing now, bless his heart, and

wobbling like he'd been gassed as he stepped into the dress while Maddy held one bony elbow. He used to have a proper six-pack under his little green frocks, but the only ridges I could feel as I slid the gown up to his shoulders were his ribs. He'd have never forgiven me if I hadn't made a joke so I did my best, but "The time you've spent on your knees, young lady, you'd think they'd be stronger" tickled him rather more than it did me.

I held him upright while Maddy did his zip, carefully holding the material straight through her latex disposables. I knew from the weekly weigh-ins that he was shedding pounds faster than a punter's purse on payday, but it was shocking to see how the frock almost fell off him. I used to envy how slim he'd always kept himself. My seventeen stone in a black leather mini has only ever been just this side of funny, but that's where comfort eating gets you. I shimmied round to stand behind him, pulling the box of dressmaker's pins out of my tunic pocket.

"Maddy, my love, could you fetch us two teas? Four sugars for Mr Wood, and one of my sweeteners in mine?"

She nodded and headed off to the kitchen. I'm never bothered about some of the sights they see in here – I tell them when they start that this is Torquay and if they aren't broad-minded already, they soon will be – but if I'm afraid I'm going to blub, I make sure I'm only going to do it in front of the nearest and dearest. *Dignity, Lionel, dignity.*

"It's gorgeous, Bet, it truly is," I told him, speaking softly into his ear. "A few little alterations and we'll have you looking like a queen. You know, a *real* one."

I was looking over his shoulder now and fumbling with the pin box, taking them out one at a time as I marked the side seams, trying not to spoil the hang of the fabric. All those afternoons in Dad's tailor's shop as a kid, playing with the chalk – I knew they'd come in handy. And then, just as I started on his bust darts, the coughing overtook him.

Pins scattered everywhere and I wrapped my arms round his chest and clung on, terrified he was going to fall. Outside, the wind was getting up and the net curtains were flapping in and out of the window frame. His hair blew back, all Maddy's efforts to comb over his bald spot undone. I held him till the convulsions stopped and I realised that, under his breath – or what he had left of it – he'd started to sing. That bloody song from *Titanic*, where Kate Winslet stands at the prow of the ship, all winsome and shimmery as Leonardo DiCaprio nibbles at her ear lobes.

"Bet? Please, my love, not *that* song. Not *now*."

"Oh, Lil, sweetheart, I'm so sorry. I forgot," he said, his head drooping. "Forgive me?"

"As long as you don't move a muscle. There's more little pricks on this carpet right now than you've seen in a month of Sundays."

At least that got him laughing, his ribs rubbing against my wrists, enough for us to hardly notice the knock on the door before Maddy reappeared with a tray of tea and biscuits and a schooner of sherry for Bet's nightcap.

"Maddy, dear," I asked her politely while I stifled a giggle, "I dropped the pin box. Could you be an angel while I hold on to Mr Wood?"

"It's all right, Lil," he told me under his breath as she scrabbled at his feet. "You don't have to hang on quite so tight."

As I walked back to the office, bearing the frock on its hanger like a banner in a transvestites' union parade, I could feel the laughter fading from me. It was that song, that bloody song. *Lionel, you've told yourself you're not going to cry, and you're not. You've moved on, remember . . .*

But remembering was the problem. December the fourteenth, 1997. When I sat in a cinema in Leicester Square. Just me. Suddenly, very *much* just me. Six hours Danny'd been gone, back to Australia to die with his family. He'd not even have touched down at Sydney, he'd still be airborne. I remember thinking that, and then forcing myself not to. *None of that "he's up there somewhere, looking down at us" nonsense, Lionel. It won't help.*

We'd said our final goodbye in the sister's office. The nurses on the AIDS ward had thrown him a party that morning. Tea, through a straw, and tiny squares of really soft cake. And then they'd taken us to the office so we could have some time alone while they packed his bags for him and made sure his taxi to the airport was on its way. They'd done everything – told the airline about medication and special diets, organised wheelchairs at the transit airports and nice young men to push them. Everything they could except shed a tear, though I suspect one or two had snuck off to the bogs to do it out of sight. Danny had already told me not to come to the airport, that he wanted to say goodbye somewhere more private, so I'd wheeled him to the door and waved him off in the cab with one of the volunteers.

Four hours later, still in their office while they let me help with the filing, something mindless to fend off thinking, I got my first proper lesson in the kindness of strangers. The phone rang, and I heard the ward sister confirming details.

"Yes, a Daniel Thomas, that's right. Flight QF002."

A million catastrophes ran through my mind. Plane crashes, heart attacks, seizures . . .

"And you're the co-pilot, you say? Phoning from the actual plane?"

Her voice stayed calm and professional, Aberdeen accent as soft as an auntie reading a bedtime story, but her eyebrows looked like she'd just got a postcard from the moon.

I took a breath. Still airborne. At least I knew that much.

"His dentures?" she said suddenly, as if it was the oddest thing she'd heard all year. Well, second oddest. "Can you hold on? I'll just check for you."

One of the nurses went dashing out to the ward and came running back with the black velvet box Danny'd kept his teeth in after all his real ones had gone west.

"Yes, we have them," I heard the sister saying. "A courier? You're sure?"

Twenty minutes later, Danny's false teeth hurtled across London on the back of a motorbike before the airline flew them halfway round the world and delivered them to his door. For nothing. Well, nothing more than the sense of having done the right thing by someone who didn't have much longer to have right things done.

And I'd done all I could, too, at least for now. So I sat in that bloody cinema on my own. And all I could think was, *It's going to fucking sink. Just get on with it. Don't drag it out.* Danny died six days later.

I could have gone home for Christmas, pretended everything in London was going well, never mentioned Danny, just like I never had before. Except I couldn't, I just *couldn't*. So I came down here, to a little B&B by the harbour. There was a lavish Christmas dinner for the guests, and this lovely couple, Don and Terry, working their socks off to keep everyone cheerful. I told them my story after they caught me drying my eyes over the plum pudding. Terry dragged me off to their computer, showed me this online support group, registered me. "It's not just mourning together," I remember him saying, "although that helps, trust me."

For the next year, I spent most of my evenings with a group of virtual strangers who typed at each other. All over, they came from. Any time of day or night, anyone said whatever they needed to. Everyone understood why. When I shared my pilot story one night, this Aussie fella replied. Said how he was a trolley dolly for the airline, that he'd track down the co-pilot and let him know someone was grateful. I'd thought nothing of it, till three days later I got this message from a name I didn't know.

> Hi Lionel, this is Greg. Wayne passed on your message, and I wanted to answer in person. It was the least we could do for Danny, and I'm just glad we could do the right thing. He seemed like such a lovely fella, and I'm so sorry for your loss. I'm sure there's a heap of folks on here to look out for you but, if you don't mind, I'll log on once in a while and take a gander at how you're keeping. I know Danny would have wanted you to be happy, and so do I. In peace, Greg

My legs were as wobbly back then as Bet's are now, but I found my feet eventually. The hands that held me upright might have been invisible, but they were there when I needed them. Greg messaged me every Saturday, and I sent him an update every Sunday. We still do, every week. He talked me – well, they *all* talked me – through moving out of the flat, through signing up for the nursing course, leaving London. Understood when I said I was walking through a city of ghosts.

The cute man in the fishmonger's, the French guy on the market stall. The café where Danny wrote his number on my receipt when he served me my lunch, the park where we first dared kiss in public. The flat where he blew me till I hyperventilated, and the beer garden where he said those Three Little Words. They were all gone now. And then so was I.

I left that man behind – lonely, skinny Lionel who always walked with his head down. In Torquay, the only things that could haunt me were memories, and you can drown them in an inch of gin if you're determined. Although even now sometimes, in a crowd, I see a brown-haired man with a splash of freckles and a jumper that exact shade of red, and I have to swallow hard and look away.

But I'm happy. No, that's the wrong word. Proud. That's better. I've shown respect, and I've shown it where it doesn't always get a look-in. Whenever we get a new guest, I don't ask them who their next of kin is. Sharing a surname doesn't mean sharing a life. "Who cares for you most?" is a much better question.

And it gets a different answer sometimes. Some visitors really are just brothers or sisters, but sometimes you notice something. If you know to look. Matching rings or a hand that stays a second longer on a shoulder, the way one of them calls the other one "love" when they don't realise you're listening. They're here, most of them, because they love who they're visiting, and love shouldn't have to hide itself away. Not when it's needed most.

If I can, if they seem open to the idea, we'll talk. I'll tell them my office is always open if they need a moment. That there's a comfy sofa, and there's always a tin of sweets in the bottom drawer. That I can lend an ear if they need one. Rosie and Sharon still drop in to say hello, two years after Rosie's mum passed. Mrs Galpin was so far gone, bless her, she thought both of them were her daughters. "At least she's always glad to see us both," Sharon used to say.

My own love life's been more famine than feast, you might say, but when you've had foie gras you don't feel like lemon sole, do you? Davina always teases me. Tells me "nil by mouth" is all very noble, but I could at least keep my hand in. Says it like he knows exactly where, too. Spotlessly clean hands, the doctor, but a filthy mind. He told me once that if a girl as fat as me really wanted to lose weight, she might try something more aerobic than singing.

Greg asks sometimes, too, says I deserve someone nice. I tell him I'm saving myself, even if I'm not sure what from. "It's only saving if you're getting any interest," he wrote once, but he doesn't lecture. I remember the photos of him, and then him and Peter, and then the pair of them on the beach with the dog. And then no Peter. "I'm fine, Lionel," he said, "don't you go worrying about me." He said Peter leaving had taught him something. "Caring means showing it as well as feeling it, doesn't it, Lionel?" he wrote. "But you obviously know that much already."

Greg's my little secret, I suppose. Bet's the only one I've told about him – had to really, Bet being on the online forum too, tapping out financial advice for people with more problems than pennies to throw at them. Practical activism, he's always called it. One of Lil's Little Helpers, Bet is, only now they're helping him. There's Kieran, the gorgeous Irish solicitor who comes in to do last-minute changes to last wills and testaments. Ginger Freddy at the crematorium, Big Alan at the frock shop, and lovely Lewis at the florist's in Totnes. And then there's the steady stream of exquisite young men Bet's hired over the years to serve in the bank. Uncle Bert's Humpy Dinks, Davina calls them. They've all gone the extra mile, called by to solve a problem or pulled a string or two. They know the drill – don't sign the visitors' book so an eagle-eyed mother or sister won't spot your details, and phone ahead if you want to be discreet and slip in the back way.

Bet disinherited his mother last Thursday afternoon over a cup of Assam and bowl of raspberry sorbet. Wanted it all sorted before it was too late. Knew she wouldn't visit till he was at death's door, and that he couldn't do it after he'd looked her in the face.

"I've her blood in me, Lil," he said, "and bad blood it is too." His eyes were staring a hole in the folder of medical notes under my arm.

I wasn't allowed to witness the will – we got Maddy to do it. "No conflicts of interest, Lionel," Kieran told me as he arrived. "It'd be unprofessional." But it cheered Bet up.

"That woman's always told me that people get what they deserve in this world, Lil," he said afterwards. "So she's getting the knives."

I got to meet her, briefly. She flew in from Dublin when the time came. Davina said Bet probably only had a week or so left

– bronchial pneumonia and the treatment would kill him if the disease didn't. "See how she waits till I'm too weak to answer back, Lil," Bet whispered to me. "That's how she likes it."

She certainly gave it the full Catholic number. I could see where Bet got his taste in lingerie – black from head to toe she was. Black hat and black lace veil, and rosary beads clicking like the knitting needles under the guillotines. All she needed was the scythe.

I thought I'd best leave them to it, so I made them tea in the best cups. As I sorted Bet's pillows to let him sit up a bit, something twinkled at me from under the edge of his pillowcase. An emerald-green rhinestone. It must have fallen off the dress. Just as I slipped it into my hand, she stood up to be formal, shake hands with the lower orders. It would have been rude to put my hands in my pockets, so I popped it in her tea.

After she left, I took Bet his sherry. I thought he'd need the company. And there he was, laughing so hard the tears ran down his face. "Forty-seven years I've wanted to kill the old cow, and you almost choke her to death on a rhinestone," he finally said, when he could get the words out.

"She *didn't* . . ."

"Oh, she didn't know what it was, but it gave her gyp all right. Took some swallowing. Her manners haven't improved, either. Said it was no surprise a fat cunt like you couldn't recognise a tea strainer . . ."

In all our years, I'd hardly ever heard Bet swear. Certainly nothing like that. Whatever else he'd got from his mother, it wasn't his sense of decorum.

"Yes, well, always warm and accommodating, me. Flexible," I said. I could feel myself go red. Silly old Lil, blushing at something like that.

"You know what else she said?" he asked me. I just nodded. I didn't want to guess. "What a shame it was I'd spent my life married to that bank. That I'd never met a nice girl."

I smiled at that one, stroking his hand.

"I told her I had," he said. "One who was always looking out for me. A merry widow, just not the remarrying kind."

I felt myself blush again and I let the topic go, busying myself with turning his blankets down.

"You've never said, Lil. Were you close? With yours?"

"Two hundred and thirty-seven miles. Five hours on a good day," I said, making sure his buzzer was where he could reach it. "Otherwise four."

I couldn't see his reaction, his face hidden behind his lacquered Japanese fan, retrieved from under the bedclothes now that Mother had left.

"Sleep well, Bet. See you in the morning. And if you need anything . . ."

"You too, Lil. Be good."

Bet insisted on a secular ceremony, maybe to spite Mother one last time. We all stood in our Sunday best, dignified and sombre, eyes fixed either on the floor or on the celebrant. We heard about his prowess in the school curling team, about his professional exams, what a generous and caring boss he'd been at the bank, all the money he'd raised "for charity". It was beautiful, but it wasn't him – all black lace and white lies. By the time the coffin had rattled through the curtain and we all shuffled outside to the strains of *Banish Misfortune*, the real man had barely been mentioned. We'd honour him later in the Feathers, the way he'd told us to, "once she's caught the last broomstick back to the home country".

Ginger Freddy said he'd tell me when the ashes were ready to collect, how Mrs Wood had asked that I scatter them from Princess Pier.

"Probably for the best," he said, scanning the crowd to make sure she'd left. "People never generally expect crystals, but that much Swarovski would startle anyone."

"And his dress suit?" I asked him, paranoid she'd find out one day what he'd really been cremated in.

"Lovely bit of schmutter, don't you think?" he said with a wink, showing me a flash of its brilliant-green lining. "Big Al let the shoulders out for me."

I didn't stay long in the pub. Only the one ghost, maybe, but he was everywhere I looked. Not just the old posters on the wall, but every corner of the room. I'd never been in there without seeing him, and I couldn't stop seeing him now. Davina and I stumbled our way through *Love Hurts* like he'd requested, and then I told the others I needed a bit of fresh air. I could hear them still singing as I left. *Sisters, sisters, there were never such devoted sisters . . .*

Kieran came to find me, leaning on the pier railings under one of the lamp posts where I could blame a wet eye on the seaspray.

"I have the ashes, Lil, if you want us all to come and scatter them," he said, putting his arm round me, giving me a gentle squeeze, "but I think you should open this first. Bet left it with me for you. For when . . . well, you know . . ."

He handed me an envelope. Mr Lionel Bonniface c/o Clearview Hospice, it said, neatly typed across the front.

I opened it as carefully as I could, hands trembling. As I unfolded the letter, I could see there was something else. A plane ticket. An open return to Sydney, first class. And a thousand quid in fifty-pound notes.

"I think you should read the letter, Lil," Kieran said, taking a step backwards so he didn't block the light.

It was Bet's writing, a little wobblier than I remember it. Silly sod must have written it very recently.

> Dearest Lionel,
>
> I'm so sorry that the time has come for you to read this, but you've always helped me keep my secrets so I've always kept yours. No one ever had a sister like you, and I wanted to say more than thank you. I wanted to leave you with a bit of hope, and make sure you know that you've earned it.
>
> It's Mardi Gras in February, and Greg says the spare room's all yours. He's retired now and you can stay as long as you want. He says you're to get yourself down to Bondi Beach with him and make a big splash.
>
> Oh, and don't forget your dentures.
> All my love,
> Bertrand

"The act of writing is a way of tricking yourself into revealing something that you would never consciously put into the world."

Chuck Palahniuk

Arrowtown

STEFANIE SEDDON

I don't need to look through the lenses to recognise him, but I zoom in anyway, as if a close-up on his familiar features might explain how he's come to be down there, and I've come to be up here, the two of us not one hundred yards from each other in the same rocky gully, several thousand feet above Arrowtown.

Golden tussocks scatter the gap between us. I need to keep perfectly still, lying as I am on my stomach, behind this cluster of rocks, elbows dug into the hard, dry earth. I hold the binoculars steady and see him clearly now, framed in a perfect black circle. His hair is still dark, but worn long, falling to his shoulders with a lankness I suppose is in keeping with his current situation. He's wearing jeans and a black T-shirt with the sleeves ripped out. His thin, hard arms are scarred with prominent veins and swirling tattoos. He doesn't look cold, yet, but he will be. The light up here deceives you. It blinds and burns, but it won't keep you warm for long. I watch him unroll his sleeping bag and fold it in half beside him. He undoes his laces and eases off his boots. Then he sits heavily on the bag and leans back against a rock, chin up, eyes closed.

He reaches for his backpack and instinctively I shrink into the dust. He pulls out a plastic Coke bottle and drinks from it, for a long time. The fingers on his other hand tap an irregular beat on his knee.

It's a funny thing, when, after so many years, you see someone's face again. Some, you wouldn't recognise at all. I'd say that would be true of most of the people I went to school with around here, and I doubt they'd recognise me now, either, if I didn't tell them my name. Most of us suffer a little hair loss, a little weight gain round the middle, an extra chin or two, depending upon the angle. A lifetime's experience can completely change a person's identity and it can show in their face. But others just don't seem to change at all. It's like that now with him, with Jimmy. It must be at least thirty years since I last clapped eyes on him. But I guess then he knew I'd be looking at him.

Now, as I twist the focus wheel a little more to the right, I can see the angular features that always made him look older than his years, more serious than the rest of us. He still has his high cheekbones, a product of his Maori mother, but now they leave shadows on sunken cheeks. I always thought he had the face of a boxer – battling and battered, but the guy you'd probably be cheering for. I guess you'd still say he's more handsome than the rest of us. He'd have had his pick of the girls later on, if things had turned out differently.

Jimmy stows the bottle against the rock and begins rolling a cigarette. He still makes it look effortless. As the rest of us would be picking loose tobacco shreds off our tongues and wiping soggy, disintegrating paper from our fingers, Jimmy would be blowing rings from a perfect rollie. I can picture him, a masterclass in eighties cool, sitting on the bonnet of his brother's red Valiant, skinny legs in black jeans stretched out across the metal hood like it was a sofa, hooting at us as the last precious grams of our stash blew away in a gust of wind.

"C'mon, Jimmy, just roll me one," Richie would beg, defeated by numerous fat-fingered attempts.

"Jeez, you guys," Jimmy would say, shaking his head.

Then he would patiently, generously, roll another, making us watch and learn as he measured just the right amount of tobacco into the Rizla, gently massaged the paper back and forth between his practised fingertips, and, with just a glisten of spit on the end of his tongue, wetted the glue before sealing it into a perfect white tube.

"Dudes," he would say, "you *need* me."

And we did. He was the kid that Richie and I wanted to be,

but it didn't come naturally to us like it did to him. My father was the deputy sergeant at the Arrowtown police station, and Richie's ran the dental practice, and in a small town hemmed in by mountains, that pretty much defined who we were from the day we were born until the day we moved away. Jimmy didn't fit that mould. He really did have a tough older brother with a criminal record and a car that Jimmy could drive, unlicensed, during the brother's frequent disappearances. Jimmy had the sort of chaotic home life that enabled him to go out whenever he liked and not return if he didn't want to. He could buy tobacco and vodka from Harry's bottle store without anyone thinking to tell his mother. Jimmy's home sounded the sort of place that a fourteen-year-old boy might dream of living in, even though he never invited us back after school, and never wore a winter coat, and never mentioned his birthday. We envied him his freedom, his independence, even when we overheard our parents whispering behind their local paper about court dates, about domestic violence, about that poor nice boy and what a shame it all was.

If you want to be cynical about it – and I find myself, these days, cynical about many things – you could say that the three of us had, for a time, a mutually beneficial relationship. Jimmy's cool rubbed off a little on Richie and me, and our influence probably stopped him from getting into the sort of trouble that he might have, if he were hanging around with a different set of kids. The kids from the social housing by the railway tracks, or the kids who got bused in from isolated, insular farming communities; these were the kids who reached thirteen and got expelled, or got pregnant, or got expelled for getting someone pregnant – the kids who would spend the rest of their lives scratching out a life around Arrowtown. Jimmy wasn't top of the class or anything, but he probably cared a little more about his school work because we did, and, like us, he planned to leave one day. Go to uni, get a job in the city, travel overseas. He seemed to share our ambitions and that was a good thing for him.

I shuffle on my stomach. There's a lot more of it than there used to be and it's pressing hard into my belt buckle. The ground is getting cold, so with my free hand I untie my fleece from my waist and lay it underneath me. Jimmy's getting cold now, too.

He holds his hands tightly over his arms and I realise that he can't have a jumper in his backpack, or he'd be taking it out right now. He should know better than this. We used to come up here with our air rifles, shooting rabbits with my dad, and it would get damn chilly on the long walk back down the mountain, especially after the sun went down. "Cold enough to freeze the balls off a brass monkey," was what my dad used to say. Jimmy would pack something warm to wear, back then. He looks out of place up here now, unprepared, which is not how I like to remember him. Even at the end, the very last time I saw him, he looked like he was in control of things, like he was the one calling the shots.

My dad and Jimmy got on pretty well in those days. Jimmy's own dad was never around – at least, we never met him if he was – but looking at Jimmy now, climbing into his bag, curling himself into a ball in the dirt, it's hard not to assume that they ended up the same. I guess that's why he spent so much time at my place. Every Saturday evening we'd be at my house, or at Richie's, watching music-video shows late into the night or rifling through our parents' VHS tapes. Jimmy was more interested in what was on the bookshelves. There were a lot of unread books to choose from, and they were slowly turning dog-eared thanks to Jimmy.

One Saturday night, though, we made other plans. There'd been talk at school about a party down by the river, a big party – the sort with no invitations, on a lonely stretch of beach, kids in cars drinking, the usual routine in our town. Jimmy had said he would drive us out there and suggested we take Richie's tent. We could camp the night, then he wouldn't need to worry about driving back. I knew I would never be allowed to go, so I had told my parents I was going to the movies with Richie and would stay over at his house, and Richie did the same. After tea, I put on my hi-top sneakers, stonewash jeans and a baggy white shirt with rolled-up sleeves. Thinking I looked pretty good, I went off to meet Jimmy and Richie at the Pines. I moved quickly through the centre of town, across the park and past a long strip of wooden-clad bungalows with porches whose reclining occupants watched me go by. I kept my collar up and my head down. Back then, everyone knew my dad – he'd helped or arrested most of them – and if I'd been clocked walking in the opposite direction to the cinema, there was a high chance someone would happen to mention it to him later.

At the top end of town, I turned down a dirt track into the trees. The track led to a neglected playground, where I found Jimmy at the wheel of the Valiant, revving the engine, with Richie beside him on the bench seat. Jimmy wasn't short for his age but I could barely see him over the dash of that big old car. It's hard to believe we were only fourteen that day. Looking back, I see us as older, almost men and not boys. It's funny the way you remember things.

When he saw me coming, Jimmy cut the engine and got out of the car. Richie got out, too, and I saw he was dressed the same as me, his almost new jeans and neatly ironed shirt undoing the impact of his mirror-perfected gangland swagger. Jimmy was wearing what I guessed he'd found on the floor that morning, and managed to look better than both of us.

"Dude, you made it," he called. Jimmy always appreciated the efforts we went to in dodging the strictures of our homes.

I was excited and nervous about the party. The kids were mostly older than us, a mixture of rugby boys from school and their hangers-on, young farm workers, and school drop-outs. We didn't fit into any of those groups. Richie and me, we just felt lucky to be going and we knew we wouldn't be anywhere near it if it weren't for Jimmy. We climbed into the car, sitting three-up on the stitched-leather seat, and skidded off down the track. On the back seat, two six-packs glinted under Richie's canvas tent, and when I turned to throw my sleeping bag alongside them, I saw dust trailing behind the car, puffing out thick and red like a cloud across the setting sun.

We turned down a bumpy road a few miles north of Arrowtown, and passed through a cluster of weeping willows that drooped their stringy branches into a wide, slow-flowing section of the river. A shingle beach ran down to the water; several wooden picnic tables seemed to be sinking under the weight of the metal beer kegs that covered their peeling tops. We arrived to the sound of Bruce Springsteen roaring across the river, and pulled up alongside the rusting frames of cars that had seen better days; Hillmans, Plymouths and dusty utes sat next to souped-up Fords and Holdens, while a line of motorbikes, mostly small farm runabouts, leaned on stands. Around the cars, in front and back seats, sprawled on bonnets, sitting on beer boxes, spilling across the beach, were sixty to eighty teenagers, drinking, shouting, dancing.

We took the beer to a flat patch of grass beneath a willow, where Richie and I laid out the tent. Jimmy produced a packet of tobacco. *"Born down in a dead man's town, The first kick I took was when I hit the ground,"* blared the speaker. We sat on the tent, drinking from cans, while Jimmy went to talk to some friends of his brother's; lean, weathered boys who worked for a local shearing gang. They wore ripped vests and tight black jeans and on their arms were the kinds of tattoos that made you cross the street, but they were friendly enough to Jimmy. They made Richie and me look like a couple of little girls, so we stayed put and drank our lukewarm beer. Jimmy smoked a joint with them – something he never did with us – and by the time he came back, carrying one of their six-packs, we were already pretty drunk. Some kids in the year above us came over to talk, but as soon as Jimmy went off again, they did, too.

The next few hours passed quickly. Our beer ran out, and Jimmy brought over some more cans from the shearers. The bass got louder and louder until vibrations overtook the lyrics; more cars arrived in the dark. When Richie threw up, we thought we'd better pitch our tent, so Jimmy turned on the Valiant's headlights so we could see. I was grinding the first pole into the grass, when, through the rumble of engines and the speaker noise and the shouting, a different sound came to me – a high-pitched siren, that made my stomach lurch.

"Jimmy, did you hear that?"

He must have thought I was asking him about the music because he looked up, grimacing.

"Yeah, is this Kajagoogoo? Who the fuck listens to Kajagoogoo?"

Then he heard it, too. For me, the siren meant more than just the police turning up to wreck a good night. It meant that my dad was here.

Cars scattered and kids ran into bushes. Without a word, Jimmy helped me snatch up the tent and poles, which we bundled into the back along with a dazed Richie. I scrambled around for the sleeping bags and slid across the front seat, slamming the passenger door as Jimmy jumped in from the driver's side and started the engine.

"It's OK, mate," he said. "Let's just get the fuck out of here."

The car was facing the river, and he was heavy on the clutch as he forced the clunky stick shift into reverse. Perhaps his foot hadn't been on the clutch properly. The next thing I remember was us jolting sharply backwards and then a hard thump. Then someone screamed – and I particularly remember the screaming, because I heard it just as flashing lights appeared in the distance through the willows. I was looking over Richie, through the rear windscreen, and I could see a girl standing behind the car. She was looking down, then she was looking up at me through the screen, and she had a terrible expression on her face. Jimmy sat very still, staring out over the black river. His face had a hollow look about it.

He killed the engine and we got out of the car.

I saw him in court, back then, before they took him away. They let me meet him in a side room. Richie didn't come. His parents didn't want him involved in any of it, but my dad let me have five minutes. Jimmy's social worker sat next to him, across the table from me, studying her cup of tea. It wasn't easy to have a regular conversation. Plus, he was wearing clothes that looked weird on him. They were a little big for him, a little too clean.

I tried to say things I thought he might want to hear. That I'd write, send him stuff – books, tapes – and that when he came back, things would be exactly the same as before. I kept my head down most of the time, sneakers digging into an imaginary crack in the floor, because I really didn't want to cry in front of him. Jimmy tapped his fingers on the table and hardly said anything at all.

After that, I only saw him in the courtroom, when they gave the verdict, and I saw them take him away, alone, in the back of a police van. He was looking out through the tiny window and I wondered if he saw me there, looking back at him. I don't think he did, because he didn't raise his chin up in a nod, like he would have.

I heard one or two things about him after that – how he wouldn't be coming back to school, how he'd moved to the city with his brother's crowd. Things were different between me and Richie, too. We stuck out the next two years at school, studying for exams, staying in a lot. We didn't see as much of each other. I hung around with some kids from the tennis squad and Richie got more into rugby. Then his family moved to Australia and I never saw him again; just like that, he was gone. I went to uni up north and trained as a maths teacher, and life seemed to tumble along past me. I stayed away from Arrowtown, until a divorce took its toll on my finances and friendships and I felt I'd run out of options. So I applied for a job at the local school and bought myself a property up here on the mountain, not far from where we used to shoot rabbits with our airguns.

To be honest, any thoughts of Jimmy have been pretty few and far between. An old school friend once told me he'd seen him in Christchurch looking pretty wasted. It sounded to me like he'd lost his way. And sure, since I've been back, I sometimes see places we used to go. Or I notice the way certain groups of kids at school act when they're together and that reminds me of him, of the three of us. But I've tried not to dwell on things and it all seemed so long ago, until I got the call early this morning from a Sergeant Seymour down at the station.

"We need some help up the mountain," he said.

I wasn't so sure I was interested. Then he told me that someone had run off up there. A junkie, was the word he used.

"He held up a bookie's in Christchurch with a sawn-off shotgun. Frightened the life out of the girl on the counter. We had a report of him hitchhiking through the Waitaki Valley and then someone spotted him in town a few hours ago. I'm guessing he wants to lie low for a while, but he's pitched up in the wrong place for that."

Seymour's voice became sober and insistent.

"The thing is, he took off out your way, on foot. We reckon he's probably headed up the mountain. By all accounts he's just a messed-up druggie, but these things get a little serious when there's a weapon involved."

He told me that they had to drive up the track behind my land and they needed someone to show them around.

"You know what, mate?" he said. "I think you'll know him. He lived here once, a long time ago."

He gave me the name and I did know him. Just like I knew the route up.

The sun was coming over the hills when they arrived at my house with pistols strapped to their waists. Seymour said the armed offenders' squad had been called out from the city but would take some time to get there, so it would be down to us to locate him and radio through his whereabouts. I took them across the back of my property and it hadn't been hard to get sight of him, a skinny figure marching up into the distance, a good mile or so ahead. We followed him to this gully, where Seymour and his men crept down a level, closer to where Jimmy had settled. I stayed back on the ridge, tucked in between the rocks and feeling like I'd got myself into something I'd rather I hadn't.

A day feels like a long time on the mountain. I'm losing the light now, but can still make out his shaking form. Jimmy, down there, freezing half to death in his sleeping bag, and me, up here, in the half-light of a high-country dusk. Though we're the same age, me and him, it feels like I'm looking at a boy, not a man.

And now I hear the scuffing of boots on the ground. I move my binoculars across a little and see, just to the west of Seymour and his men, several black-clad figures, wearing helmets and carrying automatic weapons, creeping in through the rocks.

But Jimmy hears them, too. He jerks up in the sleeping bag, turns his head in their direction and snatches his backpack. He takes out a gun, lifts his arms towards them. Then four quick shots, and I'm flat in the dirt, eyes squeezed shut. My face is in the crook of my elbow, hand clamped down on the back of my head.

When I lift my head to see what has happened, all I can make out is a cloud of dust, rising up from the bottom of the gully.

"Time moves in one direction, memory another. We are that strange species that constructs artefacts intended to counter the natural flow of forgetting."

William Gibson

An Elephant

DOMINIKA CHMIEL

It was an early September morning in a post-Communist town. Lech and Jedrek hid under an aluminium gazebo, protecting themselves from the sluggish rain.

They were alone under the metallic roof. Four residential buildings, which together created a square, surrounded them. Lech knew the area by rote now; he had been living there for five years and sometimes felt a little bit tired of the predictability. No matter which angle he looked from, he always felt trapped by the heavy-boned blocks. They were solid yet impatient, like pawns in chess before the first move of a game. Each building had five floors and was divided vertically into five parts, each one in a different shade of mucky brown and with its own entrance. The space in the middle of this tedious architectural design was filled with a shabby playground, a small shopping mall, an off-licence, one newsagent's kiosk and finally a metal gazebo, where Lech and Jedrek squatted.

It was Jedrek who dragged them there every day, sometimes more than once. Usually, Lech had nothing against it. He was too old for running, so he enjoyed just sitting there, encircled by the giant concrete blocks. Once in a while he went for a piss, as the gazebo was providently bordered with some intimate shrubs and flowerbeds for those who needed a moment of solitude.

Jedrek's right foot suddenly twitched. His boots were worn and dirty. Flakes of filth and dust fell onto the ground. Suspecting

155

that he was being observed and judged, Jedrek looked at Lech with a goofy smile. Lech snorted. They didn't exchange much information, but it was easy to tell that they belonged together. They were synchronised at some basic, animalistic level.

The raindrops falling on the gazebo roof were gathering strength. They sounded like bullets.

Laundry dangled from balconies, swinging back and forth, and wrinkling in the rain. Here and there, a random door cracked open and a woman, looking tired although the day had just begun, stormed outside and snatched up the wet shirts, bras and panties, moist streaks of hair taping her eyes and mouth.

Jedrek undid his trouser belt and sighed lazily, positioning himself more comfortably on the bench. He looked around suspiciously. Lech understood this look in a second, as a can of lager was briskly removed from a cotton bag. Jedrek opened it with a hiss and took a greedy swig, then placed the drink on the top of his beer belly.

"Would you like some?" Jedrek was evidently on track to a better mood. "I know you would, buddy." Lech didn't respond. He had tried beer once or twice and it did nothing for him but help him to appreciate the handy closeness of the bushes even more.

Entrances to the four buildings started opening more regularly now and soon the shrubbery around the gazebo was filled with umbrellas and dogs. Some canines jogged meekly by the legs of their companions while others fought back, pulling madly on their leashes in the opposite direction to the one in which they were being led. The neighbours were circling the aluminium shelter like natural satellites around a planet with no intelligent form of life.

Jedrek kept drinking his beer, unaffected, as his neighbours threw quick glances at him. There were also embarrassed "Good mornings" and bashful nods. Lech suspected their neighbours wanted to get this part of their day over with as fast as possible, a generation of permanent avoiders.

Lech walked outside the gazebo. The smells of wet world penetrated his nostrils. He felt the raindrops stroking his naked skin like cold noses. It was nice, soothing.

He stretched out his tongue and scratched behind his ear.

"Come . . . on . . . Lech . . ." Jedrek's pauses were stressed with rhythmic belching. "You're going to get wet! Come . . . back . . . here!"

Lech barked and wagged his tail. He ran back inside and rested his paws on Jedrek's muddy shoes.

Karol was fifteen years old and about to encounter his first psychedelic experience. It was a regular school day but he told his mother he didn't feel well and she pretended to believe him. His mother was unrivalled at faking.

Three anorexic beams of morning light managed to creep inside Karol's bedroom. Three long, thin lines split the dark floor into sectors. There wasn't much space or furniture to divide, though. A wooden bedside table next to a chest of drawers. A bed that Karol – tall and silent, the universal definition of a mildly disturbed teen, as his mother once told him – spent most of his time on. A decent pile of old music albums: Tool, the Black Keys, Nirvana. T-shirts, all of them black, rested on a plastic chair; a silver boom box was economically stowed beneath it. On the yellow-greyish walls there were no posters, only a big sign, hand-written. The letters were fragile, shaking as if they had a fever, although the text was written in capitals. EVERYTHING IS A FREE PLAY OF THE MIND was stretched along one wall, parallel to the bed Karol lay on. He turned his head and looked at the caption, adjusting his headphones so that he couldn't hear the annoyingly optimistic YouTube laughs coming from the next room.

On the bright side, Ewa, Karol's mother, was so much into the YouTube beauty vloggers that she probably wouldn't notice that he was tripping. One of the biggest tragedies of Ewa's existence, Karol thought, was that his mother didn't have a daughter to dress in fancy clothes and put fab make-up on. That and the fact she was failing in life in general.

Since she started working afternoon shifts at the supermarket, Ewa kept her mornings busy in front of a computer, watching twenty-something girls making extra-surprised faces to the web cameras of the MacBooks their parents had paid for. Luckily, Karol had different priorities.

He was prepared for his journey. Ready to explore the psychedelic realm with just a little help from anti-coughing pills named Acodin. It was quite an innocent drug, the sort you could buy over the counter. The secret was to be generous and take a few more pills than prescribed. In fact, a lot more.

Karol lay on the bed thinking about the tips his older and more experienced friends had given him on how to get trashed with these little round wonders. The entire preparation before actually taking the pills was like an urban ritual. Karol bought two packs so he visited, just as advised, two pharmacies in different parts of the town. It was the best way not to raise any suspicion. He also performed some dry coughing in front of a pharmacist and confirmed that he would never exceed the prescribed dosage. Now the pills were scattered on the lid of a laptop lying on the bedside table, like dots waiting to be connected, and Karol was getting ready to open the door that could lead him anywhere. He had heard about Out-of-Body Experiences and trips that culminated with encountering The One True God. He'd read about time-travelling and chatting with weird creatures from different dimensions. It sounded like fun.

Karol swallowed the pills, one by one, reaching the total amount of forty. The journey would last about five, maybe six hours but DXM, the chemical compound in Acodin responsible for inducing different states of consciousness, needed some time to spin up and break the ice of both body and mind. Karol looked at the rest of the pills on the table. They had no distinctive taste or aroma. White and smaller than the tip of a pinkie, they looked innocent, almost like curled-up sleeping puppies.

Karol smiled. His mum had work and his father probably wouldn't show up until the end of the day. He had heard that DXM could be nasty and moody. As his friends had told him: "Dude, your mindset is everything." Karol didn't feel anything yet; only his throat was a little sore from popping all the candies.

To boost his Zen, Karol pressed the Play button on his CD player. He listened to Bill Hicks describing his most amusing drug experience, but mostly offending the audience, as usual: "How much do you smoke, sir? Two packs a day, is that right? Pussy. I go through two *lighters* a day. That's right, two lighters! You're a health nut compared to me."

Poor Hicks, Karol thought. Of all the politically incorrect

things the comic praised it was his passion for smoking that killed him in the end.

Suddenly, Karol realised that the words in his head stretched like an infinite chewing gum and that he had no idea where they might have stopped.

The drugs were soaking in. Karol's body was gaining more and more weight. He was a souvenir magnet and his bed was a fridge. The bedroom was gently rotating, with countless colours changing their places, as if he was locked inside a kaleidoscope. He was breathing deeply, trying not to panic. Then his bowels started singing. He put his hands on his stomach and felt the vibrations. For the first time in Karol's life, his physical awareness expanded and went deeper, under the layer of his pallid skin, behind the shapes of his anaemic torso and rickety limbs. His guts were yodelling, their voice growing louder and louder, as if they wanted to break through and have their share of the Out-of-Body Experience, too.

Jedrek was sure. His wife was cheating on him. Each gulp of lukewarm beer filled him with more certainty. Ewa was not a gorgeous woman, at least not any more, but she was still able to pull it off. She had been a dancer in high school. Even now, almost forty and always with a cigarette sticking out from her thin lips, she managed to move gracefully between a sink and a fridge. As this kitchen performance was charming in its innocence, Jedrek had no doubts that in some man's bedroom Ewa's swinging hips would move with definite purpose – synchronised with the sound of horns being put on him.

"Fucking life!" Jedrek doused the fire inside him with another gulp of lager. It was eight in the morning and he was officially walking the dog. But as Lech was rather a lazy kind of creature, the word "walking" was an unnecessary exaggeration. Lech was sitting next to Jedrek looking at his owner with a mixture of sympathy and respect. The dog did its morning pissing just after they left the house and now it was ready to go back home, especially since the weather wasn't on its, or actually any other dog's or living creature's, side. Unfortunately for Lech, Jedrek had other plans. He opened another can.

"Mummy, look!"

A boy around four years old, with a backpack twice his size, stopped in front of Lech and pointed his plump finger in the dog's face. "What happened to doggy?"

Lech didn't react. It wasn't news for him. It wasn't news for Jedrek, either.

The boy's mother, a spindly, dull-haired woman around thirty, looked at Lech and quickly turned her eyes away.

"It's nothing, baby. The doggy is just sick."

Then she forced a smile as if Lech were a hero of some charity event she had to attend because her boss's wife had a thing for crippled kids. She pulled her son harder by his hand. The boy was almost running now, trying to keep up with his mother's vigorous pace, the rucksack jumping up and down on his narrow back.

"The dog's not sick, lady!" shouted Jedrek. "His skin is just thicker, but Lech can still hear you, you know!"

The rain got smaller. Jedrek took another sip of his cheap beer. The bubbles were gone. He glanced at the dog furtively but Lech didn't seem to care.

Jedrek's dog wasn't the prettiest creature alive, certainly. He and Ewa took him to see a vet one day, after Lech, then still a puppy, lost his hair and the skin on his back started flaking, revealing pink layers of something that looked like canned ham with a questionably long expiry date. The vet told them that Lech was suffering from a rare skin disease, something similar to elephantiasis.

"You know, just like the guy in that old artsy movie," the vet said, stroking Lech with a rubber glove. "It shouldn't get any more serious than this. I'll give you some pills and a cream. We can do vitamin injections, too, if you are interested? Eventually, Lech's skin will start to heal."

"Heal?" asked Ewa hopefully and Lech, as if on command, immediately started licking her palm.

"Well . . . it will never look normal – I mean, like an ordinary dog's. The bare skin will probably stiffen with keratosis, kind of."

"So maybe we should just put him down?" Jedrek muttered. He had an enormous hangover. It was the culmination of his heavy drinking, soon to be followed by his "voluntary" release from the police force.

"You want to kill him?" Ewa looked at Jedrek, her pupils tiny but full of loathing. At that moment Jedrek thought he could have been the one changing into an elephant. "I'd never let you do that to Lech. Karol loves him." Her eyes were watering and Lech's tongue worked faster between her lean fingers.

"Our son calls this dog his little brother." Ewa smiled at the vet and he answered with a headshake. Jedrek was impressed that the doc was able to catch this grin as he seemed to have been pretty busy with staring at his wife's legs ever since they'd entered his office.

"Sir, I don't really think it's necessary to take such a radical step." The vet opened Lech's mouth and analysed his teeth, to the sound of minor but constant snarling. "This doggy here has an entire life ahead of him."

Jedrek would have disagreed. He would have elaborated on why sometimes the most painful measures could be the most effective ones. Unfortunately he was busy fighting his gag reflex at the time. Jesus, he thought, all of these nasty animal smells.

On their way home, Ewa was driving and chain-smoking. She used to wear short skirts back then and had jelly flats on her skinny, tanned legs. Jedrek sat in the passenger seat with Lech on his lap. He could have sworn that in the past hour the dog had become heavier, denser. Jedrek could hardly move underneath his hairless load. Lech not only looked like an elephant, now he was also turning into one.

Standing under the gazebo and inhaling the fresh after-rain air, Jedrek eyed Lech with a sudden overwhelming emotion. In the long run it turned out that hideousness touched him much more than beauty. The dog was old so its ugliness could have been excused by its age. In the human world it didn't work that way any more, but in a dog's reality this argument was possibly still valid. There was something reassuring in that. Like having a natural permit to fail.

"Come here, buddy, come here." The dog approached Jedrek, trustingly, with its tail wagging smile after smile. For a creature that could have had a German Shepherd as a grandfather, Lech was surprisingly mellow.

"Yep, boy, in the end it's just you and me." Jedrek smashed

the empty beer can between his hands. He tried to throw it into the nearby sandpit, but he missed.

"No worries," he said with a bitter smile. He had ten more of those and plans for some heavier stuff.

"Come on, Lech. Time to go home, buddy," he said to the dog as Lech leaned against his legs. Jedrek took his cotton bag with two almost intact six-packs inside. The man and the dog marched in unison towards the building where they lived. Suddenly, Jedrek turned around. The gazebo, with an aura of gleaming raindrops, looked lonely without them. Besides, his arm hurt. The bag full of beers was like a heavy anchor waiting to be weighed. Jedrek burped violently. Lech barked. The sound of a can being opened followed.

"Bastards!" Ewa heard a full-throated roar. "I will get you! I will show the whole world what you did to me, you officious pricks!"

Here we go again, she thought, and turned the computer off just to hide her head in her perfectly manicured hands. When Jedrek had left that morning to "walk the dog", she was almost sure it would end like this.

Ewa dragged herself across the living room towards the balcony door, opened it and saw her husband, outside the building, barefoot, belligerently preaching about a conspiracy that had resulted in him being fired from the police. His bare feet were proof of his innocence. That he hadn't done anything wrong – like Jesus crucified for other people's sins. At least that was what he told Ewa once, just before spitting his drink on the dinner table and setting it on fire like the burning bush.

Windows were opening; people stuck their heads out, looked down, and drew their heads back in. Shouting drunkard Jedrek from the fourth floor was old news. The residents of the estate pretended they didn't notice anything. Ewa pretended she didn't notice them not noticing.

"Ewa, Ewa! I forgive you! I love you!" Downstairs her husband was calling her name with an intoxicated affection. After thirty minutes of this barefoot performance, Jedrek mercifully tumbled inside the flat and immediately rolled into the toilet.

Then the festival of growls began. Shortly it became a creepy canon.

Untz. Untz. Untz.

"Adaaam!" Jedrek bellowed at the top of his lungs.

Untz. Untz. Untz.

"Adam, damn you! You know who it is! Kill the music, I tell you!" Jedrek screamed even louder.

Untz. Untz. Untz. Wub. Untz!

"Jedrek. Please. Stop." Ewa stood close to the toilet door, which her husband had locked from the inside. She pressed her cheek against the wooden panel. "Get out, get out right now!"

"Adam, I will kill you! You son of a bitch! Aaah . . . Aaah! My arse! Arrargh . . . Yyyh . . ."

It was a routine everyone was familiar with. When Jedrek was drunk he behaved like an asshole. The irony was, he couldn't shit because of his haemorrhoids. And when he couldn't shit, he blamed everyone. This time the easiest target was their neighbours' son Adam – an acne-prone student who was a delightful techno-listener. Jedrek didn't like it. He wanted the whole world to know.

Untz. Untz. Untz.

"Adam, turn the fuckin' music down! I need to focu-u-s-s!" shouted Jedrek in a bass voice. "I tell you, son, there is no greater pain than these haemorrrrrhoid bastards! Shut up the music, I can't shit, shut it up, I need to push it all o-o-u-t!" Jedrek's voice resonated sharply as if he were in a band shell, not wobbling on a toilet bowl. He didn't seem to get tired. Ewa did. She went to the living room, sat in an armchair in front of the TV and lit a cigarette.

Her fingernails were done following the latest online trends. At the beginning it wasn't easy – looking at these young creatures on her computer screen and comparing their smooth faces and blow-dried hair to her own, worn and used. But after a while, with this sadness came the realisation that at least she belonged somewhere, and it was better than nothing. Besides, Ewa had always wanted to have a daughter. It never happened; she had Karol. She loved him, but he was still a weird teenager, always dressed in black clothes, listening only to music full of aggression, rapid growls and questions Ewa was afraid to ask. There was a lot of screaming, too, and probably it was one of the inspirations for Jedrek and his current one-man toilet show.

"Adam, Adam, I dare you!"

The music had stopped, but Ewa could still hear her husband roaring. "The hell with it," she decided. There was no point in hiding in front of the telly. Ewa stood up and screamed back, "Stop it! Stop it right now!"

She stormed out of the room and knocked passionately on the toilet door.

"For God's sake, Jedrek, stop yelling!"

"But I can't, it hurts so much, so much . . ." Jedrek's muffled mumble. "So much . . . A . . . a . . . aaaa!" Animal sounds of fighting with natural destiny leaked outside the toilet and penetrated her ears.

Ewa sighed. At least he was sitting there locked in, just a little more annoying background noise. It was still better than the alternative – Jedrek's never-ending monologues when he sat cross-legged on the carpet, like a wobbly Buddha. Smelling of crude moonshine he would lean close to her, puffing and panting. She smirked then as if she had heard the best joke ever.

And just like that, the screaming was over. Ewa pushed her ear to the door. She heard a deep, multi-dimensional sound, a familiar, drunken kind of snoring that had the texture of brand-new sandpaper. Jedrek must have fallen asleep – on the toilet. Ewa smiled and reached for another cigarette. She realised with relief that her nail polish hadn't chipped off.

Jedrek sleeping had many pros. No more shouting; he would be out for a few hours, so no more anal drama. On the negative side, the toilet was out of order. In terms of peeing, their situation was not that bad – they always had the bathtub. At worst, Karol could use a public toilet in the nearby shopping mall and she was off to work soon anyway. It was handled. They would survive.

The rhythmic sound of Jedrek's snarling on the toilet seat made Ewa relaxed and drowsy. She crouched against the door and shut her eyes. The snoring, next to screaming, was the most popular lullaby in their home. The flat was calm, the silence stained only with Jedrek's drooling wheezes.

Karol has never been high – like really high – except some minor marijuana party trips, but that wasn't really doping, it was more like laughing and feeling hungry and lazy and rubbery. This time he was tripping. He was fucked!

His body was still lying on the bed with the headphones on, but Karol was somewhere else. At the beginning, when it all started, he just felt like a robot. An android. Dreaming of electric sheep. Then the avalanche flushed everything down.

Acodin took control and turned the inside of his mouth into the Sahara, limitless and full of sparkling sand, and sun, and Islamic rebels. He wanted a glass of water but it was impossible to get to the kitchen because there was a caveman shouting somewhere and his elephant stomping and hopping around the apartment, one giant stride after another.

In Karol's stomach there was this amazing feeling rising, awakening, like the first day of summer holiday, or like being on a rollercoaster, or like being in love.

He found a half-empty bottle of water under his bed and drinking it was like swallowing stones – rolling stones. Karol chuckled. Then God started talking to him. He wore a T-shirt with a huge red tongue and a halo hovering above it. God was yelling about black holes and pain and He was yelling about Adam, the First Man. "Karol, meet me in the Garden of Eden," He said. The holy road was wet and made of bathroom tiles, the galaxies of stars grew on apple trees and bloomed, twisting, when Karol found he was looking into the eyes of the Original Man. They were drains without a bottom. Adam asked Karol if he was into ribs 'cause he had some to spare. Then Karol saw a hand orbiting closer and closer to him, like a fallen star, or a deadly asteroid. He was in a disaster movie, and he was scared and screaming, "Where the hell is Bruce Willis? Who will save us?" He was screaming with colours now, an ocean of black flowed from his mouth, blinding him, and just like that Karol was back in the room.

A thin, womanlike figurine stood in the doorway. It had two heads, held a cigarette and its nails were made of rainbows. The figurine's first head was unfamiliar, with a mouth like a time-tunnel. The other was Bill Hicks, who looked greedily at the cigarette in one of its hands and twisted his short chubby neck to get closer to the fag. It wasn't Bill's luckiest day; the hand was stretched far behind so that the smoke wouldn't fly into the room. But Karol could see the smoke anyway. It was conquering the bedroom. The nicotine mist filled the space with ghostly skeleton silhouettes of morbid barbecue grills.

Karol felt sick, uncomfortable in his skin, uncomfortable in this very moment.

"Where's Lech?" the first head asked.

Karol didn't know what it meant.

"Where is the dog, you crackhead?" said Bill Hicks. He finally landed the cigarette and was chewing the filter with dedication and a lot of lip smacking.

Karol couldn't acknowledge any creature of that kind. He wasn't really sure what a dogyoucrackhead even was. Bill's smacking got louder. Karol interpreted it as a suggestion to start searching for whatever was missing. Because he still couldn't move, he made himself useful by looking around the room. Oh boy, he thought. Everything was vivid yet blurred at the same time. He got the feeling the furniture didn't like him that much. On the other hand, his guts were very talkative – he couldn't stop burping. His sweaty body was shaking. He was seriously afraid of what would come out of him next.

"Yo, psychonaut, get your head out of your ass!" Bill Hicks aggressively spat out the rumpled cigarette butt. It landed on the floor with a whizz.

"Karol, for God's sake, have a sip of water and help me. Is Lech with you? He didn't come back with your father. Lech is missing."

Ewa eyed Karol's room. Everything seemed abnormal, just like usual. Karol was immobile on the bed, his forehead oily with sebum. Her son's eyes were like glass, two empty jars of sauerkraut. She had to admit it. Karol was very convincing in the role of a student who had come down with flu and couldn't go to school.

"You're good, Karol. You're really good. Only it's me again who has to deal with all of this . . . shit." Ewa closed the door behind her. Sounds from the toilet marked her every step when she entered the living room. She glanced around. The TV was off. There was nothing to look at.

The dog was gone.

Ewa felt fear drilling somewhere deep beneath her belly button. Once again that day, she looked through the window and down at the entrance.

Then she noticed him.

Lech was sitting in front of the door to the building, barking randomly. No neighbours were staring. He raised his head; the dog's eyes shone like green ambers against the background of his chopped-pork naked skin. Lech barked again as if he wanted Ewa to know that he was waiting for her. That he was still there.

"There's a moral
force in a sentence
when it comes out
right. It speaks
the writer's will
to live."

Don DeLillo

1 Up
ALISON HITCHCOCK

1 Across We can neither slow it down nor speed it up, or
can we? (4)

Ken tipped the point of his biro onto his tongue, hovered it over
1 Across and then stopped. Can't speed it up or slow it down,
or can we? The words ran through his mind but the answer didn't
come. Mary would have known; she'd have got it before Ken had
even finished reading out the clue.

Love a crossword but never have one, that's right, isn't it,
she'd say, and then be on to the next clue. Let's get a move on, just
because you're retired doesn't mean we have to go in slow motion,
I've housework to get on with.

1 Across still didn't come to Ken. He tried 1 Down.

1 Down You do the sums, it's not one or three (7)

Got that one, Mary, got that one, he said into the empty room.
TWOSOME. Now we're getting somewhere. He nodded towards
the empty chair by his side. She'd be sipping her tea now, telling
him to drink up. Too hot for me yet, he'd reply. She'd have finished
before he'd even started. Asbestos lips, he called her.

Ken missed their comfortable morning routine. Up at eight, her going downstairs to make the breakfast, always a pot of tea and a slice of toast, while he walked into each room to draw back the curtains. The newspaper always waiting for him on the doormat.

After breakfast, showered, shaved and dressed, Ken would sit in the living room with the newspaper while Mary busied herself in the house. Feet up, she'd say over the noise of the vacuum as she ran it into the room. What are the headlines? When Ken told her about an impending strike or a new threat of war in a country neither of them had ever heard of, she'd ask, Who'd want to be Prime Minister? and shake her head. This would make Ken smile. Mary had given up work when they got married. He sometimes wondered whether he should have encouraged her to go back, especially after Tony had gone to university, but she always seemed so busy at home.

By mid-morning, Mary would have peeled potatoes for lunch, washed bedding and hung it out on the line, and given the kitchen floor a good scrub.

They had lived in the same house since they were married. Don't mend what's not broken, Ken heard her say to Tony on the phone when he occasionally called to see how they were. Me and your dad don't need a bungalow, we're fine here, and anyway, you might want it one day. Ken would smile; Tony was never coming back to live their way.

4 Across Is it mind, clothes or money? (6)

Ken repeated the clue out loud. That one wasn't coming to him, either. Do one of the ones across from TWOSOME – Mary's voice. At least you've got the first letter.

6 Across There's only one singer in the choir today (4)

Oh, that's easy, said Ken, chuckling. He wrote in SOLO. Mary'd had a lovely voice and had once been in the church choir but she'd stopped going. She said she was happiest just singing as she pottered around the house, and that God didn't need her to be in church to hear her singing his praises. She'd have enjoyed the hymns at her funeral; he'd picked out her favourites, although they could have done with a few more voices to do them real justice.

By eleven, Mary would be ready for a sit down and she'd bring Ken a cup of tea and a biscuit. Keep us going till lunch. That's when they'd start the crossword, but Mary could never sit for long before there was another job to do in the house and she'd up and off again. Devils and hands, she'd say as she disappeared into the kitchen.

Since she'd gone, Ken had stuck with the same routine, up at eight, breakfast, bathroom, peel the potatoes for lunch, go round with the hoover, a quick dust if anything looked like it needed it, and then start the crossword. He'd look up at the clock. Nine thirty.

So this Friday morning Ken was pleased when he heard the doorbell chiming. He wasn't used to visitors. Since the initial stream of neighbours, with warmed dinners and home-made cakes, in the month after the funeral, the doorbell hadn't been much used. Probably the postman with something for next door, he said out loud. He'd noticed he said a lot of things out loud, but he didn't try to stop himself because it was as if Mary was still there to hear him. First sign of going mad. He smiled as he carefully put the folded paper and pen onto the coffee table, took off his reading glasses and went into the hallway.

On the other side of the opened door a young man in a grey, shiny suit thrust his ID card towards Ken.

The man grinned widely, letting the card fall back to his chest as he stretched out his arm.

"John Thones," said the man, giving Ken's veined and mottled hand a thorough shake. "From Insulation Verma Limited. Can I come in? I'd like to talk to you about the heat that you're losing from your roof. We're government contracted."

"I didn't know I was losing heat." Ken looked up, squinting into the rising sun.

"I know." The man shook his head. "All this street's the same. You may as well be throwing money into the sky. That's why the government's doing something about it."

He pointed to his ID card but as Ken had taken off his reading glasses the words were a bit of a blur.

"You better come in." Ken stepped aside to let the man pass. "Would you like a cup of tea?"

"I wouldn't say no."

Ken followed him into the living room.

"Nice place you've got here. Just you in today, is it?"

Ken looked over at Mary's chair, and across to the solitary mug of half-drunk tea on the coffee table.

"Yes, that's right. Milk and sugar?"

"Just milk, thank you. I'll show you on this." He held up what Ken knew to be an iPad. Tony'd had one when he came up for the funeral. "I can show you how much money you'll save."

In the kitchen, Ken filled the kettle with fresh water and took a mug and tea bag from the cupboard. He looked over at the three, peeled potatoes covered with water in the saucepan. They looked lost. When Mary'd been here the potatoes filled the pan. He supposed he should use a smaller one.

Behind the stove was the china teapot. If he brewed a fresh cup of tea for himself as well as his visitor, he could use it. He smiled as he took the tea bag from the mug and dropped it into the pot.

Always warm the pot first: secret of a good cup of tea – Mary again. He removed the bag and swilled the pot with the now just boiling water. It would be nice to be drinking tea from a teapot again.

Carrying the tray loaded with mugs, teapot and milk jug into the living room, Ken noticed that the man had placed pieces of graphed paper on the coffee table.

"I can show you on the iPad," the man said, lifting it up in front of him. "But I thought you might prefer to see it on paper. No Mrs . . . er . . . today?" He pointed to Ken and Mary's wedding photograph on the mantelpiece.

"Sturt. Mary Sturt, that's my wife. No, she's not with us any more."

Ken poured the tea, still feeling the unfamiliar vibration of his last sentence.

"I'm sorry to hear that, Mr Sturt." The man reached over to take his mug. "Very sorry."

"Who did you say you were again?" Ken sat back in his chair, glancing up at the clock.

"John Thones, sir. Work for Insulation Verma Limited. We're government contracted. Here's our website." He offered Ken the iPad.

Holding the screen a little away from himself, Ken could make out pictures of men in white protective clothing crouched down in small spaces.

"Look, I'll be honest with you," said the man. "I can see you're a bright gentleman and you're not going to want all the sales chat. Basically what it is, the government pays us to insulate people's lofts – helps the environment and all that, and you get cheaper fuel bills, which is what we all want, isn't it?" He chortled as he took a sip of his tea. "Oh, that's nice. Yorkshire, is it? Yorkshire tea?"

Buy Yorkshire, and when you can't buy Yorkshire buy British, Mary would say.

"It is," said Ken, smiling as he put on his glasses and bent forward to look at the graphs. "I've heard about this insulation. And it's free, is it?"

"It is. You just claim it back with this form." The man passed Ken a piece of paper with the words Department of the Environment in bold letters along the top. "Now, if I could just get up into your loft, we can see what's what."

Ken and Mary had never used the loft much. The stepladder was rickety and Mary hadn't liked Ken going up there. It was a big space with little in it. Tony had once stored some boxes there after his divorce, but Ken couldn't remember if they'd ever been moved.

"No need for you to be coming up here," the man shouted as he pulled himself through the hatch. "If you can just hold the ladder. I've got my tape measure."

"It'll be a bit dusty up there," Ken called. "Watch your suit."

A few minutes later the man was dangling his leg through the hatch, searching for the top rung of the ladder. Ken held on to the bottom.

"Right, well that's all easy," said the man as he descended the ladder. "I'll get back to that cup of tea now." And he darted down the stairs, leaving Ken standing on the landing, peering up into the dark loft.

"Now, can I get you to fill in this form?" the man asked as Ken walked back into the living room. The papers had been cleared from the coffee table. "I don't want to rush you but I get paid by the house so I need to crack on, and as it's free . . ." He handed Ken the contract.

There wasn't much to fill in, the man had already completed most of it: his name, company name, loft measurements, proposed date for work to start. Ken signed at the bottom and handed it back, placing his pen onto the folded newspaper.

"You like a crossword, do you? Give me a clue if you're stuck."

"Oh, right," said Ken, picking up the newspaper. "We do like a crossword. What about this one?"

7 Across Beware all that glitters (5,4)

"Easy, Mr Sturt," the man said. "Fool's gold."

"Very clever, very clever." Ken wrote in the letters. "You'd have been a match for my wife."

"Now, all I need from you, Mr Sturt, is a cheque. You pay me now, we come and do the work, and then you claim back from the government." He handed Ken another form. "You'll get the money back in fourteen days. It's a very good system. Unusual for government." He laughed.

"Oh. Right," said Ken. "How much?"

"Three hundred and ten pounds. But we shan't cash it till we've actually done the work. That way, we're all fair and square, as it were."

"Did you want another drop of tea?" Ken leaned towards the pot.

"Thank you, Mr Sturt, but I won't. As I say, I get paid by the house. If you give me your cheque then I'll not be bothering you further." He was putting the signed form in his briefcase and closing the lock.

"I see," said Ken, pushing himself up out of the chair.

As Ken opened the front door to let the man out, the sun streamed in, catching the man's suit. The glint from the material reflected into Ken's eyes.

The man turned to shake hands as Ken dropped his head.

"Pleasure doing business with you, Mr Sturt."

Ken, about to extend his hand, suddenly moved it to his forehead, creasing the folds of skin between his fingers.

"You did measure up for both sides of the loft, didn't you?" he asked, lifting his head to look at the man's face, his hand shading his eyes from the sun.

"Both sides?"

"Yes, there's a small door, through to the other side. We had a false wall put in years ago when we thought we might need an extra bedroom. You'd better come back in."

Ken ushered the man out of the doorway and back into the hall, closing the door behind him.

"I wouldn't want only half of it done, would I, what with it being free? The ladder's still there. It'll be no trouble for you, will it? To measure the other side?"

The man put down his briefcase, wiping a newly formed bead of sweat from his brow.

"Certainly not, Mr Sturt. Obviously I'll need another cheque for a bigger area."

"Not a problem," said Ken, his arm guiding the man to the staircase.

"Watch the dust on your suit," Ken warned again, as the man disappeared once more through the hatch. This time Ken climbed up a few of the steps behind him. As soon as the man got himself to his feet in the stooped space of the loft, Ken brought down the hatch door and with a speed that surprised even himself, turned the lock, stepped down the rungs, closed the ladder, moved it back into Tony's old bedroom and scurried down the stairs.

Never trust a man in a shiny suit, he said out loud. That's what you'd say, isn't it, Mary.

When he reached the bottom of the stairs, he could hear cries coming from the loft. He fetched the tea tray from the living room, looked at the clock and walked into the kitchen.

We'll be needing a few more potatoes, Ken said as he glanced over at the saucepan. There's not enough there for two. He closed the kitchen door, muffling the shouts and banging, and took three more potatoes from the bag at the side of the sink.

By the time Ken had peeled more potatoes, walked to the supermarket to buy an extra piece of fish and moved the man's briefcase into the cupboard underneath the stairs, it was almost eleven o'clock.

Time for a cup of tea and a biscuit, he said, putting fresh water in the kettle and emptying the cold tea from the pot.

At eleven, Ken once again sat down in his chair, placed his mug and biscuit on the coffee table, put on his reading glasses and picked up the paper and pen.

He studied the grid. What was that, 2 Down, second letter O from SOLO?

2 Down Con my pa (anagram) (7)

Ken tipped the point of his biro onto his tongue and wrote in the answer.

The Year of the Pig
CLIVE PARISH

You can never be sure how people will react when you tell them you've lived with a pig. Some are surprised at first, but will then quiz you closely about the animal's supposed intelligence. While others, the vast majority, are shocked that anyone would keep one in the house. Then, what happens when they realise you're serious, is they frown and crimp their nose, like you've made a bad smell. My God, they say, what were your parents thinking?

Most people don't appreciate that pigs won't shit on the carpet or chew the furniture, any more than a well-trained dog. My mother was one of those; she hadn't a clue. I was still a young lad, about twelve at the time, and me and my brother, Michael, we were watching telly with Mum when in walked Bazza carrying this yellow plastic storage box.

"Look what I've got," he said, as he laid the box in front of the fire and pulled out this wriggling bundle, all black and pink and wrapped in an old bath towel, her little snub nose and ears peeking from among the folds. I could see her tiny eyes, wide awake, staring out at us, and her nostrils twitching and flaring as if she could smell something cooking.

"Oh my God, it's a bloody pig," gasped Mum. I can still see the look on her face. "What you going to do with that?"

"We're not doing nothing," said Bazza. "*It* is a *she*, and she's our new pet."

Now had Bazza known my mother better, he might not have risked bringing home a new pet without asking, let alone producing a pig out of a box. But Bazza hadn't been with us for long and we all liked having him around.

"We need to keep her warm, that's important, and feed her a bottle when she's hungry – just like a baby," he said. "We can all manage that, can't we?"

Then he reached inside the box and drew out a baby's bottle, teat and all, and a tin of formula milk.

"Here, Carol, stop fretting and make this up, like you used to for these two."

Off she went to the kitchen looking none too sure, but soon she was back with a bottle full of milk and Bazza passed her the piglet to hold. We all gathered round, real close, and watched as she guided the teat beneath the quivering snout and let a few warm drops trickle into her gaping mouth. The piglet began to suckle, tentatively at first, then in great gulps.

"Oh, the little darling," Mum said. "Am I going to have to wind her too?"

She sat down in her armchair and watched the piglet drink.

"Can we keep her, Mum, please?" said Michael, pulling on her arm and looking pleadingly into her eyes.

"Well, I don't know," she replied. "I never heard of anyone keeping a pet pig before."

"It'll be fine, babe," said Bazza reassuringly. "You house-train them and take them for walks, and she can even have her own basket – just like keeping a dog.

"Except, with a pig," he continued, "you can always eat her if you get short of cash."

The three of us looked at him aghast.

"You shouldn't joke like that," said Mum. The piglet had almost finished her bottle. "She's far too sweet to eat."

Bazza came with the house, or so it seemed back then. One day we came home from school to find our bags packed and waiting in the hallway. An hour later a white van drew up and out stepped this tall, lanky man with pockmarked cheeks and a ring through his ear.

"Boys, this is Bazza," Mum announced, although we learned much later that his real name was Barry. "Bazza's going to help us move into our lovely new house."

I don't know whether she intended Bazza to stay, but he did. And at the time, Michael and me agreed it was all for the good. He was the first man we knew properly, apart from Grandpa, who we saw very little, and some teachers. As for our real dad, Mum never spoke about him – and she always changed the subject if we asked. But with the arrival of Bazza our lives improved considerably. For a start, he had a Nintendo, and he bought loads of games, which we used to play early in the morning before they came downstairs, and we got to see action movies on telly and other stuff that Mum never watched.

Bazza never told us where the piglet came from. Just that a mate owed him.

"So what shall we call her?" he said, after we found her a blanket and tucked her up in her box that first night.

"Why don't you let the boys choose a name?" Mum suggested.

Bazza ignored her. "I think we should call her Stella, after Stella Artois. Because she's beautiful, like the beer."

"You can't call a pig Stella Artois, stupid," said Mum.

"I think she's beautiful, too," I piped up. "Can we call her Princess Leia?"

Compared with our old place, Number 9 Laburnum Drive was a proper house. It was owned by the council and had two bedrooms, and was sat in the middle of a row. And if you looked out the bathroom window you could see our new school across the playing fields, which backed onto our garden beyond a tall chain-link fence.

Michael and me shared the smaller bedroom at the front of the house, while Princess slept in her yellow plastic box in a corner of the living room, at least for the first few weeks, until she didn't need to feed from the bottle. I'll say this for my mother, she treated Princess like a new baby in the family. She even made her nappies out of some old towels she bought from the charity shop; there were at least three hanging on the line every day.

When we were watching telly we'd take her out of the box and feed her, except when Bazza's mates came around and then we'd have to go to our bedroom while they drank beer and played on the Nintendo. Princess didn't like the noise, or the smoke, so we used to take her box upstairs and sometimes Mum let her stay the night in our room. We'd put her on the bed and cover her in the duvet and then roll her over while she tried to escape. She liked having her tummy rubbed, too; but best of all she loved being tickled behind her ears.

Princess took to eating solids so quickly she must've been a few weeks old already when she arrived. House-training was more of a problem. That job fell to Michael and me, mainly because Mum and Bazza couldn't be bothered to take her outside every couple of hours. God knows what a mess she'd have made if it hadn't been the school holidays.

As it was, our back garden never recovered. To be fair, it could at best be described as a square of concrete with a patch of grass at the bottom, which quickly became a strip of mud beneath Princess's probing snout. She nearly dug a hole under the fence and might have squeezed under and onto the school playing field, but fortunately we caught her in time and Bazza dug a trench and buried a couple of long planks along the border to stop her burrowing through. Unfortunately, it was the only place she could poop, which was in clear view of the bull terrier at Number 13, two doors down. When the dog barked, Princess would start shaking, even when she was indoors. Sometimes she would pee on the kitchen floor rather than go outside.

By the time the summer holiday came to an end we were looking forward to going to our new school.

"You'll make lots of new friends there," Mum promised. It was one of the best in the country, she said. The government gave it extra money.

The school gates were a five-minute walk from our front door, which was great for Mum. On the first day she walked us to the entrance and waved us goodbye. After that we had to get up in the morning, prepare breakfast and make our own way to school. We didn't mind, except when we were late and the teachers put us in detention.

I started in Year 8 and Michael was two years above, which meant everyone already knew everyone else except us two. He used to meet me at break and lunchtime, which was really useful, because people would lay off me knowing I had a bigger brother. Despite Mum's promise, there weren't many of the other kids we liked, except for this one girl in Michael's year called Sadie, who we agreed wasn't up herself like the rest.

One day we asked Sadie over to play at our house. We didn't tell her about Princess; we wanted it to be a surprise. And, anyway, Mum had told us not to go around school telling people we owned a pig. Princess was lying asleep in her box when we took Sadie to see her, and she gave quite a squeal as Mikey grabbed her by the back leg and presented her for Sadie to stroke.

"I'm not sure I like pigs," she said, nervously. "It's got a snotty nose . . . and lots of teeth."

"Don't worry, she's doesn't bite," said Michael, taking hold of Sadie's hand and running her fingers along Princess's back and under her chin. Princess responded by stretching her neck out to be tickled.

"Ooh, it feels rough," Sadie said, giggling at the coarseness of the hair sprouting from Princess's cheeks and flanks, "but, she's so-o cute."

I remember thinking that maybe Sadie liked Michael holding her hand more than she enjoyed stroking Princess.

It was noticeable how Mum began to lose interest after Princess stopped feeding from the bottle. Some people should never have pets – they're just not prepared for the commitment. I mean, I was still just a child and there I was reminding them both we didn't have a single carrot or apple in the house.

"I don't know why she can't eat pizza like the rest of us," said Bazza, when I voiced my concern.

He was just winding me up, of course. Bazza was like that. Give him his due, he saw we couldn't keep Princess in a box in the corner of the living room for much longer. Mum was becoming too tetchy.

"That bloody pig keeps getting under my feet," she said. "And that box is beginning to stink."

Next day Bazza returned home with a huge metal cage, the kind they use to lock up guard dogs, and two buckets for her food and water. The only practical place to put the cage was in the kitchen: Bazza said it would be easier to clean, and we could always bring Princess into the living room when we wanted to play with her.

So we all went to watch Princess settle into her new home. With a shove from Bazza, she fell through the door and began to snuffle around the thick blanket that lined the bottom of the cage. Then Bazza locked the cage shut. Finding nothing else of interest, Princess turned to stare at us through the metal bars. I swear I'd never seen her look so sad. I promised to give her a bath later; she always enjoyed a good soak.

As time went by there were two things that got on Mum's nerves more than most. One was the way Princess would start squealing in the kitchen and scratching at the door while Mum was watching telly. The other was Bazza's friends.

Mum didn't mind his regular mates so much. When they came round she used to send Michael and me upstairs, and they'd smoke and drink and make a lot of noise. I bet the neighbours heard them, too. But it was the ones that showed up at the door, any time of the day or night. You could tell they weren't Bazza's real mates because they only stopped for a quick smoke, and then left again. We could smell it upstairs. I thought that was what a forest fire must smell like.

"I don't want them coming here any more," I heard her screaming at him one day. "And I don't want that stuff in the house. Meet them down the pub – or anywhere but where we live. You hear me?"

Of course he did – we all could. But Bazza's reply was too quiet to catch upstairs. The tirade continued: "What about the bloody kids? You're not on your own now – you've got a family to look after. All it would take is for one of the neighbours to send the police round and you'd be back inside."

The next thing I knew he was roaring at her like some jungle beast. There was a thump, like something heavy dropping on the floor, and then the sound of the door slamming. It wasn't the first row, and it wouldn't be the last. Afterwards we heard Mum coming upstairs. I thought I heard her crying as she went into their bedroom.

I crossed the landing and gently pushed open the door so I could see through the crack. She was lying on the bed, her face buried in the crook of her arm.

"You all right, Mum?"

There was no reply; just the sound of her breathing, fitful and deep.

"Mum?" I didn't really expect an answer. We'd seen her like this before, in the old place. Some days she used to stay in bed all day.

I went downstairs to the kitchen. Princess was lying stretched out across the cage. She pulled herself up and pressed her nose against the bars, her little tail wagging away. I opened the door and squeezed inside. We gave each other a long cuddle.

Then word started to go around school about Princess. People I'd never spoken to before would come up to me in the playground and ask if it was true. And there was this one bloke, Garth White, from Year 10, who turned out to be a real cunt. He and his mates caught me on the way home one afternoon, just outside the school gates. First I knew, I heard these snorting sounds coming from behind.

"Hey, Pikey, is that pig shit I can smell?" called White.

I looked around and saw them coming towards me, fists tight. Any chance of escape was disappearing fast. I knew I couldn't count on help from Michael – he'd gone off with Sadie, probably to the rec or her house, as he'd been doing most days lately. There was only one thing to do – leg it.

I guess that was one advantage of living so close to school. I gained myself a much-needed second or two before they gave chase and, pulling out my house key as I ran, I managed to reach our porch as they drew level with the garden gate. My legs and arms were shaking like trees in a gale, but I held it together long enough to give White the finger as I closed the front door. Inside, Mum was watching TV in the living room and must have seen everything through the window. I crumpled in her lap and broke down in tears. She put a hand on my head and rubbed my hair.

"Just hit him next time. Hard as you can."

That was all she said, and then went back to watching telly.

When Michael came home he found me playing with Princess in our bedroom. If it hadn't been for him, I doubt whether I'd have had the courage to step foot inside school the next day. But as he pointed out, there was less than a week until the end of term, and he promised to meet me every day after class. And that's what he did, waiting with me in the library until we were certain everyone had gone home.

It was around that time that Princess started to pull up the carpet in the living room. We came back from the supermarket one Saturday afternoon to find the Christmas tree, one of those artificial ones, lying on its side, with tinsel and baubles strewn across the floor.

"Who left the cage door open?" was the first thing my mother said.

Michael and me looked at each other. The toppled tree wasn't the only present Princess had left. The kitchen was a complete mess. Both buckets were lying upturned and water and vegetable peel were sprayed across the vinyl floor. And there was a pile of shit by the back door.

"I thought this bloody pig was house-trained," she said. "Bazza, you and the kids get this bloody place cleared up, or that pig won't be the only one walking the streets this Christmas."

Not long after, Mum said she couldn't stand Princess under her feet any more.

"It's no good, she's too bloody big," she said. "She's going to have to go – it's either her or me."

I couldn't believe my ears. We'd only had her for a few months, but Princess had become a huge part of my life. To lose her would've been almost as bad as someone taking my brother away. I refused to come out of the bedroom for the entire day, and I screamed and cried until my throat became sore and I ran out of tears. I was lying there on the bed, exhausted, thinking of where I could go if I ran away, when Mum finally came upstairs and sat on the bed beside me, and said we could keep her, providing we kept Princess in her cage or out in the garden.

As it happened, that winter turned out to be one of the coldest. We were all wrapped up in our coats and woolly hats, even in the house. We couldn't afford the heating so we were only allowed the fire on in the living room. But I couldn't sit and watch telly knowing Princess was cold and stuck in her cage, so I took the thickest blanket I could find and wrapped her up as best I could, and fished out some socks from the washing basket to pull over her feet.

I remember it was so cold that year there was still snow on the ground in March. One time I woke up in the middle of the night, shivering under the duvet. Then I heard men talking in the garden, below our window. There was something in the tone of the men's voices I didn't like. I whispered to Michael to wake up and we both crept over to the window and looked out. The front door was open and a light from downstairs cast a wedge across the snow. We couldn't see anyone below, so we tiptoed onto the landing and knelt at the top of the stairs.

Bazza was standing at the front door with his back to us. He was holding it half open, but wide enough for a cold draught to sweep up the stairs. Whoever he was talking to was swearing loud enough to wake the neighbours. All of a sudden Bazza slammed the door and for a moment I thought he was going to turn round and catch us, but instead he bolted through the living room and we heard a rattle of metal from the kitchen as he opened the cutlery drawer.

The next thing there was a crash of broken glass and Bazza was back at the front door and charging outside with a kitchen knife in his hand.

Just then Mum appeared out of her bedroom. "What the fuck's going on? What are you two doing?"

She looked at first like she could barely open her eyes, but must have felt the draught coming up the stairs because she almost immediately noticed the front door was open. Her look changed in an instant, like she'd stepped into a cold bath. She grabbed us both by our pyjamas, dragged us into her bedroom and threw us onto the bed.

"Don't make a sound, either of you."

She sat down with her back to the door, and that's how we

all stayed until we heard the front door close and Bazza's boots stomping up the stairs. Mum got up and opened the door. I don't know why she looked relieved to see him: he almost knocked her over as he strode into the bedroom, breathing hard and with this mean, ugly look on his face. He went straight to the wardrobe and started to pull out the clothes and boxes piled at the bottom.

"Get those fucking kids out of here," he shouted at her, and Mum led us back to bed. The last thing I remember was hearing Bazza in the bathroom, flushing the toilet over and over.

The next day everyone at school had heard about the disturbance in our street. The kids in my class were asking me what happened, and I told them what Bazza told me to say: wasn't anything to do with us.

Michael warned me there might be trouble and said he'd meet me at lunchtime rather than see Sadie. Me and my brother had always been close, and I wouldn't say he ever went looking for a fight, but that day he said to me, "Sam, don't let them see you're scared. You and me, we're not going to take shit from anyone."

And I wasn't scared, even when I saw Garth White and his mates coming across the playground towards us. Not with Michael around.

"Hey, Pikey, what's all this about your old man chasing a bloke down the street last night?" White said to Michael, looking cocky in front of the others.

"None of your fucking business, White."

"Come on, Pikey, why don't you share with us what your crackhead dad's been up to? Nicked stuff off the wrong people, did he? Took all their gear?"

"You don't know what you're talking about, White. Fuck off and leave us alone."

But I could see a flicker of doubt cross Michael's face, and so could White.

"So where's your real dad?" he said, like he's plucked the question out of nowhere. "Couldn't stand living with a fat pig like your mother?"

Michael looked nonplussed by the unexpected switch in attack. And with his attention focused so intently on my brother,

White didn't see it coming. I hit him. I hit him as hard as I could, just like Mum told me. Within seconds arms were flailing and boots flying, and an elbow caught me square on the nose. I fell to the ground and lay there dazed, my arms wrapped about my head to deflect any further blows. But none came. The sound of scuffling suddenly died down and, when I peered out from under my arm, I saw Michael standing beside me and Garth White and his mates backing away.

I looked up at Michael, relieved he'd fought them off. In his hand was Mum's kitchen knife.

To this day, I've never understood why people were always picking fights with my family. Michael was in big trouble over the knife, of course, and so was I, although rather unfairly I thought. The police arrived, and then my mother, and we had to wait in separate rooms, being watched all the time, while they talked about us in the head's office.

If it hadn't been for the kitchen knife, we might have stayed in the house at Number 9 Laburnum Drive. But the school declared Michael was permanently excluded and I was lucky not to be so too, and Mum insisted she couldn't stand all the talk among the neighbours and we were going to stay at Grandpa's for a few weeks while she sorted herself out and found a new place for us to live. All except Bazza. She didn't want Bazza with us in the next house.

The arrangements for Princess, she said, were only temporary; there wasn't enough room at Grandpa's for a pig. I wasn't to worry because Princess was going to stay at an animal sanctuary, which was like a hotel, where she'd be fed lots of nice food and meet other pigs, and if we wanted to we could go and visit her at any time.

I don't know how long it took me to realise I'd never see Princess again, but hardly a day passed in the months that followed without me thinking about her. Eventually, Mum told me to stop my nagging; we'd go and get her when she was good and ready.

But, of course, she never was.

"We'd never expect to understand a piece of music on one listen, but we tend to believe we've read a book after reading it just once."

Ali Smith

Intervention
DAVID SAVILL

April 25th, 2004
London

Anya walked out of the lift to find the wrong picture on the corridor wall and a pot plant out of place. The lift had gone up, not down, and from here, the quickest way out of the building was onto the roof. At the top of the fire escape she barged through the smokers' exit and marched across the peeling bitumen, stopping only when she came to the rails. Over Exmouth Market pigeons scrapped on the scaffolded tower of Our Most Holy Redeemer. William had called the office. He had called her actual phone. Three years. And now he says, "Hello you, what have you been up to?" Pleasantries. Questions about her work, and "How have you been?" And "Are you still living on Church Street?" The fact she answered his questions annoyed her more than the questions themselves. The way she played along. The way she tried to vaguely impress him by mentioning her new place in Walthamstow, her interest-only mortgage, her very slight promotion, whom she saw from the old days. They were chatting about Bethany fucking Aldridge's bloody pregnancy. (*No*, the husband wasn't a guy William knew. *Yes*, Anya had been to the wedding.) Like this, she had babbled on. She had always found it easy to talk to William. Perhaps that was the problem.

She smelt smoke, then saw the man sitting by the air-conditioning unit and realised, too late, she had been muttering under her breath. Not a Dignity Monitor man (he was clearly over fifty for a start), more likely one of the chartered surveyors from the fourth floor. She loosened her grip on the rail, and trying to affect a casual posture, put her hands in the pockets of her jeans. She was someone who came up here to take in the view every day, that was all –

"Smoke?" The man held out the packet as Anya headed back for the roof door.

"There is nothing I would like more than to smoke a cigarette," she told him.

"Oh dear. I shouldn't tempt you, then."

"Let's say it's been one of those days."

"Always is," the man said.

"Thank you anyway."

Anya was closing the door when she added with her best smile, "You never know, tomorrow might be better."

But today was not. She tried to pay attention to a young solicitor from one of the new agencies scooping up asylum cases. The woman had come to tell Anya the story of her Serbian client. What the solicitor really wanted was a human rights researcher to act as an expert witness. But Anya needed to see if the story added up first, and the solicitor clearly hadn't done this before. For a start, she had come without the client. The client was a man from Serbia, claiming a threat to life in the form of homophobic bullying. He came from the village of Slatina, but when Anya pointed out there were at least two Slatinas in Serbia, it appeared to be news to the woman. In telling the story, the solicitor kept referring to 1998, but when Anya looked at the affidavit, the client had written 1996. They tried to call the client but he wasn't answering, and the difficulty of matching any information held by Dignity Monitor with the times and places in contention made Anya late for her regional-desk meeting with the programme director. Last through the door, she had to perch on a filing cabinet next to the old television, facing the backs at the table as Rhidian Keller talked about the effects of the Kosovan riots on regional funding, and the need to redistribute further funds for election-monitoring activities in Moldova. She tried to follow, but the woman sitting in front of her was texting someone who wanted to know whether to pick up cereal at the supermarket, and for some reason, this was a more compelling drama.

Yes, we are out.

The Shreddies, or The Cheerios?

Shreddies. NO MORE CHEERIOS.

Kids?

TOO MUCH SUGAR!

William had once tried to drown Anya's mobile phone. In Brecon. A rare moment of anger. But he had chucked it over a stream so small it landed on the other bank, and Anya had been able to cross over the stepping stones to retrieve it. The cracked screen was something she had come to regard with some affection. William really did hate mobile phones.

"Can we work with that, Anya?"

It was Rhidian.

"Sorry?"

Her seated colleagues had all turned their heads and were looking up at her with the eyes of people anxious for a meeting to end.

"The Kosovan riot report?" Rhidian said.

"Yes –"

Anya intended a question but Rhidian carried on.

"Good. So, unfortunately," he said, "we haven't yet got the green light to pick up on the Kosovan returnees project."

Anya stopped smiling. She had come to the meeting to challenge this very point. The returnees project was hers. But before she could gather her thoughts, someone was talking about the new liaison for the Council of Europe. She had to wait until the meeting was over before she could catch up with Rhidian in the empty room.

"Would it help if I wrote a paper?" she started.

"The report on returnees?"

"I think the time to finish this is now."

"Can you complete it from here?"

"I can't get the same buy-in."

Rhidian turned from his screen. "We've had Abu Ghraib, the

report on the riots – financially, I just can't get them to prioritise the returnees. Maybe if you do it from your desk, but another field investigation – I don't think so."

It was no use making the argument alone. She should have caught him during the meeting and co-opted the other members of the team. Her arguments had the tired sound of lines well rehearsed. It wasn't always right to divert funds for emergencies, the bigger picture was more important. Once committed it damaged their reputation to scale back on a report or do it half-arsed. But Rhidian could nod in sympathy all day, the programme director was just a messenger when it came to money. It was the divisional director she needed to be talking to.

She stood up. "Well I might just have to take a holiday in Pristina."

"Anya, the way you work, you should take a holiday in the Bahamas, on a beach."

"And have my nails buffed by Haitian migrants who get beaten up in detention cells?"

Good old Anya, Rhidian's smile said, *there's always Anya to do it*.

"And the riot report," he added as she left. "You'll add something to it? About Svinjare?"

Dignity Monitor had told Anya to leave Kosovo when the March riots began. On the phone from London a man from the emergencies team asked if she could recommend a fixer. Not only were they taking over, they also wanted her staff. But now, as the report was prepared for Legal and due to be published, they needed her. When she saw the draft it was clear why.

The account lacked testimony from the first day of the riots. This made Anya essential precisely because she hadn't left the country like a good girl, but asked her fixer to drive straight to Svinjare. On the radio there had been news of Albanians burning down Serbian houses.

What was it they were saying in the report's Introduction? Numbers: 2 days, 550 homes burned, along with 27 churches and monasteries. 4,100 people displaced. From the UN secretary-general to the head of NATO, around the diplomatic table it had been decided: "organised extremists" were to blame. When you had fucked up as badly as the United Nations Mission in Kosovo, it was better to paint the enemy as organised.

But it wasn't organised. And this was the point the report needed to make. The Albanian rioters had been stoked for months. They were reacting to the lousy way in which the UN were running things. The UN's Kosovo forces could do nothing about it because they lacked any coherent policy. Anya had seen it herself. She had stood at the roadblock in Svinjare, five hundred metres from a French military camp where hundreds of vehicles were still lined up in perfect military order, and going nowhere. She had watched as the rioters walked straight past a handful of KFOR troops and the single UN civilian police car that had troubled to turn up.

She returned from the water fountain in the office. The water was always too cold and it numbed her teeth.

In the village of Svinjare, she typed, *Albanian boys were seen torturing the livestock of Serbian villagers.*

Then she deleted the sentence. There was no room in the report for what she had seen behind the burning barn, for the boys who stood with flaming torches, lighting a pig hung from scaffolding and doused in petrol. The suffering of an animal didn't add anything to the main argument here. The problem in Svinjare, was that the French in KFOR saw their role as the protection of people, not property. And so all the UN troops had done was bus the Serbs of the village to the sports hall of Camp Belvedere, leaving the rioters to do as they liked. By early evening, the base had registered 206 of the villagers and Anya's notes were filled with their voices.

She found the one that needed to be heard and added it to the report first:

> "If I had a euro for every international who has come around here and observed what is happening. For every foreign soldier who has walked through my village and done nothing. All this 'help' that doesn't *help*. All these cars, and these helicopters, and all this money, and still they can walk into our village and burn our homes, when the whole lot – the whole lot of you who are supposed to

bring 'peace' and 'security' – are sitting here doing nothing. Worse than nothing – you're getting rid of us, and helping *them*, helping *them*, take what they want . . . If I had a euro for that!"

It was a voice loud enough for one moment to drown Will's out.

She was still messing with the punctuation when the office intern appeared at her shoulder and, like a schoolboy, asked permission to go home.

"Do you feel like getting drunk?" Anya said.

If she was going to have a bad day, she might as well have a bad night. He introduced her to a craft beer called Bruised Moon, and she introduced him to gin. She didn't *really* mean to get drunk, but somehow they hadn't eaten. At one point in the evening Jack had suggested a restaurant, but she couldn't imagine the slow business of ordering food. Anya felt aged by his references. She didn't know the films and books he was talking about. He didn't know who Winona Ryder was and had never even heard of *Heathers*.

The loud carriages of the Victoria line transported them from Highbury and Islington to Walthamstow in an instant – walk in, bright lights, walk off. She couldn't remember walking down the cut, or along the terrace. They had been laughing about something to do with hipster hair, then opening the door of her house, she felt as if she were falling into the dark silence of a stranger's. When she found the light switch, her living room appeared to her like something that had been washed too many times. And Anya suddenly felt as if *she* had been washed too many times. When the door closed behind them, she was standing in her home with a boy about whom she knew practically nothing.

"I like it when they knock the rooms through like this," he said, "kitchen to lounge."

She struggled to keep things from getting away. Kettle, tap, running water.

"Yes."

"You have this whole place to yourself?" His voice seemed closer now. "How many bedrooms is this? Three?"

She turned off the tap and closed her eyes. She wanted his

breath on her neck and his hand on her belly. She wanted his fingers extended around her waist to make her feel small. But when she turned around to meet his face, Jack wasn't close to her at all. Never had been. He was as far away as possible, standing on the other side of the sofa and picking up a picture from the mantelpiece.

"Where's this?"

Anya put down the kettle and tried to walk around the objects of her house with grace. He was looking at the picture of the Roma girls in Stojnik. She took off her glasses so things didn't seem too real.

"It's from a field trip to Bosnia."

"And you're working on Kosovo now?"

She didn't hear what he said next. She pressed her nose into his arm, felt his hands make a gift of her head, his lips brushing down her face, rough over her mouth.

"Wait there." Anya took the picture out of his hand and put it back on the mantel.

Alone in her bedroom, she pulled her tights from underneath her skirt and threw them into a pile of dirty laundry in the corner. The underwear drawer offered a large pile of black knickers. She used to own something spotty – pale, blue spots – but at the bottom of the drawer she found only the straps of a suspender belt. Where was it? It was William who had bought the spotty set. There had even been a chemise babydoll thing at one point. In the sock drawer, she found a pair of canary-yellow knickers which would have to do, but when she hoicked them on, they felt a little small. There was no full-length mirror, so she had to angle the spot-squeezing mirror on her chest of drawers just to look at herself.

Her glasses. They were downstairs. In the mirror, only the vague shape of a woman.

The shape slumped back onto the bed. She wasn't going to fuck the intern. Who was she kidding? Three years. Will had not called in three years, and now he wanted to talk as if nothing had changed; as if all that silence was OK, as if it meant nothing at all. They should "catch up", Will said. She should come over at Christmas. He would show her Thailand. *Thailand*. And what she had wanted to say, what she had wanted to scream from the roof, came out now in a sad dribble. "Fuck you," Anya mumbled into the cradle of her hands. Fuck Will. Not the intern. She couldn't fuck the intern because Will had ruined that, too. He had called from halfway around the world, reached into her life, and swept it all away. And she couldn't fuck the intern, because the intern would be there in the office on Monday morning.

Will had talked as if nothing had changed. And he was right. They had been together thirteen years, and for that reason alone they would always be together in some way, and even the "other side of the world" wasn't really the other side of the world any more. It was nine hours away and –

"Hi."

She looked up. An attractive man, still young enough to look good in jeans, was standing at the door of her room.

"Is this like – the *third* bedroom?"

"Two here. And there's a loft conversion."

Jack crossed the threshold and surveyed the room like a bad actor lost on the stage. "It's so big. You could rent out the rooms."

She could. She could rent out the spare rooms of this house – this house built for the ideal nuclear family she had not yet managed to produce. "I'm looking for lodgers," Anya said. But the truth was, she hadn't even advertised.

He looked at her dirty laundry and unmade bed. "I'm going to have to say that I think this is probably not a good idea, professionally and everything."

What was he? All of twenty years old? "Professionally?" Anya regained herself.

He looked confused. "Well you didn't come back down," he said. "And I thought –"

"No, you're right of course. Too much to drink. Not a good idea. There's a bed made up in the room next door."

"Right." Jack looked crestfallen. "Well I mean if you still *want* to –"

"That's romantic!"

He held up his hands in surrender. "I mean, whatever *you* want –"

Anya patted the bed. He did as he was told. Placing her hand on a thigh that seemed inhumanly hard, she touched the stiff cotton of his jeans and walked her fingers up to the zipper.

"Is it true," he said, "that you chased off some rioters in Kosovo? I heard you threw stones at them and told them their mothers would be ashamed? Something about a pig?"

She pushed Jack back onto the bed, and climbing on top of him, placed her hand over his mouth. "For fuck's sake," Anya said, "shut up."

"Intervention" is the first chapter of *They Are Trying to Break Your Heart* (Bloomsbury, 2016)

"Writing a book is a horrible, exhausting struggle, like a long bout of some painful illness. One would never undertake such a thing if one were not driven on by some demon whom one can neither resist nor understand."

George Orwell

Arlington, Virginia

EMILY EVERETT

Jennifer

Leaving flowers on a grave always seemed strange to me. My first summer job was helping the town's florist trim back her garden, and she told me you can tell that a flower is dead from the minute you cut it. The things people do to preserve the appearance of life – a notch slit in the stem, a vase of fresh water – don't change the fact. And of course I would never have said it to anyone today, but leaving flowers that are already dead in a cemetery full of the dead seems depressing and ironic in equal parts.

Back when our family was together, when I was a kid, planting flowers at a grave made more sense. We were from good farmer stock in generations past, and replanting something from the garden was pragmatic and thoughtful, without that threat of appearing sentimental. And then you could return for a visit under the guise of "watering the weed" or "just starting it off", armed with a jug of water or bag of fertilizer to fend off anyone who might suspect purer motives, or offer Kleenex. I don't have to deal with any of that, now that I live in the city. Not a cemetery in sight.

But I saw a sprinkling of withered wreaths and wilting bouquets dotting the blank sea of white headstones today, nothing growing at all but the perfectly trimmed and fluffed hedges, and strategically placed oak trees. That the groundskeepers find a way of stretching out their maintenance into a forty-hour work week astounds me. Still, it would be hard to picture the plain graves at Arlington National Cemetery hemmed in by uneven lilac bushes and straggly marigolds. Walking up the hill towards the newer graves, I thought how the rows of identical white stones would be a wet dream for my photographer friends, all the geometric lines shooting out to the horizon no matter where you stand.

We were headed up there for my brother-in-law's funeral – "memorial service" is such a lovely euphemism. Killed in combat, the obit said. Of course it had to be the stickiest, most humid day of the year, and everyone in our small group was dripping sweat inside their best black polyester. My newly widowed sister, Lisa, was leading the charge up the winding pavement, with the family and friends drifting wearily behind her like the Israelites.

She walked purposefully up the hill with a crumpled cemetery map in her hand and the same "thank you for coming, yes I'm fine" expression she'd been wearing since the taxis pulled up just below the Welcome Centre. I stayed back and away from her, to make things easier for both of us – no talking necessary. They had no children, and everyone else had left theirs with sitters, so at least there was no whingeing about the heat.

I hoped that this would be short and standard. The beauty of a military funeral is that you can smooth over the messy grief with a bit of jingoistic rhetoric, and after some gunshots and a nod to He who has those pearly gates upstairs, you're home free with the hors d'oeuvres and the air conditioning.

It was just when we were coming up to the marked grave site that I felt it, a tremor in the air and ground that was too small for anyone to comment on. And then, in an instant, there was painful sound all around, too much and too loud, and too near. Even knowing now that it was really a military flyover, just thinking about it still makes me jumpy as hell. I've seen them before, of course, but this, high on a hill in the sky, with the planes only a few hundred yards away from us, was paralysing. Because of the trees you can't see the jets until after the sound has broken and surrounded your head. It sounds silly now but I did think that I was ending in some cataclysmic way; it was only when the jets slid away on their trails of cloud that I realised what had happened and shut my gaping mouth.

I learned later that it was for the funeral, up top by the Tomb of the Unknown Soldier, of the last of the Columbia astronauts.

As the roar of jet engines drifted away, we all sat gratefully and shakily on the white plastic chairs provided. People smiled giddily and laughed softly to each other. Oh how silly, we thought we were dying but it was just a flyover.

Lisa

While everyone settled themselves and pointed skyward, shaking their heads, I had to sneak away. My high heels sank into the soft grass as soon as I stepped off the pavement, so I wrenched off my shoes and held them in one hand as I slipped across the hill in my sweaty stockings. I knew that as soon as the flyover conversation had worn itself out heads would turn and eyes would scan for me, the widow, over the tops of the graves. I hurried to cover behind a big granite structure, some odd hybrid of a sundial and a low mausoleum.

Ducking down I immediately slipped and landed on my hip and elbow in the damp grass. It was like having two thoughts at once, the surface part of me thinking how lucky to be wearing black so the grass stains won't show, the other part of me thinking of the feeling in my gut when the jets shook the air and my ears roared. I was suddenly crying pretty hard with little quiet gasps, and the shaded ground felt like the only comfort I would get on this long, miserable day.

The surface part of me reasoned that it was nothing to hide, not strange at all, to be crying on the afternoon of one's husband's funeral at the National Cemetery, if just a little unorthodox to do it flat on the grass in one's stockings behind a sundial. But the other part of me knew it was dredged-up memories of someone other than my late husband that loomed up from nowhere, from the solid ground and air still echoing with sound. I went over again the feeling of the flyover, the way it came straight from silence and shook my nerves and bones and organs, the way it had felt as though the bottom of my body was gone and that everything inside had dropped out while I stood frozen. It is not something I had ever experienced before, but I knew about that feeling because our mother had described it to me, many years ago, using those words and then saying, This is what my seizures feel like.

I have never had a seizure but I have seen them. As a kid at a mall in Delaware, I saw an epileptic, whipping and twisting while people waved for help. But more often I have seen the other kind, the kind that is still and desperate, terrifyingly internal. Our mother had this kind of seizure many times when I was fourteen and fifteen, before they knew what was wrong with her.

She would look up from whatever she was doing, reading the TV guide or fixing a necklace, with an edge of panic and surprise, and my father would spring for the bottle of pills and pass her two as fast as he could tip them out. Sometimes the bottle would be forgotten in the car or in the pocket of someone's coat. Then the pills wouldn't be there soon enough and my mother would curl on the couch and my father would push us out of the room. It was after one of these times that she told me what a seizure feels like. I know she told only me because Jenny was barely ten or eleven at the time.

While the honest part of me admitted this, that the flyover had loosened those protected, pretend-forgotten thoughts from their safe place in my gut, the surface part of me was trying to get things together; wipe snot from nose and mascara from eyes. The granite stone was cool, or at least cooler than the air, so I pressed against it while tugging on my shoes.

Standing now but stalling a little, I could read the inscription on the memorial; it was for the *USS Maine*, blown up in Havana Harbour at the start of the Spanish-American War. The thing I had thought was a sundial was the mast from the ship, the only thing they salvaged before they sank it for good out at sea. All this was explained on the stone and I read it quietly to myself, breathing each word in and out like a yoga mantra. Finally I had reunited surface-me and other-me into one still, composed face that I would call "thank you for coming to my late husband's funeral".

I walked back by some low trees, carefully, leaving little stiletto puncture marks. Since a few of the dutiful mourners were still dragging themselves up the hill, no one noticed my quiet return, or else they pretended not to. Some stood in groups, talking, with their backs to the casket, but most were already seated. My sister was squinting at her phone in the sun and noticed no one around her, and I wondered again, with a mix of confusion and annoyance, why she had come. Beyond the obvious rationale of family duty, of course, since familial obligations had never directed her behaviour in the past. I envied her naked shoulders and bare legs; her silky sleeveless dress looked heavenly cool compared to my layers of fabric. Jenny appeared, as always, too artsy and metropolitan for the rest of us, with the hard fact of distance to protect her. Miles and miles between her and everyone else, her and Hopwood, Pennsylvania, and certainly between her and me.

Jennifer

I drove myself the five minutes from the cemetery to the hotel where the reception was. It felt nearly miraculous to just be alone for a few moments, bathing in the ice-cold AC, ears still ringing dully from the gun salute. As if our eardrums hadn't been traumatised enough by the flyover. The hotel was called the Watergate – a fact that only I seemed to find funny.

The hotel restaurant was closed and coolly bare, with dim lighting and evenly spaced blank white tables. We were shuffled through it to a brighter private room at the back, scattered with cut flowers and framed photos of the dearly departed. Lisa looked quiet and present as she spoke to each cousin and college friend, so I tried to stay well out of her way. I guess I knew we'd eventually get into it all, for better or worse, but as long as I could avoid it, I would. After the flyover I had watched her lean weakly on the back of one of those flimsy plastic chairs, but she had laughed it off like everyone else a minute later. Cool and collected, always.

An oddly flirtatious waiter poured me a glass of yellowy Chardonnay from behind his draped table. I drifted through the room quietly for a while, and a few people stopped me long enough to say hello, before turning back to their low conversations.

No one was too excited to talk to me, unsurprisingly. Without ever having done anything truly outrageous or psychotic, I had still become a cause for wariness over the years. When we were younger, Lisa had always been better at hiding her uneasiness behind a face of perfunctory pleasantness. My inability, or unwillingness, to put others at ease led to the now popular view that I was the fragile and unpredictable one, the artist, and whispers of my Prozac days most likely still abound. It only bothered me that people still connected this with what happened to my mother, since I really didn't.

I sipped at my wine, and watched with interest the people who were obviously funeral pros – my older aunts and uncles, neighbours, striking a practised balance between apologetic and affable, moving to each group with a mix of Hopwood gossip and remembrance. In snatches of talk, I heard an odd jumble of names from my small home town, jobs, kids, graduations, deaths. The idiotic phrase "it was suicide, so tragic" floated up to the surface of conversation, spoken by a middle-aged woman I didn't know, the phrase tied to a name I also didn't know. I looked up from my glass to see Lisa set down hers, and slide out into the empty restaurant.

That was a sore subject for us, you might say. After about a year and a half of sickness and suffering and treatment, my mother had swallowed all the pills she could reach from her bed, and died before they could get her to the hospital.

Even in the chilled hotel, Lisa hadn't ever stopped sweating, so I thought perhaps she was just leaving to patch up her melting make-up. My initial lifelong instinct to avoid, avoid, avoid was overtaken by a vague impulse to follow her; maybe to help with her dripping face and wayward eyeliner, or maybe to finally have that one-on-one we'd been headed for, but delaying, all day.

I slipped between the glass doors and followed her out into the restaurant and down a hall past the main entrance. Instead of turning at the ladies' room, she continued into the next room. Lurking by the bathroom, I wondered whether avoidance might not be the best policy after all, easier and gentler on both of us. Probably Lisa was just glad that I had come, and wanted to leave it at that. There was also a possibility that she wasn't glad.

A minute or two later I heard, just audible above the piped music in the hallway, hesitant notes played on a piano. As the notes formed themselves into arpeggiated chords, and the chords into a familiar progression in D major, I inched to the doorway. Inside I saw Lisa with her back to me at the glossy black piano, in a tall room with a table set with shining silver for a dozen absent diners.

If anyone in the other rooms heard Pachelbel, they pretended not to. I suppose they would have thought it strange, anyway, since the piece is now standard fare for wedding processions, not funeral receptions at unfortunately named hotels. I, on the other hand, had heard it played at one funeral, my mother's, almost two decades ago. Lisa had played it then as well. My mother was sick for six months before they even figured out what was wrong. The shadowy something in her brain that they had promised from the start could not be cancer, could not possibly be cancer or she'd already be dead, was in fact just that.

The idiot oncologists had said six to eight months, but of course they'd been wrong about that, too. After a year she couldn't speak without confusion, and couldn't sleep because of the steroids she was taking. The medication they gave her to calm the effects of the steroids made her disoriented and upset, so there was another pill for anxiety. Her favourite thing, as it all got worse and worse in our little house-turned-hospice, was listening to Lisa practise the piano before her Tuesday lessons, and her favourite piece was Pachelbel's *Canon*. Lisa played it all the time and told Mom it was for a recital in a few months, but her teacher didn't believe in recitals and I knew Lisa never played in any.

It didn't make sense for her to be playing it now, after she had worked so hard to seem cool and aloof all day, and after we'd both worked so hard to leave Hopwood in that distant untouchable past. She had taken off her heels to better reach the pedals, and I saw smudges of green and brown on the bottom of her stockings.

When did she get grass stains? It felt like an odd little opening, a chink in her well-crafted mourning armour. I stepped forward into the room impulsively and she stiffened her shoulders at the sound, so I put on what I hoped was a friendly attitude and settled on the edge of a chair.

"So I guess old habits die hard?"

One sentence in and I'd already managed to say "die" at a funeral. I'm so good at this family stuff. She looked hard at me for a second and then grimaced, her fingers sliding into her lap from the keys.

"It's the only thing I can still play from memory. Without sheet music, I mean."

"That's pretty good after so long."

She shrugged. "My fingers remember it. We don't have a piano at home, so I couldn't resist trying this one." The "we" seemed to echo around the room.

"Well it sounded nice," I said lamely.

"I didn't think I would see you here, Jenny."

"I had time off from the museum. Summer is our slow time." I lost momentum. "I thought I could help out, or something."

"Help how?" She swiped my excuse out of the air with an impatient flick of her hand.

"Isn't it obvious?" I laughed and leaned forward in my chair. "I'm the diversion. Everyone's so busy worrying about the crazy sister, they have hardly found time to wonder about the dry-eyed widow." I hadn't meant to say that at all, but I felt very defensive already and I was rambling.

"I'm not dry-eyed," she whispered through her teeth, "and I don't need a diversion. Did you orchestrate the dramatic flyover too?" She stood up and closed the piano with an aggressive thud.

Moving to one of the mirrored pillars, Lisa checked her teeth for stray lipstick and wiped at the black make-up that had clumped in the corners of her eyes. All business.

"Lisa," I said quietly. Whispered at the piano, conciliatory. She huffed and came back, perching on the edge of the piano bench as if she were just about to leave. "Don't make me explain. You must have known I'd come. We may not be good sisters or even decent normal ones but we can still show up at each other's major life events, right?"

"I guess you came to the wedding, too," she said hesitatingly, as if she thought I was leading her into some trap.

"I created a diversion there as well, if you remember." I'd drunk too much, danced hilariously, and left just after cake, but it certainly gave everyone something to talk about.

Lisa laughed, just a tiny guilty one. I pressed on.

"But I was nothing compared to Dad and his hiccupping speeches. I thought you would hide under the table it was so mortifying."

She smiled, nodding, and ventured, ". . . and then the bouquet toss? With all the desperate divorced cousins out there? I thought Sarah would kill herself diving for it."

So, just another funeral where you accidentally mention people offing themselves. Lisa opened her mouth and shut it quickly again, surprised. I could see the old panic bubbling up in her like a flooded drain.

"It's OK, Lis, that's not what you meant."

I rummaged in my purse and held out a make-up wipe, and she blotted her face and swiped under her eyes. Chin up, she shyly tipped her face left and right for my approval, and I nodded the all-clear.

Why was she so upset about that one little verbal slip? While it was true that both of us typically bristled when anyone made a comment about suicide, it was also sort of old news now. It had been the secret of our little family unit ever since that day; my father had been so careful to explain it to Lisa and me that same morning, so that we would know never to tell, so that the rest of the family, and our teachers, neighbours would be able to sigh, and nod, and say that it was just her time to go. A pat on the back and a glance skyward, and off you go, girls.

As years passed we'd both pulled it together a bit for appearances, and I figured it took a lot to shake Lisa these days. I tried to keep our conversation moving to gloss over it – her sudden sensitivity confused and even irked me a little. I wanted to shake her.

"Busy day, Lis? Have you eaten anything? The food in there is good, really."

"I ate right before the memorial, I should still be OK. I just . . ." She started to say something, swallowed, moved on. "I've just been so tired. It's been crazy the last few weeks, and I think about Mom a lot."

"I know, funerals always do that. Memorials. It's OK."

"Yeah, you're right about that. But this one especially. I can't shake it. And I feel bad because I shouldn't be focused on her now."

This was more emotion than we'd exchanged in about ten years, and it made me antsy as hell. But I tried to meet her halfway.

"It's OK, though, we're just like that. I get times like that, too. You know it'll pass once this is all over and you can go home."

"I know, Jenny," she said, sighing, "you're right. It just wears me out." She put the tissue to her eyes again, started to say something else, and shook her head instead. It felt like there was a gap between us, a tenuous bridge that couldn't quite make up for the distance and the time. She was trying, I was trying. I wanted to reach across the space, but couldn't bring myself to when it seemed such an impossible distance. There were so many years of keeping quiet, keeping my own secrets, and they sprawled between us like physical space.

In my mind I could tell Lisa what I'd always meant to, the second secret: that I had handed Mom the pills myself, that she had asked me for them and explained it all to me, and I had let it happen anyways. But in my mind I just saw Lisa's anger at me, saw her throw her years of hard, quiet, secret suffering at my feet, and I didn't say a word, like I hadn't a hundred times before. Every single day that she hadn't called me to talk, that I hadn't phoned her from New York; there isn't a bridge for that kind of distance.

Lisa

I walked Jenny to her car, and we stood in the open door while her AC churned and *Graceland* played on the speakers. Our old road-trip mixtapes for family car journeys had always included Paul Simon and that album in particular, the perfect travelling music.

I could easily make her excuses to the others, who'd probably be grateful that they hadn't had to talk to her anyways. It was funny how everyone assumed we were so different; I the dutiful success story, pleasing and pleasant, she the unpredictable and unfriendly little sister. Back home no one saw her city life and her success, just the emotional girl she had been that set everyone on edge. Really we were exactly the same, except perhaps when it came to keeping up appearances. To me it was always part of keeping the secret, but Jenny had kept it just as well by making everyone around her a little uncomfortable and distant.

We hugged a real goodbye, crushing the light smell of sweat and perfume from our damp clothes while Paul Simon sang that losing love is like a window in your heart. I wanted her to stay so I could hug her longer and tell her every detail, but I knew the sooner she left the sooner I could shove it all away from me again. Jenny did seem to know that she could help by leaving; we secret-keepers understand the worth of silence.

Earlier, crouching at that granite memorial, I had pictured myself telling her quietly, showing her the letter of condolence I got from the army. Usually widows and mothers get a signed letter from the President himself, but not for soldiers who die by suicide. But in the end I couldn't tell her or anyone, because then that would have been the one thing they knew about him. I wanted Jenny to know only the good things about him. I wanted to keep them separate, the tragedies at both ends of me.

"You're never going to kill storytelling, because it's built into the human plan. We come with it."

Margaret Atwood

The Window
REBECCA ROUILLARD

Deirdre's ground-floor flat jutted out perpendicular to the main body of the block and as she stood at the sink doing the washing-up she could see a window open on the second floor. Her own window was only open a crack but she could hear voices – a strange acoustic carried the sound, if not the substance, of the conversation down quite clearly into her kitchen. Even if she could have made out the words it was unlikely that she would have understood them. She didn't know the people who lived in Flat 24, but she'd seen them. She'd nodded hello in the hallway as the shrouded mother, clearly pregnant again, struggled with shopping, children and a buggy. Where did they fit all of those children in a two-bedroom flat?

Deirdre's eye was caught by a sudden billowing and fluttering of curtains out of the second-floor window, and then a small head appeared. Two sets of knuckles framed the head and then an elbow. At first she thought the child was just looking, trying to see out of the window, but then her stomach lurched – she saw a small foot appear next to the elbow. The child was trying to climb out. Surely someone would appear to take the child away from the window? Surely someone was there? She hesitated for a moment. It would be embarrassing to shout, to run – to make a fuss unnecessarily. The little leg hooked over the sill and a small bottom appeared.

"Hello!" she shouted and banged on the window. Washing-up

water splattered over the pots of herbs on her windowsill. It was useless – they wouldn't hear her from inside the flat. And then, before she had even decided to run, she found herself running. She ran through the living room, panic fluttering high up in her chest. She unlocked the door with a shaking hand, imagining a little body hitting the ground hard and a small skull cracked and leaking. She stumbled and fell over the step into the gravel walkway that separated the building from the back garden. Even as she fell she was still moving, crawling, scrabbling for purchase in the stones. She managed to get to her feet, her heart beating loudly in her ears and dreading what she might find as she came around the corner of the building. There was nothing on the ground yet. She looked up – two little legs were dangling out of the window and still no sign of anyone else. It was typical. There was probably a horde of relatives in there but not one to notice that the child was about to fall. She was almost there. She ran, still trying to shout but unable to say anything other than, "Hello, hello."

And then she saw one of the child's hands slip – saw it hanging by one hand for a second and then falling. As it fell she felt a rush of relief; it looked so weightless – surely it was just a toy after all. The child must have dropped a toy out of the window. But even as she had this thought, her arms stretched out to catch it and something hit her hard, knocking her to the ground and winding her. She clutched the thing tightly to her chest as she struggled to take a breath, but it started to wriggle and then to cry. She looked down and found that she was holding a small boy in her arms. He looked about two years old; he had thick, black hair and a heavy fringe of black lashes around his eyes. She realised that she was still wearing her yellow washing-up gloves and that there was someone screaming and hanging out of the window; it was the mother, reaching her arms towards the ground in a fruitless delayed reaction – all she could do from that distance. Then she disappeared from the window and two other brown faces appeared, gazing down at Deirdre and the child.

And then before Deirdre had time to think about what she would say she was surrounded by a crowd. The child was dragged out of her arms. The mother was saying "Thank you" over and over again and squeezing both of her yellow-gloved hands. The hydrangeas needed pruning, she noticed. She should speak to the garden-service people about that. The child had disappeared into the embraces of his family. There didn't seem to be anything else for her to do or say so she walked back inside and locked the door again. She took off the washing-up gloves and washed her hands. She walked from the kitchen to the living room several times without knowing what she was looking for or what she had meant to do next. She went to her computer and opened the draft of an email she'd been writing earlier – before she'd started on the breakfast dishes. It was addressed to the board of directors of the block:

> The children from Flat 24 have been picking the flowers in the garden again – not just picking them but pulling the petals off and dispersing them all over the lawn. It's messy, destructive and very frustrating considering the substantial levy we pay for garden services. Perhaps they should be prevented from playing in the garden altogether if they cannot behave. At the very least they need to be properly supervised.

She had complained to the directors about Flat 24 several times before; the issue of the children playing in the garden had been discussed at a board meeting and the family had been warned to supervise their children, but nothing more had been done. She moved the cursor to the Send button but didn't click on it. She saved the email.

At five o'clock there was a knock on the door. She opened it to find the child's mother holding a large Pyrex dish.

"It is vegetable biryani," the mother told her, offering the dish. "For you. Thank you."

Deirdre had accepted the dish before she had time to think about it, and then the mother put her hand on Deirdre's arm and squeezed it gently. "Thank you," she said again, her eyes shining with unshed tears.

"Thank you, it was really not necessary," Deirdre said. "Goodbye, then," and she shut the door quickly before the woman could start crying.

She carried the large dish through to the kitchen and set it down on the side – it was enough food for six.

The next morning, just before ten, the phone rang.

"Hello, is that Deirdre Morris?"

"Yes, who's calling?"

"My name is Mark Roberts, I'm phoning from the *Surrey Comet*."

Deirdre wondered if they were trying to get her to subscribe to something. Surely the *Surrey Comet* was a free newspaper?

". . . you saved the little boy's life," the journalist was saying.

"Oh that." Deirdre realised what he was talking about. "It was nothing. I was in the right place at the right time."

"Could you tell me a bit more about what happened?"

"I was washing the dishes yesterday morning, and I looked out of my window and saw the boy climbing out. I ran out of my flat and fortunately was in time to catch him before he . . . landed."

"That was a great catch – are you a sportswoman?"

"No, I was standing directly below, I couldn't have missed him. It wasn't that high."

"I think you're being modest. You're quite the heroine. Would you mind if I sent a photographer round to take your picture a bit later?"

"No thank you, I'd rather not."

"Are you sure? People love these kinds of stories."

"I have to go. Goodbye." She put the phone down quickly.

The phone rang again. Deirdre didn't answer it. She went into the kitchen instead. It still smelt of unfamiliar spices. She'd eaten a plate of biryani for dinner the night before; it had tasted all right but she hadn't enjoyed it. She took the dish out of the fridge, scraped the leftovers into a Tupperware container, washed the dish and walked upstairs to return it to Flat 24. She knocked on the door and a different, older woman answered – perhaps the child's grandmother.

Deirdre held out the dish. "Thank you so much, it was delicious –"

But the older woman did not let her finish and instead pulled her inside and shut the door. She was led into the living room and shown a seat. The child's mother stood up to welcome her. There was another woman there, too, and an older man.

"My sister –, my father –," the mother introduced them. Deirdre didn't catch any of the names.

"I will make tea," the older woman announced.

"Oh, no thank you, I must go . . ." Deirdre started, but it was too late. The grandmother had disappeared. Everyone sat down. The upholstery was stiff and scratchy against the back of her knees. She realised that the boy was there, too – she hadn't noticed him before – holding on to his mother's legs. The other children were at school, Deirdre supposed. He looked fine; he probably didn't even remember falling.

"Is the boy all right?" Deirdre asked. "No injuries?"

"He is OK," the mother reassured her. And then she pushed the child towards Deirdre as though she would want to examine the child herself.

Deirdre leaned towards the small boy. "No more climbing," she told him. "You frightened your mummy."

He looked at her blankly then ran off. Everybody else was nodding and smiling.

The grandmother came back with a tray. She handed Deirdre a cup of tea and offered a plate of home-made biscuits. They had dried fruit in them and were cloyingly sweet. She drank some tea quickly to get the biscuit down.

"Did you make these?" she asked the grandmother.

The grandmother indicated the child's mother.

"Lovely. The biryani was lovely, too. Too much for me, though, I'll be eating it for a week," she said. "Because you gave me so much," she added quickly, in case they thought she was asking for more.

They were all still smiling at her. Nobody said anything. She ate her biscuit and sipped her tea. It was still very hot and scalded her throat, but she drank it down as quickly as she could. The main wall of the living room was covered with an intricately patterned tapestry in rich tones of teal and gold. She thought about mentioning it but then hesitated; if she admired it perhaps they might try and give it to her. She turned away quickly and looked at the window instead – the ill-fated window. It was shut now. She wondered how long it would take before they grew complacent again – forgot to close the window, forgot to watch the child.

"I really must go now, thank you so much," she told the group. They each gripped her hand, one at a time, in farewell.

The phone rang again several times that day. Deirdre didn't answer it. She thought about going out but she didn't. At three o'clock she heard people talking outside her flat. She peeked round the side of the net curtains and saw a photographer taking photos of the boy and his mother. She went quickly to sit in the bedroom in case they looked for her through the living-room windows. She tried to read but her ears were straining to hear the conversation. It was hardly news – only a second-storey window. She didn't understand why people would want to publicise their bad parenting anyway. Ten minutes later there was a knock on the door. She ignored it and held her breath. There was a second knock and then silence.

At five o'clock sharp there was another knock on the door. Deirdre was half expecting it; it was the child's mother. She had a plate of the same sickly-sweet biscuits Deirdre had sampled earlier; they were warm – just baked.

"It's really not necessary," Deirdre said. The mother squeezed her hand and thanked her again – her face glowing with gratitude.

She shut the door and took the plate to the kitchen. She ate one biscuit and then tipped the others into the rubbish bin. She washed the plate and walked upstairs to Flat 24. She left it on the mat outside the door.

She reheated a portion of the biryani for her dinner and then scraped the rest into the bin.

The next day Deirdre heard the flap of her letterbox and she half expected some kind of baked goods to have been forced through the narrow slot, but instead it was an advertising flyer for a local estate agent. She turned it over and looked at the selection of properties available in the immediate area. She looked at the flyer for a while before she dropped it in the paper-recycling bin.

She sat down at her computer and reopened the draft email she had been writing to the board of directors before the window incident. She deleted it and began a new one:

> I'm not sure if you have been made aware of recent events. On Monday morning a small child

fell out of the window of Flat 24. Had I not been looking out of my kitchen at exactly the right moment and managed to run outside and catch the child, there could have been a terrible tragedy. I hardly need mention the potential decline in our property values if the block had been the scene of such a horrible accident. In addition, the tenants of Flat 24 then invited the local paparazzi onto the property to report the story, and since then I have been harassed for interviews and photographs – a serious invasion of my privacy. I propose that the eviction of the tenants of Flat 24 be discussed at the next board meeting.

Deirdre clicked the Send button.

The phone rang several times during the day. Deirdre didn't answer it.

At five o'clock someone knocked; Deirdre didn't answer the door. There was a second knock, slightly louder and more insistent. She didn't answer.

Ten minutes later, she checked. Another dish on the mat outside.

She locked the door of her flat carefully behind her and carried the dish, still warm, up to the second floor. She laid it down outside the door of Flat 24 and walked away without looking back.

"Delay is natural to a writer. He is like a surfer - he bides his time, waits for the perfect wave on which to ride in."

E. B. White

Are We Nearly There?

KATE SMALLEY ELLIS

"Clear your mind, Jen." Mum is chewing gum fast, itching for a cigarette Dad won't let her have in his car. "This is an easy start. You know the route to Granny's."

Her words are to soothe herself as much as me but she's more reassuring than Dad, whose driving-instructor technique is to fall asleep in the back "to show he trusts me". Well he shouldn't trust me. Neither of them should. There's no way I should be allowed on this three-lane motorway surrounded by lorries and motorbikes and people carriers even though my plastic card is pink now and I only got three minors on my test. I shouldn't have my whole family's lives in my shaky, hung-over, no-longer-a-virgin hands. It's not that it blew my mind. It didn't. I don't even think I came. He said he loved me and I said "Oh" and peeled my stomach away from his.

"When are we going to be there?" Shelly whines from the back. She pulls on my headrest, jolting my swollen brain inside my skull. I'm in the fast lane because my real instructor, Tony, said I should "blend in with the traffic", and everyone else is in the fast lane. The middle barrier dips in and out of the grass like a beige snake. My stomach loops. I taste tequila every time I swallow. When I looked in the mirror this morning my tongue was yellow and had a new layer of texture on it. I didn't know tongues went yellow.

Tony told me that if you're still drunk from the night before they can find the alcohol in your blood. He said they'd ban me from driving if I was caught but I've been bugging Dad for this motorway experience for so long now I couldn't back out. He spent ages on the phone booking the insurance. Then the whole of Monday's dinner he flapped spaghetti from his fork, moaning about how expensive it was because I'm only seventeen and that he knew I wouldn't crash anyway because I'm so sensible.

Mum is leaning towards me checking the speedo. I can smell her last cigarette on her breath. New white hairs spring from her temples like worried antennae. My eyes lock onto her tense profile.

"Eyes on the road!"

I flick back front. There is a lorry ahead that's so tall I can't see its roof. A moving skyscraper. Plastic green side panels flap in and out with the wind like sideways trampolines.

Simon cried when he found his cat. I guess it's good that he's got a sensitive side but technically that means he had sex with me then started crying. She was just old I think. He came back in to his bedroom after going to the toilet and stood there naked, holding it up in his palms like a plate.

"She's stiff," he said as he lowered her down to me in bed.

I was so drunk I saw two dead cats so prodded at one to see which was real. He started shaking with tears. I watched goosebumps form on his thighs then suggested more tequila. He slid her into an old Adidas shoebox as I poured. We drank to her, Dorothy. He talked fondly about when she got stuck up a ladder and how she'd start meowing whenever the *EastEnders* theme tune came on. I noticed for the first time how long his eyelashes were.

There is a car in front now and I'm concentrating on its number plate, keeping exactly the same distance between R546 HUX and me at all times. We're not crashing. My arms are moving only with the car. I can feel its rhythm like it's part of me. It trusts me, it can tell I have a full licence now. I'm wearing blinkers, zoning out. This is what ultimate concentration must feel like. I'm invincible, a sexually active, invincible woman behind the wheel.

"Are you deaf or what?" Mum shouts and I jump. The needle is edging towards 85 mph. There is a gust of wind and the deep connection between me and the car is severed abruptly.

"Only a fool breaks the two-second rule." Mum loves a mantra.

The lorry bulges back in front and the steering wheel jerks. I turn it back but too much and we're nearly in the middle lane. I can see Mum twitching out of the corner of my eye. Dad is snoring loudly behind her. A wet blob of tissue lands on my lap and bubbles of spit leak onto my jeans.

"Shelly, you stop that right now. Your sister is driving, do you want her to crash? Slow. Down." Mum has gone pale.

I put the brakes on.

"Not that much! Someone's behind you. Always check your mirrors! Derek, can you –" Mum looks back at Dad. "Oh for . . . Wake him up, will you, Shelly?"

There is a slap then Dad snorts and Shelly giggles. I focus on a strap whipping the lorry in front and on keeping the car in a straight line.

"What the . . . ?" Dad's voice is thick and croaky.

"Derek, help me out. Jen's struggling. Are you shaking, Jen?"

"I'm fine, I . . . How do I change lanes?"

"Mirrors!" Dad is awake now.

"Mirror, mirror on the wall, who is the prettiest of them all? Meeee." Shelly laughs at her own joke.

I can hear her teeth squelching on another clod of tissue.

"Quiet, will you?" Mum is holding the dashboard as if it might fall apart.

"I'm bored." Shelly starts stamping on the floor. I feel the rhythm through my seat. Hot saliva gathers in my mouth. I think I might be sick.

I remember Simon balancing the tequila bottle on top of a postbox on the walk home. He had to hold my hand steady as I opened the front door because I kept missing the keyhole.

"Careful now, Jen. We need to get in the slow lane." My hands jerk the wheel to the left. "Not yet." Mum is pressing herself back into her seat, pushing her feet forward on invisible brakes.

I slow down and see a massive Land Rover getting bigger in the rear-view mirror. I see Simon's wall moving closer and further away again. I see myself on top of him, surprised it's really me in that position. I imagine I'm in *Pretty Woman* and we're in a penthouse suite and he's a millionaire and we've just eaten strawberries not Wotsits and –

"JEN!"

"What?" I swallow. It tastes bitter. My mouth is dry and I can feel the ridges of its roof with my tongue.

"Watch where you're going! Slow lane, remember? Take. It. Easy."

I flick my head back and forth from the side mirror to the front and see flashes of cars and road and Mum but no information, never any space. My hands are gripping the wheel tight, my elbows locked straight. Every time I move I'm scared the wheel is going to spin out of control.

"Stay in the middle of the lane! Shit, Jen. I thought you were ready for this . . ."

The lorry in front wobbles and my head swerves with it. Shelly pulls on the back of my seat. A horn sounds from close by. Cars overtake on both sides.

The car smells of the cake Mum has made for tea, gooey chocolate with the icing that clings to your tongue like peanut butter. My palms are sticking to the wheel.

"Change lanes, come on. There's space . . . now!"

I watch as someone else moves my hands. The left one taps the indicator. They manoeuvre the car into the slow lane. We don't hit anything.

"Now, Jen! Exit's coming. Indicate."

My arms are moving again and they seem to remember the driving lessons for me. No one knows I've done it yet. I need to get off this road. The speedo says 75 mph, 80 mph. The car in front is getting closer.

"Brakes!"

"Slip lane. NOW."

"Jen's gonna cra-ash." A glob of tissue thuds on the ceiling just above my head.

"Shut up, Shelly." Mum's voice has a tremble in it. "OK, so

remember to slow down when you get off, OK? The roundabout will come up unexpectedly."

Like Simon's cock. He was ready before I'd even thought about it. Curiosity allowed him in more than anything else and he did do some licking first but I don't think what we did can be full sex. I mean, he moved himself in and out but none of the other stuff happened. No weird noises came out of me. It felt OK.

"OK, you know these roads, don't you? Don't straighten out the roundabouts. Take it nice and slow."

I nod. I'm on a fairground ride and clinging on to the safety bar, screaming in my head. Shelly is squealing in the back, or is it singing?

"Shelly, I told you to stop that. Derek, can you . . . ?"

"Listen to your mother."

Everything is hazy like the moment just before he did it last night, as if something was about to happen and I didn't want to miss it. He poked me then slipped out but tried again and I shut my eyes in case it hurt.

I blink. I passed the roundabout. We're on the hilly road now, driving through the forest. I used to love it when I was a kid. I'd scream at Mum to drive faster down the steep stretches and put my hands up like I was on a ride at Chessington World of Adventures. I let the car roll down faster and faster and dark pine trees either side of the road are blurring out of the corners of my eyes and everything is too fast and filling up my head with flashing lights and white lines and –

"Jen, slow down!"

I push my foot down and lean forward, bracing myself against the wheel. The car slows and it's still moving in a straight line.

"Down here on the left."

I shift into third then second as we approach the final turn of the journey, but a wave of sickness hits me before we get there and I have to stop, so I take a turn before, too fast. It's not a road but a track and there is a wooden gate right in front. I brake hard and jerk forward. Shelly screams and we bump back into our seats.

I turn the engine off, unclip my seat belt and open the door, then run over to the gate and throw up. Holding on to the rough wood for support, I watch the yellow liquid sink into the grass. I slowly stand upright and everything is brighter and focused now, trees are waving new leaves from across the field. I feel Mum rub my back then peel the keys from my fist. I remember Simon steadying my drunken waist last night, his fingers still so nervous on me they almost fluttered.

Crow Harvest

GILLI FRYZER

Gwyn Williams moved stiff-legged towards his father's old gun box, wall-bolted at the far end of the kitchen passage. No need for light, the thick walls and uneven flagstones as close to him as the furrows beneath his silvered stubble. He located the chilly weight of a double gun barrel, scrabbled for the cartridge belt, and bore his findings back towards the warmth. Beth's ears twitched at his return, her tail drumming in the dirt.

Gwyn's arm swept across the kitchen table, sending unopened invoices, bank statements, and dirty crockery crashing onto the flags. A single light bulb fizzed under its layer of dust as he began to clean, rodding and oiling the barrel, buffing the action, rubbing imaginary deposits from its surface, running the bolt to check for friction. He cocked the gun, then sighted along its barrel, the smooth wooden stock nestling hard back into his shoulder. Satisfied, he began to load fresh cartridges one by one into the belt, pushing each tube under the canvas so that its brass head showed clear. As the last cartridge rammed home he reached for the switch on the wall, his strength blinking out with the light.

Da's old chair creaked as Gwyn settled back to wait for dawn, the uncocked gun bent across his thighs. The narrow hands of the old oak clock pointed to half past three. The urge to sleep dragged hard; Gwyn sat straighter, shepherd's instinct still alive, still watchful.

Dai Williams' unforgiving face floated in front of Gwyn, weathered and remorseless, and behind it the shades of other men who had dug a living from the mountain, and who, like his father, lay crumbled under name-scratched slates in the chapel yard.

"Fiddle's put away, Da," he said, sighing, his voice too weak to strike an answering sound from the walls.

The collie lay on the mat in front of the stove, her grizzled muzzle resting on his sock. Daft bugger, thought Gwyn, but he left his foot where it was. A wave of nausea reminded him of Doc Evans' tablets, lying untaken beside the sink.

"Don't need doping when there's gun work to do," muttered Gwyn to the empty air.

A spark winked, vanished as the logs in the burner broke to greying ash. His calloused palms rested on top of the gun, its comforting solidity pressing him down into his seat, anchoring his depleted body to the chair, the dying warmth of the stove, the ticking clock. Gwyn felt that without that steel weight his body would simply detach itself from its surroundings and float away, its pinprick consciousness spinning into a maelstrom of beak and claw. The fiery ache deep in his belly forced his eyes open again.

The outlines of table, sink and stove stood firm against the night, but the dizziness remained. Before him loomed the great bulk of the far wall, cracked apart by the stairwell. It was a good few years since anyone other than Gwyn had climbed that steep flight to his tiny bedroom with its sagging roof, and in a harsh winter, weeks might pass uncounted before he bothered to make the solitary trip.

There had been that one time, though. What was she called? Barmaid with hipbones like a skinny heifer's, a rump that swayed its empty promise up those narrow steps. Years back, anyway. Not a pick on her, whoever she was. Poor choice of breeding stock, Da would've grunted, not worth the price. He remembered lying on the bed and watching as she tugged her flowered dress up over her head; the sudden disappointment of her tiny breasts, little bigger than the feeding teats of his ewes.

The clock hands shuddered past the hour and Gwyn closed his eyes. The June dawn would rise soon enough.

* * * * *

That winter gone had been savage beyond memory; thick snow choking the mountain pastures well past Easter. Man and dog struggled to save even half the flock; the thaw was well under way before the others could be reached.

A bitter sun had tinged the trampled snow with ruddy streaks as Gwyn rolled the last ewe over with his boot. The matted fleece was rank with the stench of ditch water, eye sockets scraped to yellow bone. She'd gone in labour, bloody afterbirth and dead lamb frozen to her legs. The crows had feasted on them both before the snow blew in. Grunting, he dragged the bloated carcass down the muddied grass towards the pick-up and heaved it onto the rest, tossing the final pecked-out scrap of skin and bone on top.

Spring always turned up, but this time too damn late for anything. Too late to save the mountain ponies, the brown hares, the sheep that froze against the drystone walls. Christ, even the birdsong was missing now. Nothing wanted to settle this high up any more. Only the carrion crows thrived. As the white tide receded he had seen countless black spots fluttering high on the hillside, feeding on exposed remains, tiny portents of disaster dancing from one point to another.

He chewed his lip and stared past the stinking fleeces, seeing salvation rotting within every swollen belly. Gwyn wasn't one for looking in the mirror, but he sensed the chill had reached him, too. He fastened the tailgate of the truck with leaden arms, as though the weak spring sunlight had come too late to warm his bones.

"Here."

Gwyn summoned the old collie back from the wall where she was still nosing the trodden slush. She sprang onto the passenger seat and settled herself for the jolting ride back to the yard, pale eyes fixed on her master. The truck ground its tyres deep into ruts as Gwyn forced it down the mountain; the air that whistled through its cab dispersing the cloying stink of decomposition. Beside him the dog's calm gaze stung like a rebuke.

Back at the yard the fetid carcasses slid silently onto the stones, and the weight of their loss dropped hard onto the old man's shoulders.

*

Like the decrepit walls that divided the hills, the thick stone blocks of the house had shifted haphazardly, settling it inexorably back into the landscape from which it had risen. Four tiny, cross-paned windows, deep-laid beneath sagging slates; a squat chimney at each end, a bleached wooden door tucked under a central porch. The tattered poplars behind its crumbling chimneys served as a ragged windbreak. It was hard to see where the hillside ended; rock and scree skittered to a halt where the ancient yard wall leant, grass-topped, against the wind. Dewi had called with the mail; a red-inked envelope lay tucked under the iron boot scraper.

As Gwyn lifted the latch he could hear the roosting jackdaws squabbling in the disused chimney. Behind its heavy door the house was silent, its air musty and undisturbed. Only in the darkness of the tiny kitchen was there any breath of life, and that came from the chipped blue range that Gwyn had been feeding since he was a little boy. Now he tossed the letter aside, unopened, and bent once more to the waiting log pile, even as tiredness rose within him. The discarded letter slid unnoticed from the cluttered table to join the heap on the flags below.

Gwyn tipped hot water onto powdered soup and stirred it, steam dampening his cheek. He lowered himself into the rubbed wood of his father's chair, its threadbare cushions stitched sixty years ago as a bridal bulwark against the walling, foddering and slaughtering of the hill farmer's daily round. Horsehair stuffing squeaked and groaned against his angular frame. Daylight had faded, but the effort of crossing the kitchen to flick a switch seemed too great. He had spent so much of his indoor life in that dim corner by the stove that its obstacles could be negotiated without light, without touch, almost without consciousness or the energy that any other form of existence seemed to demand from him.

His bones ached from the chill and the effort of locating the final missing sheep. Gwyn drained his mug and allowed his eyelids to drop.

That next morning broke cold and clear, a faint pink light softening the deep window recess as Gwyn pushed his head under the kitchen tap. A sharp pain drew his stomach up hard towards his ribs, more insistent than the sullen ache Doc Evans had located in his guts, a hunger pang that spoke instead of living, of bread and meat, eggs and honey. Da had sat at this table with laver bread, sausage and eggs piled high; Mam would've thought shame to send a man empty-bellied to work. Gwyn shrugged. Just as well they'd gone, like, with the fodder bins as near empty as the pantry shelf.

He rubbed his head with the rough towel so that his eyes watered and his sunken cheeks began to sting under their covering of stubble. Beth whined and scratched behind him. He pulled the door open to release the collie, steadying his back against the doorframe as he pulled on his boots.

Snow clouds still lingered like fading bruises above the western hills. The morning air was sharp; his breath escaped in trails as he crossed the old vegetable plot, its black soil already flecked with the sharp green of bursting seeds. Da had worked it hard, had passed buckets of berries and beans to Mam like he was showering her with flowers. It wasn't hill farming, according to a younger, more confident Gwyn, and the fruit cage had collapsed into a tangle of rotten poles and wire netting, the beds overrun with buttercup and groundsel; the ground not worth the time for clearing, until now, with his stomach empty and the bank at the gate.

The hens were clustered in a corner of the run, bobbing and clucking with fright. Gwyn could hear movement inside the nesting boxes. He lifted the shovel that propped the henhouse door shut, and leaning forward, lifted the lid. Ragged black feathers burst upwards into his face and Gwyn staggered back, swinging the shovel up and across his body. There was a muffled sound as the metal connected.

"You thievin' bloody bastard, you!"

Gwyn swung wildly again at the injured crow. It dropped the egg from its beak, and flapped against the wire netting, wing dangling. Gwyn stretched forwards and struck again, hard. The crippled bird fluttered at his feet; yolk seeped out from the broken shell beside his boot. The crow uttered a single harsh caw as Gwyn stooped and drove the shovel through.

He wedged the shovel back against the henhouse door and tossed the crow's battered remains onto the top of the yard wall.

Back in the kitchen, dog and master shared a bowl of cereal, the stone-flagged floor grave cold between them. The collie licked the last of the milk as Gwyn lifted the door latch and stepped outside into a whirlwind of noise.

A black knot of crows span above the roof tiles, their long, repeated cawing echoing between house and barn, increasing in intensity as, in twos and threes, other crows joined the circling group. Gwyn watched as the birds united in repeated waves of darkness, flying apart and then together again, their wings rolling and unrolling as they rode the air, all the time uttering strange, prolonged cries. The sky above the farmyard filled with thirty or forty crows wheeling and turning above his head until his ears were full of nothing but their harsh calls and the sound of beating wings.

He picked the dead crow up by its stiffened feathers and hurled it high over the wall and into the field. The corpse fluttered and tumbled in mockery as the mob continued to curse from the sky.

Inside the long barn, the air was heavy with the milky scent of nursing ewes. His depleted flock was restless, its anxious bleats increasing as he approached. Like his animals, Gwyn gazed through the open doors to the distant peaks. The drifts had only just melted, and the tough upland grass was as colourless and patchy as his growing beard. But under the corrugated roof the air was warming up, and beyond it, the walls undulated in ribbons of grey stone across hills that grew greener by the day.

Gwyn picked up a pitchfork of fodder, and tossed it into the nearest pen. Then he moved down the line, and did the same. A shadow moved silently across the light. He looked over his shoulder. A single crow had drifted in from the yard and perched on the rail behind him, eyeing the sheep. He took a step back, and swung with the empty pitchfork. The nearest animal started in surprise. The giant black bird fixed Gwyn with one wary eye, and then moved sideways with a tiny, almost careless, hop. Gwyn turned back to work. Pitch, toss. The hay fell heavily into each pen and the lambs bleated.

The sense of being watched became more unbearable with each load. Slowly, Gwyn rotated his head so that one eye could observe the intruder. The bird continued to watch his movements with quiet attention. Like Da, thought Gwyn, spitting into the straw. I never worked hard enough for that bastard, either.

Pitch, toss. Pitch, toss. He gripped the worn wooden handle

with both hands, felt his palms rubbing against its curve, his arms dropping and swinging with the rhythm of the task. The crow had hopped further along the rail, and was close behind him again.

"Bugger off!"

He lunged for the bird like a wind-blown scarecrow. The crow half extended its wings, and floated towards the rail in front of the next pen. Gwyn waved the pitchfork once more, but his heart wasn't in it. The space was more open; this time there would be no catching it unawares. He sensed the bird knew this too, for as he turned away, the crow just tilted its head, and then flapped its wings back into order, like a tailcoated undertaker settling respectably at a graveside.

As Gwyn left the barn that evening, he glanced up at the sky. It was silent, swollen with steel-tipped clouds that threatened April rain. Tomorrow, he thought. Tomorrow, I'll put them out. Even if I have to truck the hay up after.

Gwyn's sleep that night was fragmented, punctured by forms that massed and rose then fell back across his face in suffocating layers. Struggling for air, he surfaced with his face buried in a cushion, nose and mouth stopped by the exhausted feathers escaping through its disintegrating cover. Early light had roused the birds, the mewling of fledglings echoing from the far chimney. Unwilling to close his eyes again, Gwyn unlatched the door for the dog and watched her pad out onto the stones.

The crows were already waiting, a score or more hunched in uncharacteristic silence along the grass thatch of the old wall, black-cloaked against the biting wind. As the door rattled Gwyn saw beaks swivel his way, then settle back. One solitary sentinel lifted, stiff-winged, from the wall's end and rose backwards against a sudden gust, leaving the main group undisturbed.

Gwyn stood firm in the doorway and regarded the column of birds until the ache in his belly gripped him again, and the cold metal latch gnawed at his bony fingers. He spat, hard, onto the yard.

"To hell with you, too," he said, and slammed the door.

Gwyn towed the trailer up the hillside to where the track ruts petered out. As he dropped the ramp the returning sheep began to tumble out, frantically at first, and then more slowly as the keen mountain wind filled the trailer and the frontrunners stopped to crop the scanty grass. The barn-reared lambs quivered, tight curls rippling as gusts slapped their skin. He hunched his back and fingered tobacco into a paper as the lambs scurried away, bleating for their dams, ears pricked for answer.

Hands cupped to light his roll-up, Gwyn watched the flock move off onto the sheepways, the first ewe picking her path through the worn tussocks on the way to higher ground, the rest following.

Gwyn envied his flock its shared consciousness, the physical contact when the animals huddled together around the hay feeders, even the constant bleat of communication, just as he envied Dewi his sense of optimism, his women friends.

"You can't leave it to chance, man," had said the little postman once, his ham-pink face shinier than ever. "Lonely hearts, in the paper, like. It's all in the pitch, see. I tell 'em I used to sing club nights down in Swansea. Gets me a first date, anyway, and . . . well, then it's down to charm and a bit of sweet-talking, mostly."

Hill farmers and their women were a hardy breed, as Da had always boasted, knowing nothing else, no more capable of living those soft valley ways than sheep were of surviving rich pasture. Up on the hill Gwyn spat bloody phlegm onto the thin grass. Truth was he'd failed on the ground of his rearing, unable to find a mate hefted to the slopes as his sheep were.

* * * * *

She'd been no catch, that girl from the Woolpack, her with the fancy Cardiff ways and a well-padded bra. Thought all grass was made of gold, that one did. The old man shifted his legs to ease the weight of the gun. His collie was snoring gently, her jaw pressing down on the bones of his foot. Doc Evans' pills were making him sleepy, making it hard to remember. Hell, had he even taken the damn pills?

Turned out she was flatter 'n a boy.

The narrow stairwell swam in front of him again, a dark cleft in the pale stone. He'd followed the girl up its steep steps that night, watched her dress ride up into tight creases just inches from his face. Without its padding her body was stiffer, more angular than he had imagined; he had struggled to service her.

"Some farmer," she'd said, her own mouth a thin trap of echoed disappointment.

* * * * *

With the sheep back on the spring grass, Gwyn set to repairing fences, fighting back from winter as he fought each year, but this season he felt himself beaten, as though the savage storms had left as deep a mark on him as they had the farm.

Still he edged further across the mountain each day, forcing each line of broken fencing back upright with defiant blows. Crows performed aerial manoeuvres above his head, landing to pick over desiccated droppings, scavenging along the tussocks for the foxes' leavings, taking off when the dull smack of the mallet came too close. He saw no one else up on the hill. Some mornings a little red van would flash along the lane below, and then when he returned to the yard more letters would be tucked under the iron boot scraper.

From time to time Gwyn would stop to roll another thin cigarette and stick it to his lips to stifle a pang of hunger. Doc Evans couldn't stop that. The blows that echoed across the valley measured out his life enough. As the blue smoke puffed out Gwyn counted the crows that wheeled overhead, following his progress. With each day, it seemed to him, their number grew.

His own hunger drove him to attack the old seed beds in the growing evening light, turning the neglected soil over and then over again with his spade; to sow peas and carrots in neat rows eight inches apart, and plant potatoes and cabbages once more. As days passed, he found himself inspecting the ground for signs of growth, counting the green shoots as they uncurled into the light.

"There you go, Da," he said aloud. "There's life here yet."

The harvest would be another matter. The ache in his gut had spread to his back now; he felt too tired to head to the Woolpack any more. Dewi'd be there; he always had a tale to tell and another in his pocket, and the bar rocking with laughter. Fair enough, knew the length of his horns, did Dewi. The little postman's stories had never been diminished by his failure to keep the same girl for more than a month or two. Dewi hadn't wasted time promising a future:

he was no Tom Jones, as he admitted, "but they still tossed their ruddy knickers, boys, when I sang *Delilah*."

Gwyn added the latest envelopes to the pile on the floor and lifted the heavy kettle onto the stove.

The evening was humid for June. Sheet lightning lit up the distant peaks; a pewter mantle of cloud obscured the head of the valley, while the rising wind drove a warning smatter of rain across the yard. Gwyn downed tools as Dewi's van turned a corner and began to bump up the track. He swung the yard gate clear and nodded the postman through.

"Duw, Gwyn," exploded Dewi as he pushed open the van door. "Will you look at yourself, now. You've a beard would shame the Apostles there."

Gwyn held out a hand for the post.

"There's some official-looking stuff there, by the looks of it," persisted Dewi. "Are you keeping yourself now, man?"

Gwyn thrust the mail into his overalls. The pain would see him out, Doc Evans said. Bank would have its say soon enough.

"Come down for a square meal, why don't you?" Dewi shut the van door and wound the window down. "You can leave this place once in a while, boyo. It's not going to go anywhere."

Gwyn placed his hand on the thin rim of the van window, and bent his head so that his mouth drew level with Dewi's ear.

"You seen them crows?"

"Which is that, then, Gwyn?"

The old farmer jerked his head.

"Watching us. On the goddamn wall. Over there."

"Can't say I did. Still, there'll always be bloody crows, my friend."

Gwyn stepped back, away from the van.

"Pick the place clean as a whistle if I let 'em," he spat.

The thunderstorm had passed, leaving a morning downpour that rattled against the kitchen window and rippled in veils across the hillside. The sheep had moved, were sprinkled like daisies on the leeward slope, yet one remained obstinate, set firm in the path of the squall.

Water gurgled in the yard drain, pooled under the door. The wood had swollen; Gwyn had to wrench the latch back to get outside. The yard wall was empty, its weeds and grasses flattened by the rain.

He whistled Beth into the truck and set off up the track. The wipers pushed a wave of water from side to side, heavy drops splattering in rings between each stroke. The engine groaned as Gwyn dropped the gears, pushed the tyres up through the mud and onto the thin mountain pasture.

At the top of the track the wind snatched at the opened door, slammed it hard against its hinge. Gwyn turned his collar up and began working his dog. He caught up with the lone ewe soon enough, her body set into the wind, still bleating. Her walleye flickered at his approach; she skittered sideways a step and stopped. Beyond her protruded an outcrop of gorse and rock that sheltered the flock when the wind turned, the ground below it trampled and bare. Nothing moved. He turned his own body to the rain, and started to climb. The collie picked up scent as he began to move around the jagged overhang; she raced ahead, nose down.

He knew as soon as she had found it. Easy pickings. Dewi didn't know their ways. Snared by gorse and bramble, young eyes pecked out clear to bone, backside crow-eaten, soft and bloodied guts spilling pink and fresh over sodden yellow flowers.

Gwyn stared back across the valley. The lone ewe was still bleating, its futile note of panic swallowed by the wind. Nothing else moved this high up, but dark spots rose and fell behind the chimneys far below, looping in triumphant circles above the empty house.

Gwyn hobbled across the yard, his breath coming in short, hard gasps, his presence disturbing the birds so little that he could have stepped from under the slate-flecked grass around the chapel. The turned earth of the vegetable plot had turned to silt, and dozens of young crows squabbled in its blackened pools, tearing up the tender plants, scrabbling for the worms and bugs that rose, half drowned, to the surface. Broken pea and bean plants dangled lifelessly from netting, tops pecked out; the cabbage plants lay trampled into the mud. Canes, loosened by heavy rain, lay like fallen timber across rows of crushed seedlings. The birds hardly stirred as Gwyn moved blindly amongst them, his wet face upturned to the sky.

* * * * *

The shapes shifted into their daylight forms and Gwyn stretched in his chair. He lifted the gun from his lap, felt his breath catch in his throat, his heart pick up. Beth rose and shook herself from ear to tail, whined gently.

He dunked his head under the tap, and shut the kitchen door on the collie.

"I don't want you warning them bastards off."

The wall outside was empty, its grassy top still flattened by the heavy rain. Beyond it the muddied track bent and turned, rose and levelled, rose again. The air had cleared to leave the promise of a summer's day, and as Gwyn forced himself to climb, he watched a thin yellow light spill onto the eastern hills.

The sheep were still some distance away as he staggered onto the steep slope of the top pasture and sucked at the dawn air like a drowning man. The old house drifted far below him, pale and insubstantial behind trails of early-morning mist. Above its slates black specks fluttered as though roused too early.

Gwyn turned from flock to house and from flock to house again, and yet again, throwing his arms apart, chest open, the cocked gun held triumphant. He turned slowly at first then faster and faster, the wind dragging tears down his cheeks, the sudden sensation of freedom forcing a laugh from him that began softly and then lifted into a roar that brought him at last to his knees, gasping for breath.

"Come on, you scavenging bastards! Come on!"

The great sentinel crow, first to reach the head of the valley, stretched out its wings and rode the dawn thermal, its wary eye fixed on the hunched figure of the farmer below, panting over his cocked gun.

"Take it. I'm done, see."

Gwyn rocked back onto his heels, arms and gun outstretched, and roared once more as the early-morning sun, the circling crows, span into a black and golden vortex of fractured light.

"I'm all yours. It's all bloody yours, boys!"

The explosion ricocheted across the valley. The great crow circled higher as splinters of bone and tissue burst in a fountain of scarlet and white against the rising blue of the sky, the dew-smeared green of the close-grazed turf. From her basket beside the stove, the collie raised her muzzle and whined, soft and long.

Up on the hill the sheep bent their narrow heads to the grass as, with funereal precision, the first crows dropped to feed.

"When you read a short story, you come out a little more aware and a little more in love with the world around you."

George Saunders

Folie à Deux
KATE WHITESIDE

Helen was on the toilet in the mixed-sex bathrooms of her work when she first saw it. A fleck of red on her upper thigh, like she'd spilled her soup. She licked her thumb and rubbed over it. She squeezed it and watched it rise up on a mountain range of cellulite until she heard the polite cough of a man on the other side of the door; she pulled up her things, grabbed her bag from beside her feet and left.

Back at her desk, she could see it through her tights. Lurking darkly, 20 denier below.

"How in the hell have I got that cut?" she thought.

Later, at home, she strode around her bedroom in lamplight, taking off her clothes one by one. It was only a cut, but for some reason she felt something snag at her insides when she sat down to take off her tights. She pretended not to notice it at first, like it was a person she was feigning not to know, but eventually she had to look at it again, and she brushed over it with her finger. It wasn't huge, but it was big enough and in an intimate enough area that she felt she really ought to know where it had come from. She poured herself a small glass of wine, read her book and fell asleep.

The next day she got up for work, had a piece of cinnamon toast, black coffee and half a grapefruit. It was a breakfast she had seen on a TV advert and she ate it every day. It was how she stayed thin. Before she had time to examine the cut again, she was getting ready to shower and in the mirror caught sight of a huge welt on her ribcage. A bruise rippled out from a central point, as if somebody had thrown a stone into her. She groped for the sink with manicured hands, gripped it with white knuckles. She looked at herself in the mirror. After a few seconds, her face started to relax. She must have walked into something. On the plus side, her modest innards had worked quietly on healing the thing on her thigh, and it looked like almost nothing. She showered, pulled her hair deftly into a bun, dressed in a green silk blouse and white pencil skirt, and left in time to not bump into the maid.

"I must be beating myself up in my sleep!" she said to the girl who served her a coffee every morning.

The girl just looked away and said: "To go?"

After a few days the cut had completely gone and the ripples on the bruise had contracted. A few days later still, her side was smooth and unblemished. She had all the more reason to smile at herself in the mirror in the morning, and she smiled at herself more and more deeply as every day went by. Until there it was again, back on her thigh. Reopened, new, and angrier. Defiant. She sat at her desk and tugged at her lips with her teeth. Tapped her fingers on her knees. A colleague walked by and asked her how she had bruised her eye. She touched her face. She said nothing, managed what she hoped seemed like a polite laugh but was actually a whimper, and went straight home.

In her bedroom she hunched in front of her laptop and Googled until panic rose in her throat and spread down her limbs. Doesn't leukaemia cause you to bruise? But what about the cuts? She stripped her bed and got her face close to it to check for bed bugs. She walked laps of her house looking for any ways mice could get in. She was sure she'd heard of mice nibbling people in their sleep. And she was an exceptionally heavy sleeper. She sat up until the early hours sending work emails to clear the decks for the morning, and didn't set an alarm.

Before she could comprehend what was happening, her body was a patchwork of purples and yellows and reds. No sooner had one thing healed, another appeared. She'd go through weeks of remission, feeling fine, thinking maybe she was better, then she'd find herself sitting at the bottom of the shower, tracing concentric circles around a swelling on her kneecap. Bruises opened up like flowers and wounds sprouted like weeds. She started to eat Coco Pops for breakfast. She wasn't herself.

"I've a big bruise on my side," she told her doctor. "And my elbow is swollen."

She clenched her jaw as she took off her shirt and he touched his fingertips to her ribcage. He sat back.

"That all looks pretty nasty," he said. "I can give you something for the pain and inflammation."

He coughed. He took a big breath. He rubbed his nose. Helen buttoned herself up and he looked levelly at her for several seconds.

"No?" he said.

Helen blinked. "What?"

He shook his head and handed her a prescription.

She looked at the boxes of pills as the pharmacist dispensed them and wondered whether to "ONLY USE AS INSTRUCTED" or not.

She developed a plethora of excuses for work, if she was ever there. Down the stairs, into the door. But she stayed off more and more, walking the hallway of her pristine house, dragging sore fingers along the walls, wondering what would be next and where it could all have possibly come from. She spent her nights crouched on her haunches in an armchair, wanting to pounce on something that she couldn't see, or even sense. She bought thick waxy make-up that she coated her jawline and temples with. Everybody in her life seemed far away, as if she was a ship barely tethered to shore.

On one of Helen's days of not being able to get out of bed, the maid stumbled across her and seemed surprised to find the house she cleaned actually was inhabited after all.

"Some people work away a lot. I assumed you were that sort of people."

"It's Marta, isn't it? I'm sorry I haven't caught up with you in a while. I'm off work right now. I'm not feeling very well. I won't get in your way."

Marta ran her eyes over Helen's face, then walked out quietly and returned with a cup of tea. Helen sat in bed and drank it and watched how carefully Marta cleaned round the chair legs, handling them tenderly as though they were damaged joints. She began to engineer being in when Marta arrived, and followed her around the house, watching the way she worked and trying to extract bits of information about her in a way she hoped seemed friendly and not prying. It pleased Helen to have somebody around the house who wasn't making any demands of her. She thought this especially when she deleted the answerphone messages from work without listening to them. Marta's visit began to be the highlight of her day. Until –

"Mrs Ramsey. Are you trying to test me or something?"

Helen, in her dressing gown, pushed her hair back slowly over her forehead, where a welt had been reddening over the last few days.

"I'm sorry?"

"Always looking over my shoulder. Do I not work well enough for you?"

Helen smiled a little trembling smile. "I'm sorry. I didn't mean to make you uncomfortable. Perhaps I just want company. I'll go to the bedroom."

As Helen began to walk away Marta touched her shoulder. She was kneading her duster. Her eyes were a sort of amber brown.

"You should see your friends more for company. Or your family."

"Yes. You're right. I should."

Helen continued walking, but Marta caught her up and again touched her shoulder.

"I hope you're not expecting me to protect you."

Helen laughed. "I'm ill. You can't protect me. It's not doable."

From then on she continued to leave money out for Marta as in the healthy days, and Marta would knock quietly and say, "All finished," through the bedroom door. If the bedroom needed doing, Helen would take a long shower. And that's how it went. One time, Helen noticed there was a little pile of broken crockery that Marta had swept into the corner of the kitchen. Helen couldn't remember what had broken or when. She gathered the pieces up and put them in the outside bin.

Helen asked for a blood test. She sat for an hour and a half in Outpatients. She had a number, as though she was waiting to buy steak. Her number was 14 blue. Blue 14. Anonymous. Between blue 13 and 15. Before red 12, somehow. The nurses had their own colours. Blue must be quicker than Red. Blue stared at Helen's face.

"That looks sore," she said.

"Which bit?" Helen asked.

"All of it."

Blue called 15 before Helen had got up off the chair.

The blood said everything was fine, but that didn't stop it showing up in her urine sometimes.

"Is there really nothing you can do?" she asked her GP again.

He looked out of the window at passing cars. "There are things in life that aren't very easy . . ."

But a ringing started in Helen's ears, and she didn't hear him.

Helen took off her shoes, left them in the footwell of her car, left her car at the surgery and walked home. She walked on the outer edge of her right foot, as the inner toes were swollen, as if somebody had stamped on them. Maybe the years of towering heels, heavy earrings and hair pulled too tightly back were taking their toll, and she was finally breaking from the inside out and the outside back in again.

At home, she punched twenty or so paracetamol tablets out of their packaging and swallowed them one by one with orange juice straight from the carton. Once she'd finished she threw the carton as hard as she could and the thin orange liquid exploded over the off-white walls.

Helen went out into the garden and sat on the grass. The sunlight lit her face; she closed her eyes. It was still light when she awoke to find Marta had propped her up and was cleaning sweat off her face.

"You didn't take enough," she said. She had the packets fanned in her hand like bank notes.

"Marta," Helen said, though it sounded like somebody else. "I'm so tired."

Marta stood up, looked at Helen slumped sideways at her feet and was quiet for several seconds. Then she said, furiously: "For fuck's sake, Helen. Why don't you just fucking leave him?"

Helen squinted up at Marta, dark against the sky. She frowned, and a rivulet of blood rose over her lip and dripped onto the grass.

"The difference between the almost right word and the right word is . . . the difference between the lightning bug and the lightning."

Mark Twain

Dirty Blond
LUKE TREDGET

A scream from the middle of the pitch, and you look up from your newspaper to see the stumps violently splayed. Fielders are running to give the bowler double high-fives and Nigel is walking from the wicket, tearing at Velcro glove straps with his teeth. The throbbing in your stomach intensifies. Seven men down. Two more, and you'll have to go out there yourself.

"What's going on?" says Phil Gurney, slamming out of the pavilion to where you sit with five men on patio chairs. Phil is captain of Flitwick Town CC, and when he left to shower his team had 129 runs with two men down, comfortably chasing a target of 216. Now they are 187 for seven, and it is the fielders, from Saddleworth CC, that are starting to sound like they fancy themselves.

Some of the men beside you, whose names and nicknames you are still absorbing – Norm, Fish, Martin, Roy, Carpet – took part in the middle-order collapse, and Phil asks if they have a particular issue with scoring runs and what the fuck was the problem anyway. Then attention turns to your brother, who jogs past on his way to the pitch.

"You've got this, Dom," says Norm, clapping.

"Your time to shine, son," says Fish.

"Do us proud, boyo," says Roy.

On his way out Dominic performs warm-ups learnt from

television: he windmills his bat from each arm and does a little run with extended backlift, heels smacking his bum. Off to your right, between the pavilion and the sightscreen, your dad is slapping his hands together so vigorously you can make out his claps from thirty metres away. Dominic settles at the crease, the size of a pen lid from where you're sitting. The bowler runs from halfway to the boundary, bowls, Dominic steps forward, blocks. The solid clonk arrives a millisecond delayed.

"That's it, Dom!" says Roy.

"Nice straight bat," adds Carpet.

"You'd think him older than fifteen."

"That you would. He'll see us home, you watch."

You try to concentrate on this big talk, but it doesn't calm the burbling in your stomach, which is pressing on your bladder as well. Your fear is a constant, physical thing and is beginning to turn into annoyance, even anger. None of this is fair. Today, 9 September, is your fourteenth birthday. For you, this is apparent everywhere you look. The trees lining the pitch and the slanting evening sunlight are here for your birthday; the cows in the next field are birthday cows. Yet somehow this fact has been lost within a game that is bigger than your birthday, bigger than you.

Another ball to Dom, which he clips through mid-wicket for two runs. More clapping and shouting from the men around you – who, despite ranging from thin to fat and short to tall, seem as uniform as a pack of white apes. Then all eyes on the scoreboard: twenty-seven runs to win, three wickets in hand, seven overs left.

Also, the clock says 6.46 p.m.; the boys will be arriving for your sleepover at 8.30 p.m. Forget about the cricket; concentrate on that instead. You've been looking forward to it for weeks, and planned to spend the afternoon in your bedroom, making final preparations. But your dad said you shouldn't mope about on your birthday, and suggested you both go to watch Dom's match, which was important: if Flitwick won they'd be promoted to the Premier Division, where they'd face teams with electronic scoreboards, restaurant-quality teas and outfields like green carpet. You shrugged, said, "All right," and ten minutes later you arrived at the Vale in his van, just as the Flitwick men walked out to field. The first action you saw, before a ball was bowled, was big Howard

Moxon – youth-team coach – run from his position at square leg, jump in his truck and speed from the car park. Perplexing to the opposition, but everyone in Flitwick knows the meaning of his bolting like this. Howard is a volunteer fireman, and when his beeper sounds he runs from any task, except – he'd told you and the Under 14s with a wink – when he's sitting on the toilet.

Howard gone, and a temporary replacement was needed. Very few spectators at the Vale that early, just a handful of wives and young children, and you saw Dom say something to the rest of the players whilst pointing to where you sat, perched on the bonnet of your dad's van. Then Phil Gurney was walking over.

"How about it, son?" said Phil. You looked at your trainers. Phil Gurney was a local celebrity – he'd almost played first class and, in some exhibition match, had clean-bowled Imran Khan. "Ten overs, max. Howard will be back within the hour."

"Why not?" said your dad, nudging you with his elbow. "Something different for your birthday, eh?"

There was some logic to this. Playing your first adult sports match seemed appropriate for your fourteenth. That morning you'd been given your own television, for your bedroom, and from now on you'd be receiving a weekly "allowance", which hailed from a different economic galaxy to the "pocket money" you were given before.

"All right," you said, and your dad raced you home to grab your whites and back again in time for the third over. You took a position in the deep field, and whilst it was hardly fun standing out there, you told yourself that it was indeed "something different" and that Howard would soon return – everyone knew the Flitwick brigade didn't fight fires, they merely rushed to a state of readiness and waited until the full-timers at Bedford said they had it covered. But at the drinks break you overheard that Howard really had gone to a fire and wouldn't be back until tea. And when tea finally came – after two hours of tense boredom that erased your previous enthusiasm for cricket – you learnt that one of the Cardington air hangars was ablaze, and that every brigade in the county would be there all day. "But don't worry, son," said Phil, "216 is a nothing score. You won't have to go out there." You believed this, too. The prospect of having to bat was a speck on the horizon, but as the afternoon deepened and successive Flitwick men gave away their wicket, this speck has angled towards you, so that now it looms as large and dark as your shadow on the grass, and you can almost taste the sharp point at which you and your fear converge.

"Shot, Dom!" says Norm, as your brother drives a half-volley through mid-off. A fielder chases the careering red dot, which thumps into the billboard for Mantles Motors, New and Used. The scoreboard tumbles four runs, echoing the applause all around. You clap as well.

"Told you he'd see us home," says Fish. "He should be batting higher than nine."

"He's only fifteen," says Norm.

"Still. Shots like that."

You say nothing. Clap, but say nothing.

By the sightscreen, your dad is talking with two men whilst pointing at the pitch – he's probably explaining that Dom's been knocking half-centuries for the county Under 16s. Beside you, Fish and Norm continue talking him up as if trying to outbid each other – they'll be saying things like "professional" and "England" soon. What is it about Dominic that makes grown men swoon? That shy, gentle boy, they all say. Not much mouth or muscle on him, but have you seen him with a football or a cricket bat? It's like the textbook is wired in his head!

Of course, this doesn't mean you're *not* good at football or cricket. No one denies you have ability. But at the same time no one confuses your talent with Dominic's, which appears to make him glow slightly. You shouldn't be upset by this; you have something he lacks. Dom is polite, decent, almost transparent, whereas you can surprise people. In the last game of the football season you punched a boy in the face. He'd been kicking your heels and laughing at you all match, so you turned around and punched him. Never done it before, but no textbook needed. An instant red card and a grilling from the coach, who seemed more confused than angry, kept asking where the hell that came from. You couldn't say, but it felt good to surprise him, to surprise them all, especially that boy who, whilst still out on the pitch, was now playing with tears on his face.

"Here comes Mr Doughnut," says Roy, as Saddleworth bring on a new bowler. Roy is the only Flitwick player besides Phil that you've heard stories about, because of the fights he picks with the opposition. You almost ask why Mr Doughnut, which would be a dumb thing to say: the new bowler is fat – even by Saddleworth standards – and throws a slow, looping delivery to Mike Giddens, who grimly knocks it back.

"Come on, Mike," says Roy. "Lick your lips."

Don't watch, don't listen. Concentrate on the newspaper spread across your lap, a tabloid found in the changing room. You read a headline three times without it yielding any meaning, then shouts fly across the field. Mr Doughnut screams at the umpire, who slowly raises his finger to the sky. The fielders' shouts change from appeal to celebration and Mike turns away from the stumps, shaking his head. Out.

The sharp point lurches closer: one more wicket, then it's you.

"Time to get padded up, son," says Phil, placing his hairy fingers on your shoulder. You nod and rise from your seat, but before the changing room you visit the toilet behind the pavilion. Your cock is so shrivelled it's surprising the piss can trickle out at all. But it's nice in the toilet, and you continue standing at the urinal long after shaking away the last drops. You weigh your cock and balls in your hand; they fit easily in one palm. A long way to go, you hope. Last month you found a ripped page from a porn magazine in this same toilet, which is never locked, whilst walking home from Lee's house. You'd encountered porn before, but not like this. As well as a woman there was a man, his penis long and circumcised and like nothing you'd seen before or could imagine owning yourself. The captions were in German. You zipped the page into the pocket of your tracksuit bottoms and tramped home across the cow field, with a buzzing feeling in your stomach that was not unpleasant.

Stay in the toilet. Drink from the gushing cold tap. Lock yourself in the cubicle, sit down on the seat. Of course, you could just run away. From the pavilion it's a ten-metre dash to the road entrance, then a five-minute jog to the woods flanking the golf course. You imagine bounding through trees in your whites, distracting men from their drives and putts, and by the time this fantasy has played out you have left the toilet, entered the changing room and then retaken your patio chair beside Norm, armoured in child-size pads and gloves.

On the pitch, Roy is facing Mr Doughnut himself. Fifteen runs to win, two wickets in hand, four overs left. Norm, Fish and Carpet are leaning forward in their seats, biting nails, saying little. The pavilion's shadow has grown to engulf the collection of patio chairs; it is suddenly cold.

"Come on, Roy," says Phil, standing behind you. "Don't be a prick."

Mr Doughnut steps to the crease, delivers. Roy swings, misses, but the ball passes the stumps. Everyone groans.

"Fuck you, Roy."

"I can't bear this. I really can't."

"If he does something stupid, it really will be something else, what I do to him."

No hint of irony in this, the guys really are in pain. They're thinking about new sponsorship deals, teas served at set places, a sit-on lawnmower. They've been working all summer to reach the Premier Division; perhaps they've been working their whole lives. And yet, this particular game can't hurt them any more. They are slick-haired and smelling of shower gel; only you are shivering in grass-stained whites. You hate them for this. Beyond these apes, the crowd by the sightscreen – now fifty or sixty strong – is in a holiday mood. They stand in chatty, jokey clusters; direct sunlight is glinting off beer cans and gold watches. You hate them, too.

Tell yourself none of this matters. You don't care about cricket, don't even care about sport. Not like Dom or your dad, who don't want to think or talk about anything else. One rainy Sunday they watched three TV football matches in a row. Three! You went to your room during the second, and wound up sketching a picture of an actor called Christopher Eccleston, whose photo you found in a glossy supplement. It was the best drawing you'd ever done, and proof of its quality came from your dad, who looked at it for a long time and said: "Don't be an artist." That made you grin. You'd surprised this gruff, fearless man – shaken him, even – by showing him a drawing of the new Doctor Who. And you'll carry on surprising him, carry on surprising them all, and will look back at this cricket match and laugh at how scared you were.

These brave thoughts skim the surface of your fear, which

has now branched into every part of your body. Dry mouth, damp hands, tingling limbs, shivering skin. And the bubbling in your stomach, for a long time simmering, has now reached a steady boil.

"Want some practice balls?" says Norm. You say, "All right," and follow him to the empty space of grass between the nets and the slip catcher. Norm has been nice to you all day; he seems to be one of those people who can't help being nice. He throws the ball at your feet and you tap it back to him. He asks about the Under 14s, your school team, your party. You tell him it's just a sleepover; he says sleepovers are the best.

Simultaneous shouts of "Catch it!" shoot across the field. You follow the eyeline of the fielders up and across to the man at the far boundary, a grain of rice against dark trees, who is making slow, dancing steps with head thrown back, his hands a waiting nest.

"Roy, you silly tosser," says Norm.

The fielder falls as if speared, then rises with one arm aloft. The other Saddleworth players stream towards him, leaping and hooting as if they'd won the match already.

Norm sighs and puts his hand on your shoulder.

"Don't worry, mate," he says. "This isn't on you."

He mutters more things that you don't quite hear. The sharp point has arrived and you want to get out there, but Norm's hand is holding you in place, perhaps to give Roy a chance to walk off the pitch, or because Phil is coming over for a word.

"Don't try anything fancy, OK, son?" says Phil, crouching beside you. You wonder if he remembers your name. "Let your brother score the runs. Just don't get out, all right?"

Nod, don't try and speak.

"Enjoy yourself," says Norm, releasing your shoulder and patting your backside. "And happy birthday."

It's an elemental change, walking onto the pitch, like plunging into a cold pool or stepping before a packed theatre. Suddenly there's green, silent space on all sides. And your fear has been replaced by a new feeling that is really no feeling. It's like you're watching yourself walk – left foot, right foot – without being involved.

"Clap him in, lads," says a Saddleworth player. They all begin clapping, except the fast bowler, who just glares as you pass within ten feet of him, his lower lip hanging wetly open.

251

"You OK?" says Dom, meeting you halfway out. He is almost unrecognisable, his face red and boggle-eyed in the shadow of his cap's peak.

Nod, don't speak. Of course you're OK.

"You can do this. This guy's throwing them straight and slow. Just step forward and block. Sure you're OK?"

You try to say yes, to prove it, but only a croak comes out. Dom stops by the umpire and you head to the striker's end. The umpire says there are two balls to come this over. You look around, as if memorising the position of each fielder. What you notice instead is the crowd – now stretching from the sightscreen to the nets, one quarter of the pitch – and the sky beyond, which is ripening into your favourite kind of sunset, with slanting rays creating a complex of gold and orange and red on rippling high clouds. It must have been cooking whilst you shivered in the pavilion's shadow. Happy birthday.

"Play," says the umpire.

Mr Doughnut takes two steps and lobs the ball towards you. Step forward, bat straight, eye on the ball. A solid block.

A thumbs-up from your brother, applause from the sideline and relief blooms through you. You can do this. A second later Mr Doughnut throws another, this time drifting down leg side. Now, you have a simple rule when batting in youth games: if the ball isn't straight, you swing the bat. You've got the hand-eye to hit most and don't have to worry about being caught – most kids can't catch, they just flap their hands at the ball. But this isn't Under 14s, this is grown-up cricket with electronic scoreboards at stake. You watch it go harmlessly past.

Wild applause from the crowd, as over is called. It stings, to be cheered for just standing there, for not even playing a shot.

"That's the stuff," says Dom, coming down the wicket to bump fists with you. "Knew you could do it."

"Yeah," you say, and then shrug, as if to add, "I suppose." But Dom is looking at the scoreboard.

"Nine to win," he says. "I'll get them this over."

"All right."

You've both got your caps off; Dom's black fringe is pasted to his forehead. You wonder if the Saddleworth guys would guess you are brothers. Doubtful. Dom is dark as an Italian, like your dad; you're fair as a Swede, like your mum. Sometimes your dad's mates wink and josh him, when he introduces you as his son.

"He's got the darkness on the *inside*," he always says, making you imagine an inner filter that protects your hair and skin from some tar-like substance, a filter that is starting to buckle and fail as your hair morphs into what your mum calls dirty blond.

"Yeah, I'll try and get them this over," Dom repeats, after a pause. "And if I don't I'll keep the strike. Just wait for my call."

Two overs left, nine runs needed, and another slow bowler, this one grey-haired and lanky and for some reason reminding you of a priest, bowls to your brother. The first two Dom blocks, calm as you like, and the third he cuts away for two runs. The fourth, a full toss, he smashes to the cow field, provoking hysterics from the boundary. He blocks the fifth and then, best of all, punches the last to long-off so you can walk a single and he keeps the strike.

The crowd – which now seems to include your mum, Howard Moxon, various kids from school and your headteacher – are cheering and clapping with hands above their heads. Victory feels imminent, and they are itching to get their hands on Dominic. Your birthday, but he will be bounced aloft. This is fine. Think of the sleepover. Think of the surprise waiting for Lee, Andy and Tom when you reveal the plan: a walk to the woods with eight cans of Carlsberg and twenty Benson & Hedges lifted from your dad's duty free.

One over to go, two runs to win. The Saddleworth guys form a huddle, and when they run back to their positions it is the fast bowler, that prick, who is standing behind the umpire, holding the ball. He charges in snorting, and grunts like a tennis player when he bowls. The first two Dom blocks, calm as, but the third is fast and at his toes and he strains to get his bat down in time.

Three balls remaining, two runs needed to win. Quiet on the pitch, quiet on the boundary, quiet in the cow field. You feel a light breeze blowing in your ear.

Next comes an even faster yorker, and your stomach scrunches when Dom swings and misses. All eyes on the stumps, which are somehow intact. The bowler howls at the sky, and by the pavilion people are screaming "Run, run, run!" But Dom appears too stunned to notice that the ball has passed the wicketkeeper, and you ignore the easy runs.

It seems to take a full minute for the shouting to trail off and for Dom to settle at the crease. He has shrunk back to being a fifteen-year-old, and blinks and fidgets as the bowler storms in for the penultimate ball. This one Dom swings at and edges, the ball flying high and fast over the slips towards third man.

"Run two!" he shouts, and off you go. You touch your bat at the other end, but before turning back you see the fielder has the ball and is about to hurl it to the keeper. But Dom said run two, so you start running.

"Go back! Back! Back!!"

"Back!"

"Back!!!!"

The screams are from Dom, from the pavilion, from the crowd, and you turn again and lunge for the crease, bat outstretched, landing just before the keeper catches the ball and flattens the stumps. Not out.

Noise everywhere, the sidelines as raucous as a football terrace. You are lying on the dusty, hard-baked wicket. Get to your feet and brush yourself down. For a second, relief at not being run out blocks the realisation that you are at the striker's end and will face the final ball. Though this fact doesn't appear lost on the crowd: people have hands on chests, hands on each other's shoulders. My word! Whatever next!

By the pavilion, Norm, Fish, Phil and the rest of the Flitwick men are striking poses of distress: they have their hands on their heads as they confront this latest disaster, the disaster of you facing the final ball. Phil and Mike step over the boundary rope and are pointing at the scoreboard. The scores are tied, 216 chasing 216. Phil then waves at Dom, who skips over, chats to them, and then jogs all the way back to relay the message to you.

"A draw should be enough," he says, breathless. "As long as we're not all out, we'll get promoted. Just don't get out. Don't play a shot."

"All right," you say, and the umpire calls you to get into position. You walk to the crease, realising that you stepped onto the pitch thinking you'd reached the sharp point. And yet here you are with the whole game, the whole season, the whole world depending on you. There are sharp points within sharp points. At the crease you turn around and are struck by the number of people staring. The fast bowler, whose run-up begins near the boundary, is trying to stare you out even from there. The ten other fielders are all staring at you. At the other end of the wicket Dom and the umpire are staring at you. The cows are staring, and the crowd – which now contains everyone you've ever met – are all staring at you. Suddenly this makes sense. It is your fourteenth birthday; of course everything should depend on you. And best of all is the sunset, which has smeared further and is flecked with turquoise and flamingo pink at the edges, like a frozen party popper. It's all for you.

"Play," says the umpire. You grit your teeth and stare hard towards the bowler, who is tearing in as if trying to mimic a crazed bull. He is running fast and will bowl fast, too, much faster than anything you've faced before, but this is nothing compared to the firing synapses in your mind. You narrow your eyes as he leaps into his delivery, and when he releases the ball, a mere reddish blur, you immediately see it is going wide, that it will miss the stumps. It is there to be hit. But you have to consider the new sightscreens, the overseas players, the restaurant-quality teas, the field like green carpet, the sit-on lawnmower, the sponsored kits and the damned bloody electronic scoreboards. But it really *is* there to be hit, the closer it gets the wider it drifts. Swing the bat. Everyone is here to watch you, the birthday boy, and you are going to put on a show. Also, the bowler is a prick. There will be a time when you don't take shit from people like him, and that time will be in about two seconds. Swing the bat. Hit the winning runs. Be bounced aloft. Be photographed for the local paper: the birthday boy wins it for Flitwick. The ball hits the pitch, and perhaps it moves off the seam but it definitely straightens, and isn't going as wide as you thought. But it's too late now, you're swinging the bat, you will either hit it or not. There are sharp points to sharp points to sharp points, and here you are, the ball has arrived, and your bat is going to meet it and you will surprise them all. Hit it or not, you are not going to block, you are going to surprise them. That is your gift to them and the day's gift to you. Here it comes. Surprise.

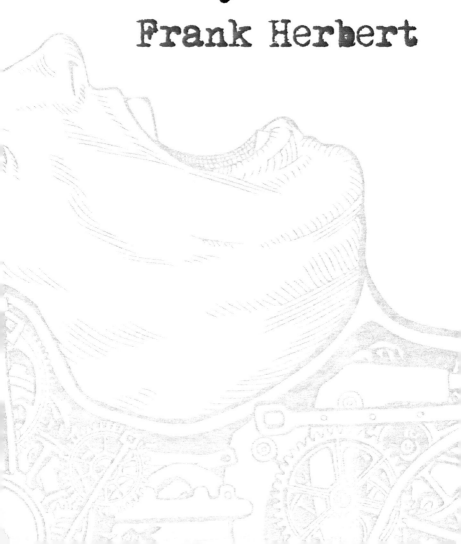

"Then there is no real ending. It's just the place where you stop the story."

Frank Herbert

Notes on
Contributors

Julia Bell is a writer and Senior Lecturer at Birkbeck, University of London where she is Convenor of the Creative Writing MA and Project Director of the Writers' Hub website. She is the author of three novels – most recently, *The Dark Light* (Macmillan, 2015) – and co-editor of *The Creative Writing Coursebook* (Macmillan, 2001) as well as three volumes of short stories, the latest being *The Sea in Birmingham* (Tindal Street Fiction Group, 2013). She also takes photographs; writes poetry, short stories, occasional essays and journalism; and is the co-curator of spoken-word night In Yer Ear.

Michael Button was born in Glasgow and lives in London. He is studying for the MA in Creative Writing at Birkbeck, graduating 2016, with a particular interest in genre fiction. During his life he has done a number of things for money – software development, DJing and teaching (swimming, English as a foreign language and probability theory). "Hardscrabble" is his first published piece of fiction. He can be contacted at michaeljbutton@gmail.com.

Dominika Chmiel is from Kraków, Poland. She obtained an MSc in Archaeology from the Jagiellonian University in 2009. After working creatively for branding and advertising agencies, she came to a realisation that her childhood prizes in literary competitions were no mistake and decided to pursue an MA in Creative Writing at Birkbeck, where she graduated in 2014. Dominika writes poetry and fiction, believing in concise, powerful forms and the force of ambiguity. Currently working at a fin-tech start-up, she releases her voice by developing two novels – in English and Polish, simultaneously.

Madeline Cross grew up in London and Wiltshire and has a BA in English Literature from Sussex University. She has worked in the non-profit sector for the past five years, in social-action and arts charities. She has just completed her final year of the Creative Writing MA at Birkbeck. "Anna" is taken from her first collection of short stories, in which she explores mental health, experiences of waiting, and our capacity to hope and endure. Madeline works at Chickenshed Theatre and lives in Peckham.

Kate Smalley Ellis is a London-based writer, bookseller and Birkbeck MA graduate. She's currently working on her first collection of short stories on love, choice, sexuality and grief. Her short fiction has been published in *Open Pen* and London/Tasmanian anthology *Transportation: Islands and Cities* (Transportation Press, 2015), and can be heard online at The Wireless Reader. She was shortlisted for the Myriad Writer's Retreat Competition in 2014. www.katesmalleyellis.com @katesmalleyelli

Emily Everett works in arts marketing, and as a freelance editor and writer. She studied English literature and music for a BA at Smith College in the US, spent a year at University College London, and completed her Master's in Literature at Queen Mary University of London in 2010. She joined the creative writing programme at Birkbeck in 2012. Her favourite authors since that time have been early-twentieth-century writers, including E. M. Forster, Edith Wharton, T. S. Eliot and, most recently, D. H. Lawrence. Forster's "Only connect . . ." epigraph was the inspiration for the short story published here, "Arlington, Virginia".

The winner of the Birkbeck 2014 MA Creative Writing Prize, **Gilli Fryzer** began to develop her first short-story collection while working on her dissertation. She has just started a PhD, also at Birkbeck, on the subject of the crone in literature, and much of her work reflects her fascination with landscape and the power of old beliefs. "Crow Harvest" was originally conceived in response to the catastrophic storms of early 2013 that brought snowdrifts several metres high across north and mid Wales, forcing its hill farmers and their animals into a desperate struggle for survival. Gilli lives in deepest Kent surrounded by dogs, hens, children and a long-suffering husband. She is merrily becoming more crone-like by the day. See more at www.writershub.co.uk/fiction-piece.php?pc=2573.

Zoe Gilbert's short stories have appeared in anthologies and journals in the UK and internationally. Her work has won prizes from Lightship and the British Fantasy Society amongst others; most recently, her story "Fishskin, Hareskin" won the Costa Short Story Award 2014. Zoe is currently working on her first folklore-inspired collection of stories, which will form part of her PhD on the short story at the University of Chichester. She lives in London, where she runs a writers' critique group and co-hosts the Word Factory short-story club.

Alison Hitchcock is Managing Editor of the Word Factory, as well as running her own business consultancy. She has just completed a Master's in Creative Writing at Birkbeck. She was runner-up in the inaugural SASH Writing Competition and is published in their anthology, *Homeless* (Stairwell Books, 2015). Her work has also appeared in *Every Day Fiction* and *The Interpreter's House*, as well as on the Writers' Hub, and she has performed at Hubbub. Alison is now working on her first novel, a story wickedly subverting the conventions of family drama when a teenage boy comes to live with his career-hungry aunt in London.

Louise Lee was once a geography teacher. When oxbow lakes no longer floated her boat, she took the next, natural step in her career progression and became a private investigator. Memorable cases include a high-functioning bigamist with three wives and six children, who was set to marry a fourth; and losing a target because George Clooney started chatting her up in a bar. She undertook the MA in Creative Writing at Birkbeck, and has had work commissioned by and broadcast on the BBC. "Stag" is an extract from her second novel, *The Last Bigamist* (scheduled publication date June 2016) – the sequel to her hugely successful debut, *The Last Honeytrap* (Headline, 2015). The books follow the cases of Florence Love, a PI who specialises in entrapment.

Deborah Martin has just completed her first year as a Creative Writing MA student at Birkbeck. She grew up in East Kilbride in the west of Scotland and studied at both the University of Cardiff and Glasgow Caledonian University. She has worked as a teacher in Canada, Thailand and Scotland, and has written for various Scottish arts magazines. Her fiction has previously appeared in *Cadenza*. Currently, she lives in Brighton where she works as a copywriter and performs poetry regularly at open-mic nights.

Heidi Nordmann was born in Bergen, the rainiest city in Europe, and moved to London to study writing. She received a first-class BA in Creative Writing from the University of Roehampton and immediately followed that up with a distinction on Birkbeck's MA Creative Writing course in 2014. Heidi is currently in Norway where she works as an editor and literary consultant, and spends her free time working on a collection of short stories.

Clive Parish is a writer and journalist who lives in the wilds of Buckinghamshire. His career began while he was still a postman, when he'd cycle around his patch after work rooting out stories for the local newspapers. He's been a reporter, sub-editor and editor on papers from London to Manchester, and on the nationals he has subbed for *Daily Express* features and for *The Times*, where he pulled the Weekend Money section together each week. He has written numerous magazine articles on popular science, and contributed features on travel and sport for the *International Herald Tribune*. More recently he worked in corporate communications for Inmarsat, the global satellite-communications company, latterly as Head of Digital. He is currently studying to master the art of storytelling at Birkbeck.

Rebecca Rouillard was born in Oxford but grew up in Durban, South Africa. She studied graphic design and worked in advertising and design for ten years before turning to writing. Since then she's had several short stories published. In 2015 she is attempting to complete the 26-mile MoonWalk London, swim the River Dart 10k, and finish her novel. The novel might be the death of her. She lives just outside London with her husband and two children. You can find her on Twitter as @rrouillard or at www.rebeccarouillard.com.

David Savill is Programme Director of the St Mary's University MA in Creative Writing. His debut novel, *They Are Trying to Break Your Heart*, will be published by Bloomsbury in March 2016; "Intervention" is the first chapter. The novel tells the story of a human rights researcher, her lover, and the Bosnian lives impacted by her work. It brings together the author's experiences in Bosnia, and in reporting the 2004 Asian tsunami for the BBC. A former journalist and documentary maker, David explores in his writing the political in our personal lives, and the dramas that play out in the teeth of international politics and globalisation. His second novel, *Disinformation*, follows a journalist into the heart of events currently unfolding in Central Europe. He graduated from the Birkbeck MA in Creative Writing, in 2008. His writing is represented by Sophie Lambert at the Conville & Walsh agency.

Frank T. Sayi is an émigré, staunch feminist, and humanist. He is a qualified nurse and a University of London and University of Portsmouth alumnus. He has an MA in Cultural and Critical Studies from Birkbeck, and is currently taking the MA in Creative Writing, with aspirations to progress to a PhD programme. His stories deal with childhood trauma, violence against women, political violence, memory and re-remembering. Frank's African background brings a non-European sensibility to his writing. "Shadows" is his first published short story and he is currently working on a novel called *Time*.

Stefanie Seddon grew up on a farm in New Zealand. She moved to London after completing a degree in English Literature at the University of Otago, and spent the next fifteen years working in the City. She currently lives in the East Sussex countryside with her young family and is studying for the MA in Creative Writing at Birkbeck. Stefanie is working on a collection of short stories inspired by the high-country landscapes and rural communities of her native New Zealand. "Arrowtown" is set against this backdrop.

Kate Seferian has just completed her MA in Creative Writing at Birkbeck, University of London. She spent her childhood in Boston and northern Georgia, and studied English literature and journalism at the University of Richmond in Virginia. Her experience in the Deep South influences much of her short-story writing, and she is currently working on a "Southern noir" novel set in Mississippi. Kate also works as an editor for an international consulting company, and she and her husband live near Cambridge. "Like Father" is her first published story.

Louise Smith grew up in the Midlands and now lives in London. She has previously worked as a documentary producer and scriptwriter. She has just completed her MA in Creative Writing at Birkbeck and is working on short stories as well as a novel.

Natasha Sutton-Williams is a playwright, singer and journalist. Her plays have been performed on the London stage at the Arcola, Southwark Playhouse and Pleasance Theatre. In January 2015 she wrote, composed and performed her one-woman show *Freud The Musical*, which was funded by Arts Council England. She is a member of Soho Theatre's Young Writers' Alumni Scheme and has been shortlisted twice for their Soho Young Writers' Award, in 2013 and 2014; she was shortlisted for the Adopt a Playwright Award 2014. She won a place on the National Youth Theatre and Shine TV's writers' programme for two years and in 2011 had her play *I AM NOT SICK* produced by the NYT. Natasha won a six-month mentorship with Alex Preston on the Inspires programme 2014/15 run by Writers' Centre Norwich and IdeasTap, where she developed her fiction writing. She is also a freelance arts journalist for londoncalling.com.

Simon Townend was born in Swansea but grew up in Windsor. He has studied at Cardiff University, Brunel University London and the University of East London, and is currently studying for a Master's in Creative Writing at Birkbeck. He was longlisted for the 2013 Bath Short Story Award and had a story published in *A Solitary Act* (Rainbow Valley Books, 2013), an anthology of Croydon writing. Living in South London with his family, Simon is currently compiling a collection of short fiction and working on his first novel.

Luke Tredget works in international development and disaster response, primarily for the Red Cross. He has been writing fiction for five years and his first novel, *Elation*, was shortlisted for the 2013 Luke Bitmead Bursary, organised by Legend Press. He began the Creative Writing MA at Birkbeck in 2014 and is currently working on his second novel.

Raised in London, **Dave Wakely** has worked as a musician, university administrator, poetry librarian, and editor in locations as disparate as Bucharest, Notting Hill and Milton Keynes. Currently working as a freelance writer, having completed his Birkbeck Creative Writing MA, he lives in Buckinghamshire with his civil partner and too many guitars. His stories have appeared in issues 10 and 11 of *The Mechanics' Institute Review*, and in *Ambit* and *Glitterwolf* magazines. As well as reading at Hubbub and Arts Gateway MK events, Dave is the MC of the Birkbeck Poets at the Duke of Wellington and blogs at http://theverbalist.wordpress.com.

Marina Warner was brought up in Egypt, Belgium, and England; her mother was Italian and her father an English bookseller. An award-winning writer of both fiction and non-fiction, she specialises in mythology and fairy tales, with an emphasis on the part women play in them. She also writes essays and reviews about art, literature and cultural history. In 1994 she gave the BBC Reith Lectures, and in 2015 chaired the judges of the Man Booker International Prize. She holds a number of academic positions, including Professor of English and Creative Writing at Birkbeck, University of London. Her latest book is *Once Upon a Time: A Short History of Fairy Tale* (OUP, 2014); a collection of short stories, *Fly Away Home*, will be published by Salt in autumn 2015; and she is writing a memoir-cum-novel set in Cairo in the fifties. Marina was awarded the 2015 Holberg Prize for her outstanding contribution to research in the arts and humanities.

Kate Whiteside was raised on the south coast and is now based in West London. She works for a prominent charity and spends the rest of her time writing prose, poetry and screenplays, along with her first novel. Her short fiction has previously appeared in Issue 11 of *The Mechanics' Institute Review,* and she is thrilled to be appearing again. Her passion is for exploring the dysfunctional in the everyday, and her style aims to create levity through absurdity.

Tom C. B. Williams is a writer and editor based in Bath, England. He has a BA in Philosophy from UCL and is due to complete his MA in Creative Writing from Birkbeck in 2016. He has been published in *Pen Pusher, Tales of the DeCongested* and *Pangea: An Anthology of Stories from Around the World,* and his short fiction has been broadcast as part of BBC Radio 4's *Ones to Watch* series featuring up-and-coming writers. He is currently working on his first novel.